Make Me Stay
Jaci BURTON

headline
ETERNAL

Published by arrangement with Berkley,
a member of Penguin Group (USA) LLC.
A Penguin Random House Company.

First published in Great Britain in 2015
by HEADLINE ETERNAL
An imprint of HEADLINE PUBLISHING GROUP

1

Cataloguing in Publication Data is available from the British Library

ISBN 978 1 4722 2817 8

Offset in 11.5/12.05 pt Times LT Std by Jouve (UK)

Printed and bound in Great Britain by CPI Group (UK) Ltd, Croydon, CR0 4YY

HEADLINE PUBLISHING GROUP
An Hachette UK Company
Carmelite House
50 Victoria Embankment
London EC4Y 0DZ

www.headlineeternal.com
www.headline.co.uk
www.hachette.co.uk

Acknowledgments

To Lillie: Thanks for letting me borrow Not My Dog.

To Shannon Stacey, Kati Brown, and especially my editor, Kate Seaver: Thank you so much for the help with the back cover copy. You were all my saviors on this one.

Chapter 1
_____

REID MCCORMACK STOOD in the middle of the main floor of the old mercantile in downtown Hope, his boots kicking around years' worth of dust and debris. The ceiling was collapsing, the original wood floor had seen years of use, and some of the floorboards were worn down to holes. He'd already been to the second and third floor to check things out. The original staircase leading to the second floor should probably be condemned. Plumbing was shit, electrical was shot, and the list of crap items he ticked off in his head should be giving him nightmares.

But Reid had a vision of what this place could be—of what it once had been. As an architect, he built from new—he'd never done work on anything historical. He was an architect, but he was also a licensed contractor. He'd done renovation work here and there, but nothing of this scope.

As he studied the blueprints for the old mercantile he'd agreed to renovate, he still had no idea what he was doing back in his hometown, or why he'd agreed to this job.

It was a big project, and he had plenty of projects with his company in Boston. Shifting responsibilities over had been a giant pain in the ass, as was taking a leave of absence and putting his company—his baby—in the hands of his associates. He'd sweated blood and risked a hell of a lot of money to get his architectural firm up and running, and with numerous late nights and damn good work, he'd made a success of McCormack Architectural Designs.

The thought of not being in Boston overseeing the business sent a shot of nervousness straight to his gut. But, he'd had to admit, when he'd come back home for his brother Logan's wedding in the spring and they'd taken a look at this old place, it had been childhood memories, plus the challenge of restoring the mercantile to its former glory, that had been too much to resist.

This was his chance to do something out of the ordinary.

He had ideas for the mercantile. A lot of them. And now that he and his brothers had bought the old building back from the town, it was their responsibility to do right by it.

He intended to do it justice.

And when the job was done he'd head back to Boston, where he belonged.

He heard a knock on the front door, dissipating the cloud of memories.

Figuring it was the general contractor he'd hired—or maybe his brothers, who were also supposed to meet him here today—he went to the door and pulled it open.

It wasn't the contractor or his brothers. It was Samantha Reasor, the owner of the flower shop around the corner. Sam was the one who'd pushed hard for them to take on this project. Or rather, for him to take it on. She was as passionate about the mercantile as anyone in Hope.

Today she wore dark skinny jeans that showcased her slender frame. Her blond hair was pulled high on top of her head, and she had on a short-sleeved polo shirt that bore the name *Reasor's Flower Shop*. And she had the prettiest damn smile he'd ever seen, with full lips painted a kissable shade of pink.

Not that he was thinking about kissing her or anything. He was back in Hope to work.

"Hi, Reid. I heard you were in town and getting ready to

start the project. I couldn't wait to get inside here again. I hope I'm not bothering you. If I am, I can take off."

"Hey, Sam. You're not a bother. Come on in. Though the place is still as dusty as it was when we did the walk-through in the spring. Are you sure you want to get dirty?"

She waved her hand as she stepped in. "I don't mind. I've been snipping and arranging flower baskets all day for an event. There are probably leaves in my hair."

As she walked by, he inhaled the fresh scent of—what was that? Freesia? Roses? Hell if he knew, since he didn't know jack about flowers. He only knew that Sam smelled damn good. And there were no leaves in her hair.

She turned in a circle, surveying both up and down the main room. "It's amazing, isn't it?"

He laughed. "Right now it's a dump."

Her gaze settled on him. "Oh, come on. Surely you can see beyond the trash and the layers of dust to what it can be. Do you have ideas yet? I mean, of course you do, because you're here to tear down and build up, so you have all the ideas, right?" She spied the rolled-up documents in his hand. "Do you have blueprints?"

"Yeah."

"Care to share? I'd love to see the plans you've worked up."

"Actually, the general contractor is due to show up here shortly, along with Luke and Logan. You're welcome to hang out while we go over them."

She pulled her phone out of her back pocket. "Unfortunately, I can't. I have a delivery to make in about thirty minutes. But I'd really like to see the blueprints."

"Some other time, then."

Her eyes lit up. "Oh, I know. Are you busy for dinner tonight?"

"Uh, dinner?"

"Sure. Why don't you come over to my place? I make a mean plate of spaghetti. If you're not busy with your family. I know you'd like to get reacquainted with them, so I don't want to step all over that."

"No, it's not that. I've been here a couple days already, so we've done the reacquainting stuff." He didn't know what the hell was going on. Was she asking him out, or was she just interested in seeing the blueprints?

"Perfect. Give me your phone and I'll put my address and cell number in it."

He handed his phone over and Sam typed in her info.

"Is seven okay? That'll give me time to close up the shop and get things going."

"Sure."

"Great." She grasped his arm. "I'm so glad you're here, Reid. I'll see you later. You and your blueprints."

She breezed out of the mercantile and he found himself staring at the closed door, wondering what the hell had just happened.

Sam probably just wanted to get a good look at the blueprints when they'd have more time. She was interested in the old building. Not in him.

And he wasn't interested in her. Or in any woman. He was in town to refurbish the mercantile, and nothing more.

But, whatever. He liked spaghetti. So he'd see Sam, she'd see the blueprints, and that would be it.

SAM WENT BACK to the shop, wishing she'd had more time to check out Reid—check out the blueprints. Not that Reid wasn't some awesome eye candy. Today he'd worn loose jeans, boots, and a short-sleeved T-shirt that showed off his tanned, well-muscled arms.

It had taken everything in her to walk out of the mercantile. Fortunately, she had a job and a timeline, and that always came first. She loaded up the flowers that Georgia Burnett had ordered for the Chamber of Commerce luncheon today, put them in her van, and drove them over to the offices. Georgia, who'd had a terrible fall last year and had spent several months laid up, was back to her old cheery, mobile self again. And since she was the mother of two of Sam's friends, Emma and Molly, Georgia was like a mother to Sam as well. Which was so nice, since the only family Sam had left was her Grammy Claire.

And family was a big deal to Sam.

She pushed through the doors of the offices, her arms filled with bouquets. Georgia was right there at the front desk waiting for her, looking slim and gorgeous as always.

"Hello, Georgia, how are you?"

"Doing wonderfully, Samantha. And you?"

"Great." She pressed a kiss to Georgia's cheek while simultaneously juggling two baskets of flowers.

"The baskets are gorgeous, honey," Georgia said. "The tables are already set up inside, so you can place them in the center of each one."

"Will do."

Sam went about her business, and once she finished, she said good-bye to Georgia and headed back to the shop. She still had several individual flower orders to prepare and deliver, which took up the remainder of her day.

Which suited her just fine. Busy was good for business, and business had been great lately. She had two weddings coming up, including that of Georgia's daughter Molly next month.

When her phone buzzed, she smiled. Speaking of the bride-to-be . . .

"Hey, Molly," she said, putting her phone on speaker so she could continue to work.

"Are you sure all the flowers we ordered are going to come in on time?" Molly asked.

"Yup."

"In the right colors?"

"Absolutely."

"And how about the lilies? Oh, and the corsages for my mom and for Carter's mom?"

"All under control, honey."

Molly paused. "I'm being a neurotic mess, aren't I?"

"Nope. You're being a bride. This is normal."

"I have a checklist of items, and then I came across flowers, and I know we've gone over this a hundred times, but you know, I just had to check."

Sam was used to this. Brides called her all the time, even

if everything was perfect. "Of course you had to check. Call anytime. But Molly? I've got this. Trust me."

"I know you do. Honest, I really do. Oh, and Sam, thanks."

"You're welcome. I'll talk to you soon." She hung up, figuring Molly would call her again tomorrow.

Which didn't bother her at all, because as a florist, her job was to keep her customers happy. And when one of her customers was also one of her closest friends, that counted double.

She delivered the afternoon flowers, then came back to clean up the shop and prep things for tomorrow morning. By then it was closing time, and she made a quick grocery list so she could dash into the store and get what she needed for dinner tonight.

She had no idea why she'd invited Reid over for dinner. First she had to go in and start blabbering at him like she had some kind of motormouth disease.

Ugh. What was wrong with her, anyway? She was normally calm and in control of herself.

Except around Reid, for some reason. Ever since that night at Logan and Des's wedding when she'd sat next to him, she'd felt an instant zap of attraction.

And ever since that zap, she'd been ridiculously shy around him.

Normally when a woman was shy, she'd be quiet, right?

But not Samantha. No, she had run-of-the-mouth issues when she was around a man she was attracted to.

So what did she do with Reid? She invited him to dinner. An impulse suggestion, sure, and only because she really wanted to see the blueprints. But was that really the only reason? When he'd been in town in the spring for the wedding, she'd definitely felt that tug of . . . something.

He'd gone back to Boston soon after his brother's wedding, and she'd ignored the zap, figuring it had been nothing more than a passing mutual interest in the mercantile. But seeing him today, that zap had been something entirely different, and totally biological.

She chewed on her bottom lip and decided to call her best

friend, Megan, for some advice. She punched in Megan's number on her phone.

"What's up, Sam?" Megan asked when she answered.

"Reid McCormack is back in town."

"I heard. So he's going to start work on the mercantile, right?"

"Yes. I popped over there today when I saw him go in. And then I invited him to dinner."

Megan paused. "That's interesting. Why?"

Sam pulled up the stool behind the counter and took a seat. "I don't know. Impulse. And, you know, I got to talking to him. I might have overtalked."

"You babbled."

Leave it to her best friend to know her so well. "Yes, I babbled. I guess I babbled my way into a dinner invitation. We were chatting about the building and he had the blueprints, which I was really interested in, and I could tell he was busy, so it was an impulse thing."

"Always go with your impulses, Sam. You're obviously attracted to him. Did he say yes?"

"He did. And why do you think I'm attracted to him?"

"Everyone saw the way the two of you were together when we all went to check out the mercantile in the spring."

Sam frowned. "What do you mean, everyone saw? What did they see?"

"Oh, you know. Heads together, wandering around looking the place over. And when you climbed up the ladder to look at the ceiling? He checked out your butt."

Sam leaned her arms on the counter. "He did not. He did? Really?"

"He did. Chelsea and I were watching. And he was not looking at the ceiling. He was looking at your butt."

"Now that *is* interesting."

"I know. So enjoy dinner. And see what happens for dessert."

"I will. But you know, I didn't invite him for dinner to have . . . dessert with him."

Megan laughed. "Sure you didn't."

"Megan, I'm serious. I just wanted to see his blueprints."

"Is that what we're calling it now?"

Sam rolled her eyes. "You're so funny."

"I know I am. Call me tomorrow with all the details."

"Okay."

Samantha hung up, grabbed her purse, and locked up the shop, then headed out to her car. Once inside, she looked at her phone to double-check her grocery list.

She was going to cook a spaghetti dinner for Reid McCormack tonight, and then she was going to look over his blueprints. And by *blueprints*, she really meant actual blueprints. Nothing involving "dessert."

But if he checked out her butt again, dessert might be back on the menu. And she wasn't talking sweets.

Chapter 2

REID DIDN'T HAVE a lot of time to ponder the mystery that was Samantha Reasor, because not long after she left, Deacon Fox pulled up.

He grinned as he walked outside to shake Deacon's hand.

"Hey, movie star," he said to Deacon.

"Fuck you."

Reid shook his head. Nothing much had changed since their high school days. Deacon still had those movie-star looks Reid used to tease him about. With jet black hair, blue eyes, and rugged good looks, Deacon had to fight off the women.

Not that Deacon had done a whole lot of fighting off back then. There'd been plenty of girls, and Deacon had never said no. Until Deacon and Loretta Simmons had hooked up. Then all other women had ceased to exist for him. But that was high school and a long time ago, and a lot had changed since then.

Though Reid had heard that Deacon was still hot with all of the women. Single, a business owner, and, though Reid didn't see the appeal, he supposed Deacon could still be considered good-looking.

If you liked the dark, rugged, handsome type.

"You had to pick the place that needs the most work, huh?" Deacon asked as they surveyed the front of the building.

"You know me. I like a challenge."

"Yeah. I know you all right. At least the outside is still in decent shape. Once we replace the porch and clean up the brick, that's all the exterior is going to need. I'll have to check out the roof, but it doesn't look to be in bad shape. From the paperwork I got, looks like the roof was replaced about ten years ago, so we should be good to go there."

"Agreed."

Deacon nodded. "Let me grab my copy of the blueprints and I'll meet you inside. Your idiot brothers coming?"

Reid laughed. "They should be here soon."

Deacon slapped him on the back. "You and me together again, McCormack. Just like old times, huh?"

"Yeah. Just like old times. Except this time you're going to have to do some of the work. You know, because I'm paying you."

"Screw you. I always worked harder than you did."

Reid shook his head when Deacon disappeared, then went inside to grab his blueprint copy and waited for Deacon. He'd hired Deacon, owner of Fox Construction, to assist him with the renovation project. In high school, he and Deacon had had English and math classes together, and had suffered through Mr. Sundford's chem class of death as lab partners.

At eighteen, it had been Deacon he'd leaned on when his mother had decided she'd rather be free than be a parent. If it hadn't been for his brothers, his dad, and Deacon, he wasn't sure how he would have survived that summer. His brothers and father had given him the family support he needed, but when that had gotten too smothering, he'd fled the house and hung out with Deacon.

Deacon didn't have the perfect family. His parents had divorced when he was ten, so he understood complicated family dynamics. Deacon hadn't judged when Reid had spilled his guts one drunken weekend out at the lake. Instead, he'd sat quietly next to him and listened as Reid had railed against his mother, against faithless women who couldn't stick it out when

times were rough. Deacon had agreed with him when necessary, and had told him he was full of shit when Reid had stumbled around in a drunken stupor and mumbled about obviously
not being worth loving.

That night was still a little fuzzy, but he remembered Deacon shoving him so hard he'd fallen on his ass in the dirt.
Deacon had told him he could blame his mother for every
goddamn thing that was wrong in the world, but none of what
had happened would ever be Reid's fault. Just like it hadn't been
Deacon's fault that his parents had decided to get a divorce.

Obviously Deacon had a lot more practical experience with
the divorce thing. It had taken Reid a while to get on board,
but he had, and his father and brothers had been his familial
rocks, while Deacon had been his Gibraltar of a friend.

He'd never forgotten it, and even though he'd left Hope
for college and then found his career in Boston, he'd never
cut ties with Deacon. So when the opportunity presented
itself to refurbish the mercantile, Deacon had been the first
person he'd thought of to help him.

"How's business?" Reid asked when Deacon came back
inside.

"Busier than a male porn star with a twelve-inch dick."

Reid snorted. "Speaking from personal experience,
Deacon?"

"You know it. It's my weekend side job."

"You wish." Only with Deacon could he have this
conversation.

He'd missed him. They'd stayed in touch over the years,
and he knew Deacon had taken over his dad's construction
business.

"This is probably a small-time operation for you," Reid
said.

"Hey, like I told you. I'm absolutely on board with doing
this renovation. The mercantile means as much to me as it
does to you. I can't wait to make her shine again."

Which was why he'd hired Deacon. They shared the same
vision.

The door opened, and Luke and Logan walked in.

"I swear we don't have tequila in here, Officer," Deacon said.

"Well, why the hell not?" Luke asked.

"Because it would take twice as long to finish the job," Reid said. "And Deacon's expensive."

Deacon shot Reid a look. "You're paying for the best, my man. That's why I'm expensive."

"You hired this joker to help with the renovation?" Logan asked, shaking Deacon's hand. "Man, you must have been high."

Deacon laughed. "Yeah, as high and sturdy as that barn you had me build for you, asshole."

Logan shrugged. "No complaints there."

Sometimes Reid really missed this camaraderie. He had friends in Boston, but it wasn't the same. He missed the people he'd grown up with, the people who knew him well, knew his idiosyncrasies and his secrets—the bad ones as well as the good ones.

Family and his best friend. His lifelines over the years.

But his business—his success story—that was in Boston.

And that's where he'd head back to once this project was finished.

Deacon looked the building over. "This place is a shithole."

"Yeah," Reid said, seeing the mess through Deacon's eyes. Holes in the walls—and the floors. Ceiling collapsing, plumbing a disaster, and electrical a total nightmare. Nothing was where he wanted it, which meant a total restructure.

The mercantile had lost her sparkle, and there was a hell of a lot of work ahead of them. She was worth it.

He shot a grin at Deacon. "But it's going to be amazing once it's finished."

Logan stepped over broken cabinets that appeared to have been wrenched from the wall by the Hulk on a bender. "This place seems worse than it did when we were here several months ago. Has it been vandalized or something?"

"No. This is pretty much how it looked back then."

Luke shook his head. "You've got your work cut out for you, brother. I'm happy to just be an investor on this one."

Logan scratched the side of his face and nodded. "Yeah, me, too. This looks like a clusterfuck in the making."

Deacon laughed. "That's because the two of you don't see beyond the mess it is now. We'll fix it, won't we, Reid?"

"Hell yes, we will." Typically he was happy to be the architect, to create the design and let the engineers and the contractors take over with the build. But before he'd hired Deacon he'd discussed his desire to be a part of the renovation, to be hands-on in turning around the mercantile. Deacon had told him it wouldn't be a problem.

They went over the blueprints. Even though Logan and Luke wouldn't be involved in the project, he wanted his brothers to know the plan. They'd contributed a lot of money—or at least the McCormack ranch had contributed a lot of money—to the renovation, so he wanted them to be on board with his thought process regarding how best to shape up the mercantile.

"Honestly, Reid, I don't know how Luke feels, but you're the talent here. I'm fine with whatever decisions you make about the building. You're the architect, and Deacon's the contractor, so the two of you know best."

Luke nodded. "I agree with Logan. If there's something you feel is necessary to have our input on, feel free to call, but this is your ball. Call it."

"All right, then. Deacon and I will get started."

After Logan and Luke left, he and Deacon sketched out preliminary project plans. They'd meet in Deacon's office tomorrow with the engineer to line everything out in more detail.

"Normally I'd stay more hands-off on a project and let the contractor handle things, but I'll tell you right now I'm probably going to be more involved than we originally talked about on this one," Reid said. He stared up at the ceiling, where it was aged and falling down. Beyond that, the original tin ceiling just begging to be shined up and showed off. "There's history here, and I'd really like to be a part of restoring it."

Deacon nodded. "You're the boss here. You can stand around and bark orders or wield a hammer and haul trash, for all I care. Up to you."

That's what he'd always liked most about Deacon—his easygoing manner. Not much ruffled his feathers.

Instead of heading all the way back to the McCormack ranch only to have to turn around and make the drive into Hope again for dinner with Samantha, Reid decided to hang out in town for the remainder of the day. He only had a couple of hours to kill, since the meeting lasted the better part of the afternoon, so he went over to the library, intending to do some research into the town's history.

He was hoping to find as much information as possible on the mercantile—and some photos.

He walked up to the research desk and found an extremely attractive brunette whose back was turned to him. Or at least her backside was attractive, since she was currently bent over the desk which gave him a great view of her curves. When she turned around, he instantly recognized her.

"Jillian? Jillian Reynolds, right?"

She frowned. "Yes?"

"Reid McCormack. We went to school together. You probably don't remember me."

She smiled as recognition dawned. "Oh, hi, Reid. It's nice to see you again. I heard you and your brothers bought the mercantile. I was so happy to hear the news. All of us—and by all of us, I mean those of us who live and work here in town—love that old building. We're so happy knowing you're restoring it."

"Thanks." She was just as pretty from the front as she was from the back, with short brown hair that framed her face and very striking green eyes. "I'm looking forward to the project, which is what brings me here."

"Sure. What can I do for you?"

"I was hoping to find some documents or books on the history of Hope, and any with photographs would be especially helpful."

"Of course. We have an entire section on Hope." She came around and led him toward the aisle marked *Hope Town History*.

"Perfect," he said. "Thanks."

"If you're looking for photos of the old mercantile over the years, you might also want to check out the Hope Historical Society and the Chamber of Commerce. I'll wager they'll have what you're looking for."

He made a mental note. "Thanks. I'll be sure to do that."

She smiled at him. "It was great talking to you again, Reid. I look forward to seeing what you're going to do with the building."

"Good to see you, too, Jillian. And thanks for the info."

He browsed the books and selected a few that had what he needed. Realizing he hadn't had a library card since . . . hell, probably since high school, he went to the front desk and applied for one.

But he didn't have a Hope address, either.

"I'm staying at the ranch during the renovation."

Jillian nodded. "That's fine." She typed into the system. "We'll just use the ranch address as yours. I don't think you're going to run off with our books."

He laughed. "Unlikely. I promise to have them back on time."

After he thanked Jillian and left the library, he put the books in his truck and checked his watch.

It was time to head over to Samantha's for dinner. He'd have to go to the chamber and the historical society tomorrow. He typed a note into the calendar on his phone so he'd remember to do that.

At least he felt like he'd accomplished something today. Tonight, after dinner, he'd look over these books and see what he could find, so he could return them to the library.

But for now, his stomach grumbled, since he hadn't had lunch.

Spaghetti dinner was sounding good.

Chapter 3

AFTER MAKING THE meat sauce and letting it simmer, Samantha went to take a shower, deciding she was going to approach tonight's dinner with Reid in an extremely low-key manner.

It was just dinner and blueprints, and nothing more than that. He had work to do, and she was very busy with the flower shop. He likely had no desire to get involved, and neither did she.

Well, actually, she'd very much like to get involved with Reid. At least physically.

What woman wouldn't? He was highly successful, drop-dead gorgeous, and, if nothing else, she'd bet he was fun to make out with. No harm in that, right?

Nothing that happened between them could ever be considered long-term, because he had a career in Boston. So they could maybe have a fling.

Except she didn't even know if he was interested in her.

Nothing like setting the flowers out before the vase, huh, Sam?

Dinner and blueprints. That was it.

She'd selected a couple of bottles of wine—a white and a

red—so Reid could choose what he liked. She'd also bought beer, because a lot of guys preferred that instead. She knew the McCormack brothers were beer drinkers, so she figured Reid might not be a wine fan.

Bread was warming in the oven. Now all she had to do was make the salad.

She was just about to start that when the doorbell rang.

Her pulse rate kicked up.

Ridiculous. This wasn't a date. It was Reid stopping by for dinner so she could get her hands on those blueprints and pick his brain about the mercantile renovation.

Nothing more, Sam. So just relax.

She opened the door and was surprised to see him standing there holding a bottle of wine.

"Hi, there," she said, unable to fight back those nervous butterflies flapping their wings in her stomach. "Come on in."

He handed her the bottle as he stepped inside. "I figured since you were nice enough to invite me to dinner, I should at least bring some wine."

"That's awfully thoughtful of you, Reid, and totally unnecessary, especially since I practically bullied you into coming to dinner."

He frowned as he followed her into the kitchen. "You didn't bully me."

"Now you're being nice. I ran at the mouth and threw dinner into the mix. You were polite to say yes. Sorry about that. I really am interested in seeing the blueprints, and I was kind of out of time and I knew you were busy and all, so this was my next best solution. But hey, you'll get an awesome dinner out of it, so there's that."

He laughed. "Well, if it makes you feel better, I'm more than a little hungry, and Des is back in town after doing a press junket for a movie. She and Logan are in reunion mode, so I'd just as soon leave the two of them alone. You actually saved me from feeling like a third wheel."

"I'll accept the savior role. Now, how about we have some wine? Or would you prefer beer?"

"Wine sounds good."

She held up the bottle he'd brought. "Let's start with this one."

She opened the wonderful cabernet, then poured it into glasses, handing one to him. "Come on into the living room. We'll sit and drink, and you can tell me how it went today."

She motioned to her small living room, so he headed that way and she followed. She tried to focus on making her way into the room, but he was right in front of her, and his jeans cupped his butt so nicely she couldn't help but look.

Reid had one amazing butt.

He took a seat on the sofa, so she grabbed a spot on the other end and set her glass on the end table, then half turned to face him.

All the McCormack men were good-looking, but there was something about Reid's dark good looks and intense green eyes that just . . . got to her. Maybe because when she looked at him, he looked back. Like . . . really looked back, as if he saw her the same way she saw him.

With interest.

It had been a long time since she'd been interested in any guy. Between managing the floral shop and taking care of her grandmother, Sam didn't have a lot of time to date.

Maybe that's why Reid sparked her interest. He was temporary, and temporary totally worked for her right now.

"This is a nice place you have here, Sam."

"Thanks. It's not exactly the house of my dreams. It's a small two-bedroom, but I bought it because it's just a few houses down from my Grammy Claire's place, so it's convenient."

"Oh, right. How is your grandmother doing?"

"She's adjusting to life without my grandpa. He died a couple of years ago, which was hard on her. I offered to move in with her, but she's as independent as they come, so my being close was the next best thing. She's eighty-three now. And she still insists on driving, which scares the hell out of me."

"I can understand you wanting to keep an eye on her."

"You have no idea. It's like trying to raise a teenager. She keeps disappearing on me and refuses to get a cell phone, so I'm constantly having to call your brother Luke or someone else at the Hope PD to locate her."

He laughed. "I'll bet that's . . . interesting."

She turned and reached for her glass of wine. "It can be downright embarrassing. One Friday night I called to check on her at nine. I typically call her in the evenings to make sure she's okay before she goes to bed. I got no answer, so I grabbed my set of keys to her house and went over there. She wasn't home. At nine o'clock, for heaven's sake."

"And of course she has no cell phone, so you couldn't call her to find out where she was."

Samantha nodded. "Right? I got in my car and started driving around, and I couldn't freakin' find her. I checked the bingo hall, because she likes to go play bingo on Friday nights, but she wasn't there. I checked the church to see if they were having movie night, which they sometimes do at the high school gym, but no one was there, either. I called a couple of her friends, who hadn't heard from her.

"By then I had started to panic. It was the dead of winter, we'd had a recent snowfall, and my thoughts strayed to her having wrecked her car or off in a ditch somewhere, freezing to death. So I called the police department. Luke was pulling a late shift, covering for a friend. He and I met up and I told him what was going on with Grammy Claire.

"Luke ended up driving around for two hours and found out from making some calls that she was having a late-night movie marathon at Esther Mansfield's house. Esther's a widow Grammy Claire met at church, so I don't know her all that well. Esther also doesn't drive, so she let Grammy Claire park her car in her garage because of the weather, which is why Luke didn't see her car when he and nearly every cop in the damn town did a sweep looking for her."

"Ouch."

"Yes. I was furious with her for not telling me where she was going. Her response? 'I'm a grown woman, Samantha. I don't believe I need to tell you my whereabouts every second of the day.'"

Reid tilted his head back and laughed, hard.

Samantha stared at him. "Not funny, Reid."

He grinned at her. "Yeah, it is. I'll bet Luke thought it was funny, too."

"First he was relieved. Then, yes, he thought it was funny. I was not amused. And after much lecturing and back-and-forth arguing, I convinced my grandmother that she needs to let me know when she's going out and where she's going."

"It really is like having a teenager, isn't it?"

She sighed and took a long swallow of wine, reliving that night of panic all over again. "I may never have children. And it's all Grammy Claire's fault."

"Oh, come on. Surely kids couldn't be as bad as all that."

"Ha. They're probably worse. Now tell me about your day."

"Nothing special about it. My brothers and I met with the contractor—Deacon Fox. Do you know him?"

"Of course. He's going to work on the project with you?"

"Yeah."

"Awesome. When does demo start?"

"Deacon and I will meet with the engineer tomorrow to finalize the plans, so demo will likely start the day after. Why? Thinking of getting your hands dirty?"

Her lips curved. "I'd love to. Living here in an older home that, as you can tell, could use some serious renovating, gives me all kinds of ideas."

Reid took a glance around the room. "Yeah? What kinds of ideas?"

"I'd love to tear out that wall separating the kitchen from the living room. The dining room is useless because I don't use it. If I opened all that up, I could have a bigger kitchen and living room. Think of the space I could use for entertaining. The cabinetry in the kitchen is fine, but it's outdated and there's no pantry. I really need a pantry, along with updated appliances. I'd also kill for a double oven and a microwave that doesn't sit on the counter, because that eats up my already limited counter space. Plus I love these hardwood floors, but they need resurfacing. Not to mention the HVAC system. I need a new heater and a new air conditioner. It's freezing in the winter and boiling hot in the summer."

It finally dawned on her that he was staring at her.

"I'm boring you."

"Actually, you're not. I'm mentally creating a design for revised space while you're talking."

"No way."

His lips curved. "Yes way."

"Really? That's amazing. I'll be right back."

She dashed into the kitchen, opened a drawer and pulled out a notebook and a pencil, then hurried back into the living room. "Will this help?"

"Sure."

He started sketching, and she took a seat next to him. It was fascinating to watch him draw, to see his imagination take fruit in lines and visuals of a cabinet here, an island there. Suddenly there were no walls, and he'd created new space with furniture and fixtures, and as he asked questions and she answered them, her dreams for this house were drawn on paper in brilliant life.

"It's a crude rendition, but I think you get the idea."

She blinked several times, unable to believe what she saw there. "It's perfect. It's exactly how I envision it. How do you do that?"

He laughed. "It's my job. Besides, this isn't my best work. I could draw it out for you in more official form if you're interested."

"I'd love it, but I can't really afford a renovation right now. Still, I appreciate you helping me to visualize what's been in my head for a while. This makes it seem more real, like it could actually happen someday."

"Oh, it could definitely happen. You have the space here. It just needs to be shifted in a few areas."

"Yeah. Shifted." And now that she'd seen what was possible, she wanted it even more.

Someday.

"Come on into the kitchen with me. I'll make the salad and spaghetti and we'll eat. You're probably starving."

"I am hungry."

He followed her into the kitchen. She made the salad and the spaghetti and took the bread out of the oven. Reid carved the bread while she mixed the meat sauce with the noodles, then Reid helped her carry everything into the dining room.

"This would be so much more informal if I had an eating area in the kitchen," she said as they dug in to the spaghetti.

"Or, with just two people, on your new island."

She waved her fork at him. "Don't tease me like that, Reid McCormack."

He laughed. "Sorry. But what you want is doable, Samantha."

"Not right now, it isn't. My budget is stretched pretty tight. And call me Sam."

"Okay, Sam. And I understand. Something to put on your back burner for someday."

"I've got a lot of those someday projects stored in my To-Do drawer."

He scooped up some pasta and slid it between his lips while she tried her best not to focus on his mouth. So instead she kept her head down and ate.

"You have a To-Do drawer?"

She lifted her gaze to his. "I do."

"Okay, now I'm interested. What's in there?"

"Secret projects and wishes for . . . someday."

"Don't I get even a hint?"

He'd likely laugh at some of the notes and scraps of paper and things in that drawer. She often wrote down wishes and put them in the drawer. Some were things she wanted to remember, others were items she jotted down just to put pen to paper, to remind herself of what was important to her on a certain date. She'd go through the drawer once a year and pull out the scraps of paper in there, checking to see if each item was still a priority. If it was, it stayed. If it wasn't, it got tossed. A lot of things remained in there for a long time.

"I want a dog . . . someday."

"You have a pretty great yard with a fence. Why can't you have one now?"

She shrugged. "Between work and Grammy Claire, that's enough to handle right now. I don't think it would be fair to leave a dog alone by itself all day long, then some nights as well."

"Oh, nights. Because of your active dating life, you mean."

She actually snorted out a laugh at that one. "Uh, no. Because I'm often over at my grandmother's house."

He cocked a brow. "You should be out with men."

"Tell that to my runaway grandmother."

He laughed.

They finished eating, and Sam pushed her plate to the side while Reid poured her another glass of wine. She thought about getting up to clear the table, then decided she'd enjoy the wine before she tackled dishes.

"So you're telling me there's no steady man in your life?"

She swirled the wine around in her glass, wondering if he was making idle conversation or if he'd asked the question because he was interested in knowing the answer for personal reasons. "No steady or occasional or otherwise. I was serious about my plate being pretty full right now. Grammy Claire enjoys her independence, but she can't do everything for herself. I do her grocery shopping and I go over there once a week to clean her house. And I know she's lonely after Grandpa's death, so I try to hang out with her at least a couple of times a week. More than just a drop in to say hello and check on her. There isn't anyone else around, family-wise. It's just her and me now. She essentially raised me after my parents died, so she's all I have left."

"Which makes you want to spend as much time with her as you can," Reid said. "I know exactly how you feel. I wish I'd had more time with my dad."

"You miss him."

"Every day."

She couldn't imagine not having Grammy Claire in her life. As much of a pain in the butt as her grandma was sometimes, she was still her family. Her only family. She loved her dearly.

They took all of the dishes into the kitchen, and, since she didn't have a dishwasher—one of her biggest complaints about her kitchen—she loaded everything into the sink.

Reid rolled up his shirtsleeves and started running water into the sink.

"Oh no. Leave those. I'll take care of them later."

He arched a brow. "You cooked. I'll clean up."

"I don't think so. I invited you to dinner. Not to do the dishes."

She tried to nudge him aside, but she might as well have tried to move a boulder. He didn't budge. Instead, he already had the scrubber in his hand, ignoring her.

"Fine," she finally said, giving up on trying to shove him aside. "I'll put the food away."

They worked in tandem, and she couldn't recall the last time any man had ever helped her with the dishes.

It was probably . . .

No. Never.

Once she took care of the food and handed him the pots and pans to wash, she grabbed a dish towel to dry and put away the dishes. Having Reid around to help was awesome. She'd have spent a half hour or longer in here doing this by herself later tonight. Instead, they were finished in fifteen minutes.

Reid dried his hands. "See? That wasn't so painful, was it?"

She hung up the towel. "You didn't have to do that."

"I wanted to. And thank you for dinner. The spaghetti was amazing. I love a home-cooked meal."

She laughed. "You get plenty of those at the ranch. Martha is an incredible cook."

"That she is. It's one of the things I'm going to enjoy the most while I'm here in Hope. I don't get a lot of home cooking in Boston."

They made their way back into the dining room and took a seat. Reid poured them both another glass of wine.

"Surely you cook."

"Not really. I work a lot of late nights, which means either microwaved meals, sandwiches, or takeout."

Sam wrinkled her nose. "Takeout is fine once in a while. I like to eat at interesting restaurants now and then, but I really enjoy cooking. Oh, and speaking of interesting restaurants, did you know that Bash Palmer is adding an eatery to his bar?"

Reid nodded. "He told me about that when I was in town for Des and Logan's wedding. I actually drew up some plans for him for . . ."

She waited for him to finish his sentence. He didn't. "You drew up plans for what?"

"I helped him refine his plans for the restaurant in the No Hope at All bar. I think it's going to be great."

Somehow she got that wasn't what he was initially going to say, that there was something else he'd drawn up plans for for Bash. But maybe it was a secret and she wasn't supposed to know about it.

She made a mental note to ask Bash's fiancée, Chelsea, about that later. "I agree. They've already started construction on it."

"I'll have to drop by and take a look at the progress. It's going to be an awesome addition to his bar."

"Agreed. And speaking of all things awesome, how about those blueprints for the mercantile?"

"Oh, right. That is why you invited me over here tonight, wasn't it?"

Not the only reason, but she definitely wanted to see his plans. "Definitely."

"They're in the truck. Let me go get them."

She sat back and finished her glass of wine.

This night had been . . . unexpected. Reid had been unexpected.

She liked him, a lot. He was open and fun to talk to. He'd sketched out a blueprint for a kitchen, dining room, and living room renovation for her without her even asking.

The man even did dishes.

Clearly there had to be something unlikable about him.

Maybe he had weird chest hair or something, though she'd never know that unless she got his shirt off.

She poured herself another glass of wine and pondered that thought with some serious imagery.

Chapter 4

REID GRABBED THE blueprints from his truck and came back inside to find Samantha—Sam—still sitting at the dining room table.

She was so pretty, in a very distracting kind of way. She had on tight jeans that molded to her curves and a long-sleeved shirt that pressed against her breasts, making him very aware it had been all too long since he'd held a woman.

Damn work had taken over all his time, including his free time, effectively putting an end to his dating life. After his breakup with Britt, he'd sworn off women for a while, and by the time he'd been ready to get back into dating again, work had consumed him.

He wasn't about to date anyone while he was in Hope. It would be a waste of time, since he had no intention of staying here. This project would last a couple of months at most, and then he'd be back in Boston again.

Plus, he knew almost everyone here, and the last thing he'd need is broken hearts and bitterness from people he'd like to think were his friends.

Still, here he was, spreading out blueprints on Samantha

Reasor's dining room table while she got up and moved in next to him, her shoulder brushing against his.

She smelled good. Something musky and intoxicating, and he really shouldn't be thinking of her as a woman he'd like to touch or kiss or anything along those lines at all. What he should be thinking about was that she was very nice and she'd cooked him dinner and she wanted to see the project blueprints.

And that was all he intended to show her tonight. Or any night.

He spread the blueprints out on the table. "Okay, so I'm not sure you'll be able to see—"

"Oh, so this is the first floor. I see what you're doing here. If I recall correctly, there are currently walls here and here. You're removing those and opening up this area on the main floor, right? Adding columns here, putting in a bathroom there." She scanned the blueprints, flipping pages as she moved floors. "Interesting office space on these floors. You've allowed for expansive space. Some larger offices, some smaller."

She knew exactly what the layout was. He looked over at her. "Blueprints are confusing as hell even for an architect or contractor. I'm impressed."

She shrugged. "It's not that hard if you read between the lines. Or rather, where the lines aren't anymore, right?"

"That's correct."

"So what are your plans for the first floor?"

"First we'll take down the walls and the old ceiling. Remember the tin tile ceiling we got a peek at underneath the dropped one?"

"Yes. It's magnificent. I can't wait to see it."

"Me, too. Once we have everything opened up, we'll take a look at the electrical and plumbing, as well as the heating and air-conditioning systems. I'm sure those will all need an over-haul. It'll be a step-by-step process from the ground up. Once we know what we're working with, we'll see what we can do with it. But I'd like the main floor to be completely open."

"And then there's upstairs."

"Yeah. A lot to do up there, especially plumbing-wise.

Architecturally it's a gold mine." He explained the concept of the office spaces he'd planned for floors two and three, and how much space he'd carved out for those floors. "But first we have a lot of teardown to do. Floors will need to be replaced on the two upper floors. The elevator is a death trap, so that'll need extensive repair. We have to add in plumbing for the new bathrooms upstairs. Well, downstairs, too. Windows will have to be brought up to this century, so those will have to be replaced on all three floors."

She swirled wine around in her glass and patiently listened to him talk as he gave her a list of everything they were going to do.

He finally stopped and stared at her. "This isn't boring for you?"

"Are you kidding? I'm so impressed, and I have to tell you, more than a little excited. Also, I have to tell you that your eyes light up when you talk about the mercantile."

"Is that right?"

"Yes. You're like a kid in a candy shop, except the candy is all locked up in the case right now and the key is lost."

His lips curved. "Something like that."

He also realized it had been all about him most of the night. "Tell me about the flower shop, Sam."

"Oh. Well, that isn't nearly as interesting as what you do."

"I don't agree. You're a business owner. That must be fun for you."

"Actually, it is. Grammy Claire owned the shop, and when she retired, I took it over. It's been a family business for as long as I've been alive. My mom worked there, too, until she and dad died in the car accident."

"I'm sorry about your parents."

"Thank you. I don't really even remember them. I was three when it happened, and Grammy Claire and Grandpa Bob raised me."

"I'm glad you had them. It must have been so hard for you."

"I remember so little of it. I just remember my grandparents. I know that I've always felt like there was something missing in my life. Grammy Claire and Grandpa Bob were older, you know? But they did their best in raising me, in giving me everything they thought I needed. And Grammy Claire was the absolute best at being a mother to me, in giving me the guidance every mother should give a daughter. She may be my grandmother, but she's been the perfect mother."

He knew what it was like to grow up without a mother's influence. But he was a guy, so he had managed it just fine. A girl needed her mother. At least Sam had had her grandmother. And from what he was hearing, a damn good mother, too.

"It's why you're so close to your grandmother."

"Yes. She's been like a mother to me. I don't know what I would have done without her and my grandfather."

"It's good to have people in your life who love and support you."

"Yes. You know what that's like. I know you had issues with your mom, but you had your dad while he was alive."

"Yeah. He was the rock of the family for sure. And we had Martha managing the ranch house. After our mother took a hike and divorced our dad, Martha and her husband Ben stepped up in a big way. They filled the gap my mom left."

She smiled at that. "Martha's amazing. We all love her."

He laughed. "Everyone does."

And this was venturing into way personal territory, when he'd meant for the night to be light and easy. He stood. "Well, tomorrow's an early day for me. Probably for you, too."

Sam got up as well. "I'm sorry. I shouldn't have kept you here so late."

"Not a big deal. I enjoyed it. Thanks for the invite."

He gathered up the blueprints and headed to the door, then turned to her. "Thanks for dinner, Sam."

"You're welcome. Thanks for giving me a peek at the blueprints. I'm looking forward to seeing what you do with the mercantile."

She leaned against the doorway, the two of them close. Closer than he'd been to a woman in a while.

God, she was pretty. And she smelled really good, and he really needed to get out the damn door before he did something stupid like haul her into his arms and kiss her.

"Night, Sam."

"Good night, Reid."

He walked to his truck and got in, shutting the door firmly behind him. He stared down the street. It was a nice street. An older, established neighborhood with a lot of tall, well-filled-in trees. The kind of neighborhood where you knew people had lived there a lot of years and everyone knew each other. He could imagine Sam really liked living there.

He'd had a good time tonight. He hadn't expected to fall so easily into conversation with Sam. To like talking to her, to enjoy spending time with her.

His last relationship had ended in disaster, and he'd sworn then he wasn't going to do another one. He'd gone out with women—one-or-two-date-only kinds of things, and that was it. No emotional attachments, no feelings involved.

Tonight he'd felt energized and excited and, for the first time in a long time—attracted.

That wasn't going to do. First, because he didn't live here, and second, because he swore he was never going to have those kinds of feelings again. Not after what had happened with Britt. Even though two years had passed, he still wore the scars of that relationship and didn't intend to ever let a woman stomp all over his heart again.

He started up the truck and drove away.

Chapter 5

TWO DAYS LATER, Reid was up well before dawn, figuring no one would be awake on the ranch.

He was wrong. When he came downstairs, Logan, Ben, and Martha were already in the kitchen. There was a full pot of coffee, and Martha was already cooking breakfast.

"I thought I'd be alone when I came down," he said as he headed over to grab a cup of coffee.

Logan shot him a look. "Man, you have been gone a long time if you've forgotten what time everybody gets up around here."

Ben looked up from where he sat at the table with a cup of coffee. "Ranchin' doesn't start at noon, boy."

Reid pulled up a spot at the table and laughed. "Yes. It's all coming back to me now. Dad rousing us when it was still dark outside to go out to the barn and saddle the horses. I was barely tall enough to get up on a horse back then."

"Gotta start 'em young, kid," Ben said. "Best time to learn that ranchin' work ethic."

"So I was told. More than once." Reid took a couple long swallows of the strong brew and winced. Ranch coffee wasn't anything like what you got at the downtown coffee shops in Boston. But he'd be damn well awake by the time he got to Hope.

"Got your crew ready for teardown today?" Logan asked.

"Yeah. Deacon and his men will meet me there."

"You plannin' on digging in and helping, or are you gonna play supervisor?" Martha asked as she laid a plate of eggs and bacon in front of him.

"Thanks, Martha. Normally I supervise a project, but this one I'm intending to dig into."

"Can't say as I blame you," Logan said. "Lots to do there, plus the sooner you get finished, the sooner you can get back to your fancy Boston digs."

Reid laughed. "It's more about what's underneath the layers of dust and debris and old fixings than getting back to Boston. And yeah, I do have a company to get back to."

"But you have someone you trust taking care of business on the Boston end, don't you?" Martha asked.

"Yes. My vice president is someone I trust completely, and he's got things well in hand during my absence."

After serving everyone their food, Martha grabbed her plate and took a seat next to him. "That has to offer you some sense of comfort."

Reid scooped eggs onto his fork. "It does. At least I know my business won't fold while I'm gone. Tim and I will be on the phone and text and e-mail frequently so I can stay on top of what's going on there."

"Peace of mind's important," Logan said. "You can't be gone from work without knowing what's going on. Otherwise it'll drive you crazy."

"Says the man who called once a day from Paris when you were supposed to be on vacation with your wife." Ben shot Logan a look.

Logan shrugged. "Like I said, peace of mind is important."

Reid laughed. He knew how important the ranch was to Logan. Though Reid and Luke were part owners in the ranch, it was Logan who had stayed and worked the ranch after their father died. Logan's life was ranching. He loved it like it was part of his soul. Ranching had never been something Reid had wanted to do. He was glad their family ranching business had been in Logan's blood. At least it would be passed on to future McCormack generations through Logan. And maybe even Luke and his wife, Emma, would someday have kids and those kids would want in on the family ranching business.

Reid, though? No way. He didn't intend to ever get married. He'd gotten close once, and that had cost him emotionally.

They all finished breakfast around the same time, so he grabbed his bag and walked out with Logan.

"Thanks for letting me stay here," he said. "I'm sorry it coincided with Des coming home. I don't mean to infringe on your reunion with your wife."

Logan frowned. "First, you're family and you're not infringing. This is your home and it always will be. Des and I have plenty of time to be by ourselves. Second, we have a bedroom with a door that locks if we want to be alone."

Reid shook his head. "And that's all the conversation I want to have about that."

"Me, too."

Several of the dogs trotted over for their morning scratches. Reid knew all the dogs. Some had been on the ranch for several years. But there was a new one that came up and pushed against him, a fine-looking brown and white mix. He bent to pet it.

"Who's this?" he asked Logan.

"No idea. He showed up here a few weeks back. He typically hangs back and doesn't let anyone pet him, but we've been feeding him. You're the first one he's allowed to get near him. I'm kind of surprised."

Reid looked down at the dog. "Aren't you just the finest damn dog I've ever seen?" He looked young, not more than a year old or so.

"Someone probably dumped him on the side of the road and he made his way here to the ranch," Logan said. "You know how it goes."

Reid nodded. "Yeah, I know how it goes."

A lot of people got dogs, then either decided they didn't want them or the dog didn't have the right temperament, so instead of trying to find a new home for them, they dumped them. It made Reid's blood pressure rise. He was glad Logan and Des took this one in.

He stood. "I'm headed out."

"Okay," Logan said. "See you later."

He headed toward the truck. The dog followed. "Sorry, dude. You have to stay here."

He opened the truck door and the dog jumped in.

"I don't think so, buddy. Out."

The dog settled in on the passenger seat and laid down.

"Oh, no. This isn't happening." He went over to the passenger side of the truck and opened the door. "Out."

The dog closed his eyes and went to sleep.

"Goddammit."

Logan laughed. "Looks like you have a traveling partner for the day."

Reid rolled his eyes. "Great."

Logan went over to the front porch and grabbed a leash from the hook, tossing it at Reid. With a grin, he said, "You two have fun today."

"Yeah, thanks."

He put his bag on the floor of the truck, shut the passenger door, and glared at the dog.

"Okay, buddy, let's get one thing straight. You are not my dog."

The dog snored at him.

With a sigh, Reid climbed into the truck, started it up, and drove off toward Hope.

SAM WAS THREE-QUARTERS of the way through a very complex floral arrangement when her cell phone beeped. It was on the counter, she had her fingers twisted in wire, and the phone was just going to have to wait.

When she finished, she stood back and admired her work.

Coral roses woven with white gardenias and just enough greenery to touch the arrangement off.

"Mark, your girlfriend is going to die of happiness," she said out loud. He'd told her what Annaleigh's favorite flowers were, so she'd managed to make a bouquet for Annaleigh's surprise birthday party centerpiece. It was huge and spectacular, and Mark would be there in a half hour to pick it up for the party tonight.

She had a spare minute to check her phone. It was a text from Megan.

Have you been over to the mercantile yet today? Dying to know what's going on there.

She typed back. No. Busy doing flower stuff. Might walk over later to check things out. Wanna come?

Megan texted back. Can't. Cakes in the oven. Report back!

She replied that she would, then hurriedly finished another order before Mark showed up. She had just finished the planter basket when Mark came in. He was super happy with the flowers and told her Annaleigh would love them. After he paid and left, she finished the planter basket and loaded it into her van for delivery, along with several other orders. It took her about a half hour to make her deliveries. By the time she came back, she was hungry for lunch, so she closed the shop and walked down the street toward the mercantile.

Busy place. Several trucks were parked outside, and a giant Dumpster had been delivered at the back entrance. And tethered to one of the outside poles on the porch was the cutest dog she'd ever seen. He looked like some kind of mix of several breeds that she couldn't make out. He was mostly brown, with white between his eyes, on his muzzle, and on his chest. He was lying down, clearly surveying people as they walked by. She approached cautiously, wanting to make sure he wasn't a guard dog. He didn't get up, didn't bark, just watched her come closer. He lifted his head and wagged his tail as she sat next to him and ran her hand over his head and scratched his ears.

"Aren't you the cutest thing? Do you belong to one of Deacon's guys?"

The dog laid his head against her hand as she petted him. It was instant love for Sam, who could have spent the remainder of the day parked right there with that adorable dog.

But just then she heard footsteps on the porch. She turned around and tried to keep her tongue from falling out of her mouth.

As an architect, she had always thought of Reid in business suits.

Right now he wore low-slung jeans, a dark brown T-shirt stained with dirt and sweat. He was sweaty. How could sweaty be so darn sexy? He also had a tool belt strapped to his hips. She'd never seen anyone look hotter.

"Hey, Sam."

She stood and swiped her damp palms on her hands.

Trying to find her suddenly absent vocal cords, she managed to clear her throat. "Hey yourself. I was just petting . . . Uh, is this your dog?"

"No. Not my dog. According to Logan, he wandered onto the ranch a few weeks ago and stayed. This morning he jumped into my truck and refused to get out. So I guess he's my assistant for the day. As you can see, he's pretty useless so far."

She laughed. "Well, he's pretty."

"Come on, don't tell him that. He'll get an ego."

She looked over at the dog, who barely raised his head to drink sloppily out of the nearby water bowl.

"I was just about to take him for a walk so he could stretch his legs," Reid said. "What are you up to?"

"Lunch break. I could walk with you, if you don't mind."

"I don't mind."

He unhooked the dog's leash, and they stepped off the porch. "I'm actually kind of hungry myself."

"Okay. How about a sandwich from Louis's sandwich shop around the corner? I could run in and get them and we could eat outside since it's a nice day."

"Sure."

They walked side by side, and Samantha tried not to notice Reid's long strides, or the way he and the dog seemed so compatible. The dog might not be his, but that dog stayed right next to him as if they'd been best pals for a lifetime.

"What's the dog's name?"

"No idea. As far as I know he doesn't have one."

"Poor thing. Was he abandoned?"

"I think so."

She grimaced. "I hate people who do that."

"So do I."

Larry Hubble, the owner of the hardware store, stuck his head out as they walked by. "Hey, Sam. Hi, Reid. How goes the teardown at the mercantile?"

They stopped. "Hi, Larry," Reid said. "Going well so far, thanks."

"Nice dog, Reid."

"Thanks. It's not my dog."

Larry looked down at the dog and grinned. "He's pretty great."

"See you later, Larry," Sam said.

They passed several people on the way to the sandwich shop. As was typical for downtown Hope, a lot of people were out at lunchtime. Though Reid had been gone since college, no one had forgotten him. People never forgot those who'd grown up and gone to school in Hope. Once you belonged, you always belonged. Plus, word had gotten out that the McCormack brothers had bought the mercantile. Everyone knew Reid was going to be working there, so they expected to see him in town.

Sam ran in to the sandwich shop and ordered them two turkey sandwiches while Reid took the dog over to the park for a quick walk around. While she was inside, Walter and Daisy Louis, the owners, asked her questions about the mercantile and about Reid. She told them she knew nothing; that she had stopped by to get a peek inside at the progress but hadn't seen anything yet.

Walter and Daisy were just as interested and excited about the mercantile as she was.

Once she got the sandwiches, she and Reid ate outside at one of the tables. The dog sat next to Reid's feet, perfectly calm and content to watch people walk by.

"He's well trained," she said as she kept her eye on the dog. "Walks great on the leash, and is very obedient."

"Yeah. Someone had a pretty damn good dog on their hands and let him go. Some people are morons."

"Yes, they are."

She opened the fruit salad she'd ordered with her sandwich. "How's everything going this morning?"

"It's . . . dusty."

She laughed. "I can imagine. Are you making progress?"

He swallowed and nodded. "We started at the back of the first floor. It's moving along well. So far, no surprises, which is a good thing."

She reached across and swiped at his jaw with her thumb. "You had a streak of dirt."

His gaze made contact with hers, and it was like she'd been struck by an electric shock so hard it made her toes curl and all the parts in her middle clench with desire. There was plenty of moisture in the air thanks to the recent rain, so she couldn't chalk it up to static electricity.

But it was definitely electric, as was the way Reid looked at her.

Finally, he grinned. "Yeah, plenty of dirt on me today, and probably will be for a while."

"It suits you."

He arched a brow. "Dirt suits me?"

"Yes. It's sexy."

He laughed. "First time I've heard that. I'm sexy dirty, huh?"

More like dirty and sexy. She took a bite of her sandwich and decided she should shut up before her mouth got her into trouble.

"I'd like to take a look at the building after we eat, if that's okay," she said.

"Nothing much to see. If possible, it's even dirtier than me, and there's more junk, wood, nails, and debris scattered around than there was before. Plus, it's not really safe."

He looked down at her slip-on pink Chucks, capris, and white polo shirt. "Trust me. You're not dressed for demolition."

"Darn. I didn't get the memo about the dress code or I'd have worn my boots today."

His lips curved. "They don't go with your outfit."

"They do go with my favorite short skirt, though."

"Now that I'd like to see," he said.

He cocked his head to the side, sliding her a look she could only describe as pure heat. Her insides nearly melted from his gaze.

The way he looked at her made her really want to wear that short skirt with her boots. She could already imagine . . .

Well. She could imagine a lot of things that had her feeling all melty.

After lunch, he walked her back to the flower shop.

"Back to work for both of us, I guess," she said.

"Yeah. Thanks for taking time out of your day to have lunch with me."

"Hey, anytime. Next time I'll bring my boots with me, so I can take a look at the inside of the mercantile."

"You do that. See you later, Sam."

"Sure. Later, Reid."

REID WATCHED SAM walk inside her shop, then exhaled, trying not to lean into her, to breathe in the smell of violets or whatever flower scent that seemed to cling to her.

While he smelled like dirt and sweat and God only knew what. Some lunch companion he was.

Though he probably smelled better than the dog, and Sam had been hugging all over him when he walked outside. He looked down at the dog, who stared up at him expectantly.

"What? I know Logan fed you this morning, and I put water out for you. We've had a walk."

The dog continued to stare.

"If you're looking for me to throw a ball or something, you're out of luck, buddy. It's back to work for me, and back to the porch for you. If you'd stayed on the ranch, you could be chasing rabbits right now."

The dog stared up at him with eyes of pure love. And if possible, he was certain the dog smiled at him.

Reid didn't get it.

He started back toward the mercantile, and the dog stayed right in step with him. Reid shook his head. This dog was well trained, able to walk on a leash.

What was wrong with people who just abandoned dogs like they were trash? He'd like to find the person who did it and have a really intense . . . conversation with them.

Deacon pulled up in his truck right as Reid made it back to the mercantile. He climbed out of the truck, a bag in one hand and a drink in the other.

"Fast food?" Reid asked as he sat on the top step. The dog settled in next to him.

Deacon took a spot on the other side of Reid and opened the bag, pulling out a carton. "Salad and green tea."

"Dude. Really?"

"Clean living, my man. You should try it."

"I had no idea you were into the healthy lifestyle."

Deacon shrugged. "I run and I try to avoid eating too much red meat. Trying not to drop dead at forty-five like my old man did."

"Yeah, I understand." Reid knew that Deacon's father had had heart problems for a long time, and he recalled how hard it had hit Deacon when his father had died. Though they'd always known Deacon's dad's heart was in trouble, losing him at such a young age had impacted Deacon— obviously more than even Reid had been aware of. Deacon tried to act like it didn't matter, but Reid knew it did.

"You're healthy, you know."

Deacon nodded. "I know. Plan to stay that way, too." He motioned to his salad. "That's why I eat all this shitty rabbit food."

Reid laughed. "So you're saying what you really wanted for lunch was a greasy hamburger."

Deacon sighed and stabbed at the salad. "I don't even want to think about it. Tell me about your lunch with the pretty Samantha Reasor."

He didn't even know Deacon had seen him with Sam. "Saw that, did you?"

"Dude, everyone sees everything in this town. You should remember that from junior year in high school when you and I got caught trying to sneak out of the gym during third period."

Reid glared at him. "That was your fault. You had a hard-on for Hailey Redmond over at Hope High and wanted to take her to lunch, and somehow I let you con me into going with you."

Deacon grinned. "Yeah. Hailey was hot."

"But those two weeks of after-school detention weren't. Plus my dad was pissed as hell."

"Mine, too. That was even worse than the detention. Still, Hailey was worth it."

"That's because you would've done anything to get laid. You probably still would."

Deacon leveled a smug smile at him. "I don't have to work so hard at it these days."

Reid laughed. "Whatever, stud. Finish your damn rabbit food and let's get back to work."

Reid brushed himself off, refilled the dog's water bowl, then headed back inside to continue demolition.

Chapter 6

AFTER A LONG-ASS, tiring day, Reid headed back to his family's ranch. The first thing he needed was a long, hot shower.

No. Correct that. First thing he wanted was a beer. Then a shower.

He got out of the truck. The dog followed, staying by his side.

"Seriously? Go get a drink. Hang out with your friends."

The other dogs came over to greet Reid, so there was a lot of petting and head-scratching. Then they all ran off.

Except the dog that was not his dog. He stayed there.

"Go on. Go play."

The dog finally sighed, then wandered off. Reid shook his head and walked up the steps, kicked off his filthy boots on the porch, and went inside, straight for the kitchen, where amazing smells greeted him.

"Oh, man, is it pot roast night?" he asked Martha.

"It is." Martha pulled her gaze from the carrots she was chopping to give him the once-over. "You're filthy. Productive day?"

"Very." He headed to the refrigerator and grabbed a can of beer.

"I'm going to assume you'll be showering before dinner."

"Yes, ma'am. I need a beer first."

"Of course you do. Now you can drink it out on the front porch."

Martha was no-nonsense about her rules, and her number one rule was you didn't drag your day's worth of dirt into her kitchen, especially when she was cooking.

"I'm out the door right now."

"You might as well grab another beer for Logan. I hear his truck pulling up out front."

She also had very good hearing, which hadn't boded well for them when they were kids. Reid's mother had ignored pretty much everything he and his brother had done as long as they didn't bother her. Martha, on the other hand, heard and saw everything, especially if it involved trouble.

She had also loved them more than their mother ever had, which was why he'd always thought of her as his mother more than he ever had his own.

There wasn't a day that went by that he wasn't grateful for her presence in his life.

He reached into the fridge for another beer, then kissed Martha on the cheek as he walked by.

She scrubbed her face. "Now I'm all dirty. And you stink."

He laughed. "I promise to shower as soon as I finish this beer."

"You'd better. You smell like you spent the day shoveling cow manure."

"Love you, Martha."

She laughed. "Love you, too, Reid."

He stepped out onto the front porch and set the extra beer on the railing, then grabbed a seat, popped open his can, and propped his feet up. The dog who was not his dog came over and wagged his tail, then sat beside him. With a sigh, Reid scratched the dog's head.

Logan was talking to Ben, who waved to Reid before heading off behind the house. Logan walked up the steps.

"Is that your second beer?" Logan asked, nodding toward the one Reid had set on the railing.

"No. It's for you, but now that you mention it, two sounds pretty good."

Logan snatched it up and took a seat next to him. "Too bad. It's mine now. You'll have to go inside and get another."

"Martha won't let me."

Logan nodded. "Because you're covered in dirt. From the looks of you, demo must have gone well."

"We tore out the dropped ceiling, pulled the cabinets, and dragged out most of the broken-down furniture and old boxes from the first floor today. The tile flooring still needs to come up—"

"Which is always a bitch," Logan said.

"Yeah." Reid took a long swallow of his beer. "We'll start tackling that tomorrow."

"What's your timeline for this project?"

"About eight to twelve weeks if everything goes well. I'm hoping to be closer to the eight-week side."

Logan took a swig of his beer and nodded. "Anxious to get back to Boston?"

"I do have a company to run."

"Yeah, I understand. But you have good people there, right?"

"I have good people there. Still, it's not like being there to do it myself."

"I know that feeling. I can't imagine not being here to run the place, but between Des, Martha, and Ben, they've convinced me I'm allowed to take some time off."

"How was Paris? And the Mediterranean cruise?"

Logan's lips ticked up. "They were good. Only because Des was there."

The screen door opened and Des herself walked out. Even in jeans and a plain white T-shirt, the woman still looked like a movie star. Her dark hair was pulled into a high ponytail and she wore black canvas tennis shoes, but there was something about her that was innately beautiful and glamorous.

"Did I hear my name?" she asked as she made her way out to the porch. She leaned over to kiss Logan. "I heard you drive up. How did it go today?"

"Good. How about you?"

She took a seat in the chair across from theirs. "Read through some scripts. Found a couple interesting ones."

"Yeah? Which ones?"

"The drama and the action adventure. That was the one you were interested in."

"I can't wait for you to tell me about them later."

It was interesting to watch the dynamic between his older brother and Des. If someone had told Reid that someday Logan would end up married to an A-list actress, Reid would have laughed at them. If you looked up *stone-faced loner* in the dictionary, Logan's picture would have been right next to it. But Des brought Logan out of his shell, and he was more animated and friendly now than Reid could ever remember.

Des dragged her gaze away from Reid's brother and onto him. "How about your day, Reid? How was the first day at the mercantile?"

"Dirty and dusty."

Des laughed. "Yes, I can see that. I can't wait to drive into town to check it out. I love that old building. Ever since Logan told me about you all buying it, I've been to town several times to check it out. It has some amazing history attached to it."

"That it does. I did a little research at the library, and got some information from the historical society. The mercantile has been everything from a mercantile—of course—to a speakeasy to an auction house to a movie theater."

Des moved over to where Logan sat and nestled down in the seat with him. He smiled in appreciation at her move and put his arm around her. "Really? That's fascinating."

"Yeah. I got the historical society to help us out by copying some of the older photos from over the years. I plan to blow them up, re-create them in black-and-white, frame them, and put them in some of the common areas of the building, along with information placards informing of the history of the building."

Des sighed. "I love that idea."

"It's good to keep the history of the place in the forefront," Logan said. "Keeps it from just being some old building."

"That's what I thought as well."

"I can't wait to see you perform your magic on it," Des said.

"I don't know about magic, but we'll see what happens."

"Either way, I sure am glad you're hanging around for a while, both in Hope and here at the ranch."

"Thanks, Des. It's nice to be home again."

"Oh, speaking of home . . . So I'm planning a dinner party for Saturday night. Just a few couples, some drinks, dinner, fun. You know."

"And you'd like me to make myself scarce? Not a problem."

She laughed. "No. Not at all. We'd like you to be here for it. It's a couples thing, though. Can you bring a date?"

"Uh . . . a date?"

"Sure. You know . . . a girl. Or a guy, if that's your thing."

"Girls are my thing. I'm just not dating anyone. Not here. Not anywhere, actually."

"I can set you up with someone."

"No." He said the word kind of forcefully, causing Logan to laugh.

Des looked over at Logan. "What?"

"He's kind of old for a blind date, isn't he?" Logan asked.

"He is not. And I know a lot of amazing single women in town."

"I'll get my own date, but thanks."

"So that's a yes? Awesome." She got up and kissed Reid on the cheek. "I'm going inside to see if Martha needs any help. You should both grab a shower before dinner."

After Des went inside, Reid sipped his beer and stared out over the property.

"Where the hell are you gonna get a date?" Logan asked.

He'd known it was coming. "I know people. Women people."

"So you're gonna call one of our cousins?"

Reid glared at Logan. "No. I'm not going to call one of the cousins. I'm going to call a woman who isn't related to us. Because I know women."

Logan let out a laugh and took a couple of long swallows of his beer. "Sure you do. I'm going to go take a shower."

"Right behind you."

Reid finished his beer, crushed the can in his hand, and lingered for a few minutes longer.

He could get a date. Somewhere.

Maybe.

Chapter 7

SAMANTHA HAD THREE birthday bouquets and four dozen bouquets of roses to finish up today for anniversaries. She also had to deliver two plants and three bouquets of flowers to Hope Hospital, along with a deluxe spray for a funeral. It was a very busy day.

She was working in the back room when she heard the door chime, so she wiped her hands and headed out front, surprised to see Reid standing at the counter. With the same dog he'd had the other day. The dog sat obediently by Reid's feet.

"Hey, Reid. I see you brought your dog again."

"Hi, Sam. He's not my dog."

She tried her best not to smile, but failed. "Of course he's not. How's it going today?"

"Busy like you wouldn't believe."

She looked him over from head to booted feet, admittedly enjoying the view. "You don't look as dirty as you did the other day. I take that to mean demolition is moving along more smoothly?"

His lips ticked up. "I guess it is. But I managed to wipe down the dust before I headed this way."

"What brings you to my store?"

"Uh . . . I need to ask you a question."

"Sure." Maybe he needed to order flowers, though it wasn't Martha or Ben's birthday. It wasn't Logan or Luke's birthday, or Emma or Des's birthday. Or any anniversaries either. The benefit of being the town florist was she pretty much had all the important dates in her head.

"Des is hosting a dinner party thing Saturday night at the ranch."

"She is?"

"Yes."

Des had already told her about the couples dinner party several weeks ago. She'd been invited, but she'd put that on hold, because that would have meant she had to scrounge up a date, which hadn't been on her radar at that time.

"That sounds fun."

"Yeah. It's a couples thing, though, so I need a date."

This was interesting, especially since Reid looked very uncomfortable. She was going to go with it to see how it played out. "Is that right?"

"Yes. So I was wondering—and you're under no obligation, of course—but if you weren't busy or anything, would you want to go?"

But now it looked like she did have a date. And an extremely hot one at that. "I'd love to come. So I'd need to bring a date?"

He frowned. "Uh, no. You'd go with me."

"Oh, I see. You didn't actually directly ask me to be your date, so I was kind of confused."

"Shit. Sorry. Samantha, Des is having a couples dinner party at the ranch on Saturday night. I would very much like to bring you as my date, if you'd like to come with me."

She knew she'd made it hard on him, but it had been too much fun to see him squirm a little. "I'd love to, Reid. Thank you for asking."

He exhaled. "Thanks. I'll come pick you up around six thirty."

"That's not necessary, since it's a long drive out to the ranch. I can drive over."

"No, you won't. I asked you to be my date, so I'll come pick you up. At six thirty."

Wasn't he being chivalrous. And wasn't she enjoying it oh so much. "Okay. Then I'll be ready at six thirty."

"Great."

She waited while he stood there and stared at her as if there was something else he wanted to say. Or do.

Like catapult himself over the counter, pull her into his arms, and kiss her.

Or maybe that was just her wishful thinking.

"So I should get back to work," he finally said.

No catapulting. How disappointing. "Yes, I should, too."

He grasped the dog's leash. "I guess I'll see you Saturday night then."

"Okay." She drummed her fingers on the counter, waiting for . . . something. She didn't know what. Just some kind of signal that him asking her to be his date hadn't been a painful experience for him.

"I'll see you later, Sam."

"Bye, Reid."

He and the dog left, and despite having been asked to be his date, she couldn't help but feel . . .

What? Disappointed? She had no idea what she felt. But whatever the sensation was, she had no time to feel it, because she had loads of work waiting for her in the back room to deal with.

Thankfully. Nothing like immersing herself in the creation of beautiful flower arrangements to take her mind off the mystery of men.

Or, rather, the mystery that was one man.

Reid McCormack.

OKAY, THAT HAD gone about as well as it could have considering he and Sam weren't dating and he'd asked her out completely out of the blue.

"What do you think?" he asked the dog as they made their

way to the park, where the dog peed on a tree, then sniffed the grass for a few minutes before sitting down next to Reid's feet.

Since it was nearing lunchtime, he figured Deacon would run out to grab a bite to eat, so he took a seat on one of the benches. The dog parked it next to him. "No opinion on my skills at asking women out, huh?"

The dog looked up at him, his tongue hanging out the side of his mouth. The dog had thoughts. Plenty of them. Reid could see that in his very intelligent, dark eyes. He was sure the dog was thinking something along the lines of *Dude, you were a total stud back there.*

"Yeah, I thought it was pretty good, too."

A police car rolled up and stopped at the curb. The window rolled down, and Reid smiled as he saw his brother, Luke.

"You know you're sitting in the park talking to your dog."

"Not my dog. He just keeps hopping into the truck when I come to work."

"That's what I've heard. Which kind of makes him your dog."

Reid shook his head. "Nope. Not my dog. What are you up to?"

"Solving crime. Saving the world. The usual."

Reid's lips curved. "Sure you are. Got time for lunch?"

"Yeah. How about Bert's diner?"

"Sounds good. Want me to meet you there?"

"That'll work best, in case I get a call. I'd hate to leave you stranded. Or have to handcuff you and shove you in the back of my patrol car."

"You're so funny. See you there in five."

He walked the dog back to the mercantile and set him up on the porch with water and the dog bone he'd retrieved from Martha this morning.

"Behave. I'll be back soon."

The dog was too busy gnawing on the bone to pay any attention to what Reid said.

He texted Deacon to let him know he was having lunch with Luke, then climbed into his truck and drove off, knowing the dog would be safe there. The best thing about a small town like Hope was that no one messed with your stuff—or your dog.

Not that the dog was his. He wasn't.

He drove over to the diner. Bert's was one of the most popular places in Hope, thanks to Bert and Charlotte, a couple of the best cooks in town. Besides Martha's home cooking, eating at Bert's was one of the things he'd missed most since he'd moved to Boston. So he intended to eat there a lot while he was working on the mercantile.

Luke had already grabbed a booth for them. He made his way past the tables, saying hello to people he knew along the way—which was pretty much everyone. He finally slid into the booth.

"I'm going to assume you're having the burger," Luke said.

"Hell yeah. With onions and mustard and pickles."

"You're so predictable."

"Hey, you can eat here all the time. This is a special treat for me."

"Not my fault you decided to up and move to Boston for no damn good reason."

Reid laughed. "I had plenty of damn good reasons, the first one being I got a great job offer after college. Which worked out really well, since I ended up starting my own business."

"Yeah. Money. Whatever. There's plenty for you to do here, ya know."

Anita, whom he'd known ever since high school, came by to take their order.

"Sure is good to see you here again, Reid," Anita said. "And everyone in Hope is really darn happy you're cleaning up the old mercantile."

"Thanks, Anita. I'm glad to be back."

They ordered their food and drinks, and Reid settled his gaze on his brother. "There were more opportunities for me in a large city and you know it."

"Hope's a growing town. You might be surprised by all there is to do here now. You've been gone awhile. You saw what they did with the town square project."

Reid nodded. "Yeah, that turned out great. The park is

amazing, and I can't believe they brought the old fountain back to life. I almost wish I had been a part of it."

Anita brought their iced teas. Luke took a sip, then pointed a finger at him. "See? That's exactly what I'm talking about. You could have been a part of the whole process if you'd been here."

Reid laughed. "I didn't say I wanted to be here. I just said it turned out great and I would have . . . You know what? Never mind. I don't live here. I'm never going to live here again. My life is in Boston now."

Anita set their burgers down in front of them. Reid's stomach growled. Loudly.

Anita patted him on the back. "Enjoy those burgers, you two."

Luke laughed. "I heard your stomach all the way across the table."

"Oh, man. I can't wait for the best burger in the world. And those fries. No one makes fries like Bert."

Luke lifted his burger. "Just remember that when you say Boston is home. Boston will never be home." Luke lifted his burger. "This is home, man."

Reid bit into his hamburger, and a little bit of him died at how good it tasted, at the rush of memories just the taste of it evoked.

Driving into Hope after school to meet up with friends, hanging out on a Friday night after the rivalry football games between Hope High and Oakdale High.

The memories clouded so thick today it was hard to see.

But this was just a burger, and Reid firmly believed in living in the present, not the past.

Today he had a life and a career in Boston, and that's what he intended to go back to after this project was finished.

No matter how damn good this diner food tasted.

Chapter 8

"IT'S NOT REALLY a date, Megan."

"Hey, I'm going to the party, too. With a non-date kind of date. And I'm wearing a hot-damn dress. So we're making a big deal of it."

Sam stood in her bedroom, eyeing her closet while Megan helped her figure out what she was going to wear to dinner.

Megan sat on her bed, cross-legged, and surveyed the contents of Sam's open closet. "Besides, in your case it's totally a date. Reid asked, you said yes. That makes it a date."

Sam disagreed. "He only asked me because he's new in town and he and I have talked a few times. I'm probably the only female on his radar at the moment. I was convenient."

Megan laughed. "Honey, he grew up here. He knows everyone in Hope. He asked *you*. Not some other woman. You. Give yourself some credit. You're a smart, successful, hot blonde with a gorgeous body, and he wants to go out with you. How convenient is it that Des was throwing a couples party?"

Sam sighed and sat on the bed. "Who's your date tonight, by the way?"

"No idea. Probably one of the McCormack cousins. Des

wanted me there and she said she'd take care of it. I'm excited to be going and hanging out with all of you, since I'm not currently part of a couple."

"I'm not part of a couple, either."

"Tonight you are. Because you have a date." Turning her attention to the closet, Megan said, "You should wear the green dress."

Sam wrinkled her nose. "It's body-hugging and a little low-cut."

"Exactly. He'll want to lick you all over."

Sam laughed. "Megan. We're just going as friends."

"You keep saying that, Sam. But I don't think he's putting you in the friend zone. And speaking of someone who's going to be in the friend zone tonight and still doesn't care, I have to go get dazzling."

After Megan left, Sam made a dash over to Grammy Claire's house. Her grandmother was seated in her favorite comfy chair, eating pretzels and watching television—some soccer match between Argentina and Brazil.

"Soccer, Grammy Claire?" she asked as she bent to kiss her cheek.

Her grandmother looked up at her with a bright smile. "Those boys have great legs."

Sam shook her head. "So what you're saying is you're ogling and you don't have the slightest interest in soccer."

"I didn't say that. I like sports. But football isn't on until tomorrow, so for tonight, it's soccer."

Sam wandered into the kitchen, which was, as usual, spotless. It was a small kitchen, much like her own, with light oak cabinets and old, worn laminate countertops. The stove was ancient, but Sam could still remember Grammy Claire fixing her oatmeal on it while she sat at the kitchen table with Grandpa Bob. Then they'd read the comics in the newspaper and Grandpa Bob would help her with her homework.

She owed her entire life to her loving grandparents. She missed Grandpa Bob, missed the sound of his big, rough laugh and the way he used to hold her hand when he walked her into school as a little girl.

Feeling oddly nostalgic, she set about the task she'd come into the kitchen for. She checked the pantry and the fridge to make sure her grandmother was stocked up on the essentials. She grabbed a paper and pen and made some notes for her next grocery shopping trip. After tucking the list into the back pocket of her jeans, she returned to the living room.

"You're fine on staples and your milk and bread should be okay until I go to the grocery store. I see you froze half a meat loaf, and there are some pork chops in there as well."

Her grandmother pulled her gaze from the television. "Yes, I have plenty to eat, honey. But I'm going out tonight, anyway, so I won't be cooking."

"Really? Where are you going?"

"Faith and I are off to the senior center for bingo."

Faith Clemons was her grandmother's best friend, so Sam knew she was in good hands. "Okay, good. So you'll call me when you get home?"

Grammy Claire shifted her gaze from the television onto her. "It's like having parents all over again. And a curfew."

Sam laughed. "Sorry. But you know I worry about you, so please call me?"

"I will. Can I hope you won't be sitting around your house on a Saturday night waiting for me to call you?"

"Actually, I'm headed over to the McCormack ranch tonight. Desiree McCormack is hosting a dinner party."

"That sounds fun. Who are you going with?"

"I'm sort of going with Reid McCormack."

Grammy Claire grabbed the remote and muted the sound on the TV. "What does 'sort of going' mean?"

"It's a couples dinner, and Reid needed a date, so he asked me."

"Then you have a date with Reid McCormack. Nice young man. Very fine-looking. And he's renovating the old mercantile. I'm very happy about that."

"I am, too. But it's not a date, Grammy Claire."

Her grandmother gave her the look—the one that said she wouldn't tolerate any BS. "He's picking you up and taking you out somewhere to eat. In my day, that was a date."

She wasn't about to argue with her. "Yes, you're right, Grammy Claire. It's a date. And I need to go get ready."

She kissed her grandmother and reminded her to call when she got back from bingo, then walked home and got into the shower. She dried her hair and put on makeup, then, against her better judgment, she went with the green dress, feeling decidedly naked. It was short and clingy and, with the bra she'd chosen, pushed what breasts she had up and over the top of the dress.

It was scandalous, but when she glanced in the mirror, she had to admit she looked pretty darn sexy. If that was the look she was going for.

Was it? She wasn't sure. Because despite her conversations with Megan and her grandmother, she knew Reid had only asked her because he didn't have many options date-wise. He'd only been here a week, and she was certain he hadn't spent that time reacquainting himself with the female population of Hope.

Still, he'd asked her and not someone else. He hadn't left it up to Des to match him up with someone. He'd come to the shop to ask her himself. So maybe it was a date after all.

She really had no idea. This whole thing was so confusing. Either way, she knew all the couples Des had asked, so she was going to have a great time no matter what.

She was just adding earrings when her doorbell rang. She went to the door and opened it.

"Holy shit," Reid said as he took in her appearance.

She smiled. "I hope that's a good thing."

He looked her over from the top of her hair down to her sparkly-heeled shoes.

"Hell yes. I mean, yes. Wow, Sam. You look . . . amazing."

"Thank you. So do you."

He wore black jeans, a white button-down shirt, and very shiny cowboy boots. His hair was slicked back and obviously freshly washed. And since he'd stepped inside her house, she caught his clean scent. He looked and smelled good enough to lick all over—a thought that sparked all her fun places.

Especially the way he kept giving her hot looks, as if his

thoughts were straying in exactly the same wicked way hers were.

But now the two of them stood in her foyer and neither of them moved. Maybe they'd never make it to dinner. Maybe they could just hang out here and spend time playing undress-each-other games.

Her mind was already awash in those visuals, her body heated from the ground floor up at how it would play out. First, her shoes. She could well imagine those great hands of his rubbing her feet. Then her calves . . .

"So . . . we should probably go," he said, pulling her out of that amazing fantasy. "Des made me promise I'd get you back there in time for cocktails."

"Oh. Sure." She'd have to quash the sex fantasy. For now.

But wouldn't it be a fun thing to ponder for after dinner tonight?

"Let me grab my sweater and purse."

"Okay."

She put on her sweater and met him back at the door. "I'm ready."

For anything that might happen.

Chapter 9

REID TRIED TO focus on the road, the speedometer, on anything but Sam's legs and that damn dress she wore.

Christ, but why was it so hot in the truck? And why had he decided to help her climb in, which gave him an eyeful of her dress riding up her thighs and that tight material cupping her supremely sweet ass?

It might have taken him a few minutes to walk around the back of the truck, count to a hundred, and get his ridiculous erection under control.

No woman had made him so hard so fast just by wearing a goddamn dress.

"Are you excited about the party tonight?" she asked, making small talk no doubt because he'd been mute for the past fifteen minutes.

It's possible that after ogling her thighs and her butt he might have swallowed his tongue and would never be able to speak again.

"Uh, sure."

He caught the slight quirk of her lips. "So, not really all that thrilled about a dinner party."

He shrugged. "I have a lot of events I go to for work. The mix-and-mingle kind of thing. This dinner party is something I've done before."

"Oh, of course. So this isn't a big deal for you. Plus, it's your family—both your brothers, I mean. So I assume Luke and Emma will be there tonight, along with Logan and Des?"

"Yeah. Otherwise, I have no idea who else Des invited."

"I see. Well, I know everyone in town. And out of town, for that matter."

He made the turn down the road that led toward the ranch. "By virtue of the fact that a florist pretty much knows everyone?"

She laughed. "Yes. I've done flowers for births, weddings, high school graduations, funerals, birthdays. You name it, if someone has an event that requires flowers, they usually call me. I mean, they could also call one of my competitors."

"But why would they do that? I've heard you're the best florist in Hope."

She shifted, causing the material of her dress to ride higher on her thighs. He tried not to groan. "You did? Who told you that?"

"Deacon."

"Really. You and Deacon were talking about my flower shop?"

"He saw us walking together the other day. Then he mentioned you handled the flowers for his granddad's funeral several years back. He said you did a really nice job."

She nodded. "That was very sweet of him. I was so sorry about his grandpa. Lovely man."

"He was. So was his dad."

"Yes. I wasn't running the flower shop when his father died. That was before my time. Grammy Claire was still in charge back then. I know it was awful for Deacon to lose his dad at such a young age."

"Yeah."

"But he's done great things with his life. He's got the construction company now. His dad would have been so proud of him."

Reid liked that Sam had such a positive outlook, that she didn't seem to dwell on sorrow. "You're right. He would be."

"Just like your dad would be proud of all you've accomplished."

Reid had always wondered what his dad would think of him owning his own business, and of him making his life in Boston. "I'd like to think so. He always told us we should make our mark on something, do whatever it was that made us happy."

Sam didn't say anything for a few minutes, so he figured their talk was over. He pulled up to the house and parked.

"And are you?" she asked.

"Am I what?"

"Happy."

"Sure."

She cocked her head to the side. "That doesn't sound like a ringing endorsement of your life, Reid."

She opened the door and got out of his truck, leaving him sitting there wondering if she just didn't get that he was content.

Or maybe he wasn't really as happy as he tried to convince everyone.

He got out and joined her.

"I would have come around to open your door," he said as he met her by the front porch.

"Sorry. I have a tendency to be independent. And I don't date much, so I forgot the whole guys-open-doors-for-me routine."

"I bow to your independence, but how about for tonight you let me open doors for you? Otherwise, Martha might smack me on the back of my head."

"We can't have that, can we?" She slipped her arm in his and nestled her body close, and Reid sure as hell had no complaints about Sam's warm body against his. They walked up the stairs together, and she waited while he opened the front door for her to walk in.

He hadn't wanted to do this whole couples dinner, but having a smart, sexy, beautiful woman like Sam on his arm tonight?

Maybe not a bad thing at all.

Chapter 10

THERE WERE WORSE things to do on a Saturday night than spending the evening in the company of some of your closest friends.

Reid had his brothers by his side, of course. And with his brothers came Sam's friends Emma, who was married to Luke, and Des, who was married to Logan. Along with them were Chelsea and Bash, Jane, who was Emma's best friend and married to Luke's best friend Will. There was also Emma's sister Molly and her fiancé, Carter. This group had always felt like family to Sam. She walked in the door and was immediately assailed by the smell of something . . . wonderful. What was it?

The doorway to the left led to the kitchen, the heart of the McCormack house, mainly because of Martha, the housekeeper and ranch manager and pseudo mother to the McCormack boys. Martha was in there with Des, who looked stunning, as always, her dark black hair piled high on her head. She saw Sam and came over to give her a hug.

"You look ravishing," Des said.

"And you look beautiful. I love that dress on you. Aubergine is definitely a hot color this season."

"Thanks. Logan just finished pouring champagne, complaining the entire time about wanting a beer. But he's suffering for me tonight because I've wanted to throw a fancy dinner party, and he thinks I'm unhappy because we don't live in Hollywood."

Sam accepted the glass of champagne from Des. "But you'd rather live here than in Hollywood."

"I know that, and even he knows that, but there's always a part of him that thinks because I'm an actress I have this desire to live in LA. Which couldn't be further from the truth. But if it gives me a win like this dinner party every now and then, who am I to complain?"

Sam grinned. "Good point. It smells amazing in here. Did Martha cook?"

"Absolutely not. She tried, but I told her she and Ben were guests tonight, so no cooking. I had the entire event catered. I flew in a chef from one of the finest restaurants in New Orleans. The menu is extraordinary."

"I can't wait."

One of the caterers waved at Des. "Excuse me for a minute. I'll catch up with you shortly. Head on into the living room. Everyone's here."

Sam wandered in to see Reid engrossed in conversation with his brothers, so she left him there and searched out Megan. She found her standing to the side of the room with Molly Burnett and Molly's fiancé, Carter Richards. And Brady Conners, who worked with Carter.

She headed over to join them.

"Hi, Sam," Molly said. "You look gorgeous tonight."

"So do you. And you, too, Megan."

"Thanks."

"Hi, Carter," she said.

"Hey, Sam. Do you know Brady?"

"I don't think we've officially met, though I'm sure we've seen each other wandering up and down the street." She held out her hand. "Hi, Brady. I'm Samantha Reasor. I own the flower shop. Everyone calls me Sam."

Brady shook her hand. "Nice to meet you, Sam."

"I forced him to come tonight," Carter said. "He spends

too much time living over my shop, working on motorcycles. I figured he could use something to eat that wasn't a microwaved meal or fast food."

Brady frowned. "Hey, I eat at Bert's, too."

"Nothing wrong with Bert's," Megan said with a bright smile. "Though I have to admit I like to cook more than I like to eat out."

"With your kitchen, who wouldn't?" Molly asked, then turned her attention to Brady. "She has the kitchen of every woman's dreams."

"So I've been hearing."

Sam counted the couples, and by process of elimination she determined Brady was obviously Megan's date for the evening. Nice call, since Brady was fine-looking.

"Every man's dreams, too," Carter said. "Especially if she's cooking for you."

Sam laughed.

"I need a refill of my champagne," Megan said. "Sam, would you go with me?"

"Sure," Sam said, since Megan obviously needed a minute alone with her.

"Excuse us," Megan said, then took Sam by the arm.

"So Brady Conners is your date tonight? Oh my God, Megan. He's hot. Tall, lean, with those smoldering, dark good looks."

They made their way into the kitchen, where one of the hired staff poured Megan a glass of champagne. "Indeed he is. But he hasn't said but three words to me the entire night, and I'm pretty sure those words were 'You look nice.'"

"So maybe he's the quiet type."

"Yes, I know he's the quiet type. I mean, I know Brady. Everyone knows Brady. Or at least knows of him. He keeps to himself above Carter and Molly's auto repair shop. He works for them during the day, then at night and on weekends he works on motorcycles. I see him riding his bike on weekends around town. Otherwise . . . nothing."

"Well, you know there was that whole incident with his brother a year or so ago."

Megan sighed and leaned against the kitchen counter. "Yes. And I know it hit Brady really hard. But still, I just don't know how to act around him."

Sam rubbed her friend's arm. "Just be yourself, Megan. You're bubbly and friendly, and I can't imagine any guy not wanting to be with you. Try and have a good time with the hot guy, okay?"

Megan smiled. "I will. And you do the same. Speaking of, where is your hot guy?"

"I hope you meant me, and if you did, I'm right here."

Sam turned to find Reid right behind her.

"Oh, hey, Reid," Megan said, her face a bright pink. "If you'll excuse me now, I'm going to find a closet and go hide in it for the rest of the night and hope to die of embarrassment."

Reid laughed. "Don't go hide. But Brady said he was looking for you."

Megan's brows rose. "He did? This is promising. I'll talk to you later, Sam."

Reid turned back to her. "So, your best friend thinks I'm the hot guy, huh?"

"Every woman thinks you're the hot guy, Reid."

"News to me." He grabbed a glass of champagne and led her out of the kitchen and back into the living room. He bent to whisper into her ear. "But just in case I forgot to mention it, you are definitely the hot woman here tonight."

She lifted her gaze to his. "Do you always say the right things, or is this just your well-practiced polite company talk?"

"In case you haven't noticed, this isn't a business function, and while Martha taught me to always be polite, you are definitely a hot woman."

The room warmed up several degrees, especially with the way his gaze lingered on her. "In that case, thank you."

"You're welcome."

He was about to say more, but then Des and Logan came in. Des clinked her glass with a spoon. "Thank you all so much for being here tonight. I hope you enjoy the meal that's been prepared by Gerard, our wonderful chef. If you'll follow me into the dining area, we'll get started."

Reid offered his arm, so she slipped her hand in there. "We rarely eat in the dining room," he said. "It's usually the kitchen, or if we have a big to-do, it's typically in the summer, so we'll set up tables outside."

She leaned into him. "Des has been talking about this dinner for weeks. She's always on the go, and now that she has a break from filming or promoting, she wanted to do something special. She's very excited about this party."

"I'm glad for her—and for Logan. He misses her when she travels. I know he's looking forward to her taking a break. And if this party makes her happy, then he's all for it."

They took seats at the long dining room table. Samantha couldn't recall ever eating in here, and she'd been to the McCormack ranch many times. The dining room was huge, with a gorgeous crystal chandelier and a solid cherrywood table that comfortably sat everyone.

"This table is amazing," she said as Reid pulled her chair out for her.

"My dad built it with my granddad a long time ago. My grandmother wanted something that would fit everyone— ranch hands and family included—for Sunday dinners."

"This definitely suits."

"My mother hated it. She called it old country hicksville. She wanted to replace it with something more modern. My dad wouldn't let her. It was a big point of contention between them."

Sam ran her fingers over the edges. "I can't imagine wanting to replace something like this—something your father and grandfather built with their own hands. It's such a stunning piece of craftsmanship."

"Yeah, well, my mom didn't much appreciate things like that. Or much of anything about living on this ranch."

She felt the pain in Reid's words and reached over to lay her hand on his. "I'm sorry."

Reid shrugged. "Nothing to be sorry about. She's long gone, and all our lives are better for it."

Reid looked across the table to where Martha sat with her husband Ben and smiled. Martha smiled back, and Sam knew that the woman who really raised him—who truly loved him as a mother should—sat right there.

Sam knew all the McCormack brothers were grateful for Martha. So was she, because she knew all the McCormacks had turned out to be wonderful men. Largely in thanks to their father—and to Martha and Ben.

Dinner was an amazing array of food—from lobster bisque to gumbo to pan-seared, pecan-encrusted catfish with the most incredible rémoulade, and filet mignon as well. Sam was certain Des had made sure to include steak just for Logan.

"My head is spinning over all this food. Also, my dress might not fit after dinner."

Reid wriggled his brows. "If you're too full, I'll be happy to help you out of that dress."

She laughed. "So noble of you."

"That's me. Full of nobility."

"You're full of something, all right," Luke said from his seat on the other side of Sam.

"Hey, shouldn't you be minding your wife, and not my business?"

"My wife is talking to Carter, and your business is so interesting, what with you offering to remove Sam's dress."

Emma shifted her gaze and leaned around Luke. "Wait. What?"

Sam laughed. "That's not really what he said."

"That's exactly what he said," Luke said to Emma.

Fortunately, dinner was brought out, so the scandalous conversation Luke had overheard was put to rest, because the food was amazing. And by the time they made it to the final course—dessert—Sam was certain there was no way she could eat another bite. Except it was a choice of chocolate layer cake or cheesecake.

"I cannot eat another bite of food," Sam said, trying to keep from groaning.

Reid leaned over to whisper in her ear. "Go ahead. I have a blanket in the truck to cover you up when I help you take that dress off."

She shook her head and tried not to laugh. And ended up

eating the cheesecake, because how could she not? It was creamy and delicious and she followed it up with coffee.

After, they all got up and wandered back to the living room, where after-dinner liqueur was served. Sam declined, so full she needed to step outside for some fresh air. She found Emma out there nursing a glass of water.

"You okay?" Sam asked.

Emma nodded. "Yes," she said, rubbing her stomach. "I'm just so full that I needed to stand for a few minutes. Wasn't that dinner amazing?"

"Incredible. I wish now I hadn't worn such a tight dress. I'm going to be miserable the rest of the night."

Emma laughed. "I know the feeling."

"At least you're wearing a dress that hides your full stomach."

"Des warned me about the menu, so I thought ahead."

"The dress is beautiful, by the way." It was a coral color, with a full skirt. That's what Sam should have worn. Something with a skirt to hide her stomach. Then she wouldn't feel like every calorie she'd consumed was on display. Oh, why had she chosen this body-skimming dress?

"Thanks. And you look stunning. Believe me, Reid hasn't taken his eyes off you the entire night."

"You think so?"

"Oh, I know it. I've been watching him. And he's been watching you. Like, constantly."

So interesting. She hadn't noticed that at all. She had to admit, the thought of Reid's interest gave her stomach all kinds of flutters. She tried to tone it down, since they weren't really a couple, but if he was interested, that meant they could at least have some fun together, right?

She and Emma went back inside. Reid was talking to Luke and Logan, so she and Emma made their way over there. Emma slipped in next to Luke, who put his arm around her waist. Logan and Reid were standing against the fireplace mantel, and the three men were talking heatedly about cattle prices, upcoming shipments, and stock, so Sam stayed back to listen for a bit. Reid saw her and smiled. Something about that lopsided smile of his made her quiver.

She didn't want to interrupt him by moving in next to him, and he wasn't her boyfriend—or, really, her date. So she went in search of Megan, but she didn't see her friend in the living room. Maybe she was in the kitchen getting a refill of champagne?

Hmm, not there, either. She wandered out to the front porch. Megan wasn't there. She went back inside to look for Brady, but didn't see him.

Maybe they had left. She thought about texting her, but that would be ridiculous. Megan was an adult, and Sam could talk to her tomorrow.

The front door opened, and Reid came out to stand next to her.

"I'm sorry. I got involved in a conversation—several, actually—with my brothers."

"You don't have to apologize to me. And I imagine you've missed being able to talk with them."

He laughed. "Trust me. I don't miss them."

It was such a nice night for early fall. Still warm, no breeze. She took a seat on the porch swing. "So you're telling me that they picked on you because you're the youngest?"

He sat next to her and stretched out his long legs, sending the swing moving. "Mercilessly. Feel sorry for me?"

"Not in the least. I was an only child, and I would have loved to have a sibling or two."

"You're not missing anything, trust me."

"Oh, you don't mean that. You love your brothers."

His lips curved upward. "Hey, I'm the one who moved to Boston, remember?"

She shifted to face him. "Why?"

"Why what?"

"Why the move?"

He looked out over the porch, into the darkness. "Opportunity, mostly. I got a good offer from a really great firm out there, so I jumped on it."

"And you did it with no hesitation, no qualms about leaving Hope and your family?"

"Not at all. My parents had divorced. Luke was off the ranch, getting his career as a police officer off the ground. Logan had already decided he was going to be a lifelong rancher. I knew being an architect was what I wanted to do, and I didn't think there'd be enough opportunity for me in Oklahoma."

She arched a brow. "Nothing to build here?"

"Okay, fine. Maybe I just wanted a fresh start. Seeing the pain linger in my dad from the divorce was a hard thing. I wanted to get away from it all. From the ranch, from my brothers, from anything and everything that reminded me of my mother."

She appreciated his honesty. Most guys weren't so self-aware, and if they were, would certainly never admit it. She could still feel that pain and anger radiating off of him. Maybe he'd run away from it and hadn't yet reconciled it. "I understand the need to run from that kind of pain. But you know, at some point you have to deal with it."

His gaze met hers and he smiled. "No, I don't. I've been doing fine all these years never dealing with it."

She laid her hand over his. "Have you?"

"Do I look unhappy?"

"Well . . . no."

"I've had a couple romantic relationships. One long-term. I don't hate women. I stayed in close contact with my father until he died. Obviously I get along great with my brothers. See? Normal."

"What about your mom?"

"What about her?"

"Have you talked to her since she left all those years ago?"

"No. None of us has."

"She hasn't contacted any of you?"

"No."

"And you haven't tried to find her."

"No."

She couldn't understand that. How could a mother leave

her children like that? Maybe a week of unhappiness, fleeing the ranch, taking a vacation or something. But . . . forever? It just didn't register with her. She'd give anything for five minutes with her parents again.

"Don't you want to see her again?"

"No. She made her choice to leave us. That chapter of our lives is closed."

"Is it?"

He cocked his head to the side. "Something you want to say, Sam?"

She clasped her hands together. "Probably, but it's none of my business."

"Go ahead. Say it."

She'd never been one to keep a thought to herself, even though it often got her into trouble. "Okay. Somehow I doubt that the chapter of your mother is closed. It seems to me that her leaving all of you has left a giant gaping wound somewhere in the vicinity of your heart and in the hearts of your brothers."

He stared at her for what seemed like a very long minute.

And then he laughed. Like a loud, long, man laugh.

"Did you read that somewhere or did you see that in some movie on one of those women's channels?"

Her brows rose. "Excuse me? Women's channels?"

"Yeah, you know. Those channels that show all those romantic movies, where there's drama and angst and then ninety minutes later everything that's wrong with a guy or a girl or a relationship is wrapped up in a neat tidy bow and everyone lives happily ever after."

She stared at him. "I cannot believe you just said that."

"So that means you watch them, right? And even worse, you actually believe that shit?"

She got up from the porch swing and turned to look down at him. "I am no longer interested in having this conversation with you."

She could still hear him laughing as she opened the door and went back inside.

She would never try to help him again.

* * *

REID PROBABLY SHOULDN'T have laughed, but honestly, he could have telegraphed what Sam was going to say from the look of concern on her face.

And okay, maybe he'd been an asshole about it, but he and his brothers had long ago written off their mother. She'd been long gone emotionally from their lives well before she'd physically left. Martha had stepped in and filled the position of mother, especially emotionally. And God knows Dad had more than been there for them.

So some deep emotional chasm? Hell, no. There wasn't a goddamn thing missing in his life as a result of his mother's departure. He'd felt bad for his dad, because for some reason, his old man had loved the selfish, narcissistic, cold-hearted woman. At least at first. And he'd remained committed to her despite her obvious hatred for everything his father had loved. Until she'd up and left and divorced him and abandoned her children.

As for Reid, he'd never received a moment of love from her, so he couldn't miss what he'd never had. His maternal needs had all been filled by Martha.

And none of that had anything to do with his decision to take a job in Boston.

Sometimes women liked to delve a little too deeply into emotional shit that wasn't there in the first place. And he damn well did blame those ridiculous TV shows that painted love and romance and family in a fake light.

Real life was nothing like that. Real life was complicated, and it didn't turn around and right itself in an hour and a half.

If it had, his mother wouldn't have been a cold bitch on wheels, wouldn't have broken his father's heart, and wouldn't have walked out on him and his brothers.

But he wasn't wounded about it.

Goddammit.

Chapter 11

WOMEN'S SHOWS. WHAT kind of moronic, sexist, archaic way of thinking was that? Sam wanted to take off one of her awesomely gorgeous stiletto shoes and shove it up Reid's—

With a sigh, she folded her arms across her stomach and continued to pace alone in one of the spare bedrooms upstairs. She needed to blow off some steam alone before going back downstairs, before facing Reid again, before she said something she would regret.

Though he had no problem letting all kinds of stupid things fall out of his mouth. And she'd thought he was perfect.

Ha. He was about as perfect as her kitchen. On the surface, yeah, it was cute. Until you looked closer and identified the flaws. That was Reid. Hot and sexy and looked perfect. Until she had a deep conversation with him and realized what a complete jackass he was.

Enough. If she kept thinking about him, she was going to find him and tell him what she really thought about him and his opinions.

She finally gathered her wits about her enough to make her

way back downstairs. Spotting Megan and Brady, she made her way over to them.

"I was looking for you two earlier and couldn't find you."

"We took a walk around the ranch to look things over," Brady said.

"In those heels?" Sam asked.

Megan laughed. "I can do anything in these heels."

Sam wondered what "anything" meant, but she figured she would ask Megan later.

"We were just heading out," Megan said.

"Great. Can I get a ride back to town with the two of you?" she asked.

"Of course," Megan said. "But isn't Reid taking you home?"

She didn't want to get into it—at least not with Brady standing there. "No sense in Reid driving all the way back to Hope and then have to drive back here to the ranch."

"Makes sense," Brady said. "I'd be happy to give you a ride."

"Great. Let me say good-bye to everyone."

The last thing she wanted was to spend any more time with Reid than necessary. She found Des and Logan and thanked them for a wonderful evening, then, deciding to be polite, told Reid she was grabbing a ride with Brady and Megan.

He looked confused. "I had planned to take you home."

"No reason for you to have to make the trip. I have a ride. Besides, there are some great women's shows on TV that I'm dying to get home and watch."

He frowned. "Sam—"

"Thanks for the invite, Reid. I'll talk to you later."

Or, quite possibly, never. She turned on her heel and headed out the door with Megan and Brady.

The ride home was filled mostly with dinner talk, though as for talk, it was her and Megan doing all the talking. Brady was generally quiet except for one-word answers like "yup" and "great." She gave him directions to her house, and he dropped her off first.

"I'll call you tomorrow," Megan said.

"Okay, great. Thanks for the ride, Brady."

"Anytime."

She went inside and tossed her purse and sweater on the table, then kicked off her shoes and slid onto the sofa.

She was tired. She should get undressed and go to bed.

But just because she felt a wee bit catty at the moment, she grabbed the remote, surfed to a particular channel, and found the perfect movie. She pulled her feet underneath her and settled in to watch the romance unfold.

Reid McCormack could suck it.

Chapter 12

"ELECTRICAL'S SHOT," DEACON said as he and Reid stood side by side in the main room downstairs. "Just about what we figured in a building this old. HVAC will need to be completely replaced, too. We haven't dug into the plumbing yet, but my guess from what my guys have been able to dig up so far is that your plumbing is shit—no pun intended."

Reid took a long swallow of his coffee, sucked in some much-needed oxygen, and glared at Deacon. "Do you have any good news for me?"

"The tin ceiling will be able to stay. We took a few of the tiles down, and there's no rot in the floor beams on the second floor, so you're good to go with keeping that ceiling intact. We'll get her polished up and looking like new."

"I'll look forward to helping with that." He had a major hard-on for that tin ceiling. Replicas were one thing. An original? That was something else.

"Now that we've pulled the drywall out on the north side of the building, we found original brick wall."

"I saw that," Reid said with a grin. "My intent is to clean

up that brick and leave that wall exposed. It'll add some historical character to the building and spaces."

"Then you're going to be one happy sonofabitch, because the walls are like that on all three stories."

"That is good news."

One piece, at least. He knew with a hundred-plus-year-old building that there would be a lot that needed to be replaced. But getting hit with that news all at once was like a gut punch. Good thing he'd already warned his brothers that there would need to be a lot of upgrades, so at least they were financially prepared for the hit.

Now that demo had been completed, it was easier to see the bones of the building. With the walls torn out and that hideous dropped ceiling gone, the bottom floor seemed much more expansive. The brick wall was beautiful. Now Reid could envision what would be, which was the potential for retail space. And there was plenty of room down here now.

"Ready to take a walk upstairs?" Deacon asked.

"Yeah."

While Deacon was all about structure, Reid was all about design. As they made their way upstairs, Reid ran his hands over the carved wood banister, itching to get it polished and gleaming, as it once was. Some of the wood planks on the staircase would have to be replaced, but they could refinish most of it. Now that they'd cleaned it off, it wasn't as bad as he'd thought when he'd given it the initial once-over.

He wanted to retain as much of the original surfaces as possible, while still keeping safety in mind.

The second floor had been gutted down to the studs as well, and now showcased tall windows, exposed brick walls, and tons of potential. Third floor was much the same. Reid could already envision office space up here, his imagination awash in visions of where he'd put a desk, where morning sun would shine in through those amazing windows, where—

"Come take a look at the plumbing issues we have up here."

Eh. Reality reared its ugly head, destroying his fantasies about ideal office space. Not that it would be his office space, anyway. But he'd sure as hell look forward to designing one kick-ass office for . . . somebody.

He and Deacon went over the plumbing on the second and third floors. Deacon was right—it was a mess and would have to be totally redone. He added that expense to his notebook as they walked the floors, at the same time letting his mind wander.

He had a plan drawn up—a solid one for space on the second and third floors. He knew where every bathroom would go, the square footage of every office.

He couldn't wait to see it all unfold. But right now? Plumbing, electrical, and HVAC.

"I've got elevator people coming in Thursday," Deacon said. "I walked in there and it's pretty cool-looking, but I haven't dared try to ride up in it."

Reid nodded. "That thing looks like a death trap."

"Yeah, no telling if it's salvageable or if you'll need an entirely new elevator."

He was hoping for the former. That elevator was a piece of history, with its cage door and manual lever. "My guess is it's probably going to have to be replaced to meet code and ADA requirements. Which is too bad."

"I don't know," Deacon said. "We might be able to do the upgrades and still maintain some of the original features."

Reid shrugged. "We have tenant and visitor safety to think about first. We'll see what the mechanics think after they review it."

"Okay. I'll make a note to have a discussion about it in our meeting on Friday."

Deacon typed that into his netbook.

"Let's meet with the HVAC and plumbing people tomorrow," Reid said as they made their way downstairs. "I want to make sure we have the plans all laid out, that the timeline is set, and materials are ordered to spec. If anything needs to be realigned on this project due to materials replacement, I want to adjust it now on the front end."

Deacon nodded. "I'll get everyone in my office that needs to be there. Eight o'clock all right with you?"

"That works."

"Great."

He left Deacon to his work and stepped outside. The dog looked up at him from his spot on the porch.

"I suppose you want a walk now," he said to the dog, who stood, shook his body from head to tail, then wagged said tail back and forth.

"Fine. But like I keep telling you, you have a mega-thousand-acre ranch you could have the run of if you'd just stay there instead of following me around."

The dog cocked his head to the side and smiled, his long pink tongue sticking out the side of his mouth.

"Whatever, dude. Let's go."

He grabbed the dog's leash and headed toward the park.

"Nice dog, Reid."

Reid nodded at Bobby Jameson, owner of the barber shop.

"Thanks. It's not my dog."

"That's what I keep hearing." Bobby bent and scratched the dog's ears. "How you doin' today, fella?"

The dog totally ate up all the attention, especially when Megan came out of the bakery and stopped to pet the dog, too.

"Hey, Reid. How's Not My Dog doing today?"

Reid frowned. "Huh?"

Megan looked up at him. "Your dog. Not My Dog."

"That's not his name."

"Really. Then what is it?"

"Uh . . ."

"Everyone's taken to calling him Not My Dog, since that's what you keep telling everyone," Bobby said, straightening as a customer headed into his shop. "Good to see you, Reid." He looked down at the dog. "Not My Dog."

Bobby headed inside, leaving him with Megan, who gave him a smirk.

"See? It's a great name, by the way. I need to run. Talk to you later, Reid." She bent down to rub the dog's ears. "You, too, Not My Dog."

Reid watched Megan walk away, then looked down at the dog.

"Not My Dog?"

The dog's ears perked up, and his tail swished back and forth.

"Oh, for God's sake. Really?"

Not My Dog moved toward him, planting a front paw on Reid's foot.

"So you like that name."

The dog wriggled back and forth as if to say, *Totally digging the name. Even if you weren't the one smart enough to come up with it.*

"Whatever, Not My Dog. Let's head to the park."

SAMANTHA DIDN'T MEAN to walk out of the floral shop just at the moment Reid and Not My Dog were making their way toward the park. She had an armload of deliveries, so ducking back inside wasn't an option. She was just going to have to suck it up and ignore him. Or worse, be pleasant.

Maybe she'd get lucky and he wouldn't notice her.

She went outside and opened the doors of the delivery van, trying to keep her head down and focus on getting the flowers inside the van.

She heard footsteps, mentally cursing her lousy timing when Reid came around the side of the van.

"Hey, Sam. I thought I saw you come outside."

She looked up and forced a smile. "Oh, hi, Reid. I was just about to leave. I have some deliveries to make." She looked down at the dog, unable to resist cradling his cute face between her hands. "Hey, Not My Dog."

"Does everyone know about the dog's name?"

She lifted her gaze to Reid's, her stomach tumbling at the way his sexy eyes were trained so seriously on hers. "Of course. Word travels fast around here. It's a great name, by the way."

"I didn't name him."

She shrugged. "You kind of did, actually."

"Okay, maybe I did, but not intentionally. He's not my dog."

She was not in the mood for his attitude. "He kind of is, actually. He follows you to work every day, doesn't he?"

"Well, yeah, but that's not my fault. He's not my dog."

She held out both hands toward the dog, and then to him. "And thus his new name is born. You should get used to the idea that he's yours. Because like it or not, he's claimed you."

Reid sighed. Sam knew she was irritated for no rational reason whatsoever, which meant retreat was probably a really good idea right now.

"I need to go, Reid. I'll see you later, okay?"

"Oh, sure. Later, Sam."

She walked around to the driver's side of the van and climbed in. Suddenly, Reid was right there, looking up at her through the driver's side window. She rolled the window down. "Yes?"

"Are you mad at me for some reason?"

"No. Yes. I don't know, maybe. I don't have time to get into it."

"Would you have time later?"

"I don't know. Maybe."

He gave her a half smile. "Okay. Can we talk about it then?"

She shouldn't do this, but she already knew she was going to, because she hated leaving things unfinished. "Come by the house after work."

"Okay." He looked down at his feet. "I'll have the dog."

"Not My Dog is always invited to my house."

"I get the idea you mean that I'm not always invited."

"We can discuss that part later as well. I really have to go."

"Sure. Bye, Sam." He took a step back, allowing her to roll up her window and drive away. He stood there watching while she turned the corner.

She was even more confused. She was still angry with him, but she had no idea why. And he was so damned attractive she had all these conflicting emotions swirling around her insides.

And now he was coming over to her house later.

Great. She made a mental note to stop at the grocery store and pick up some items to cook.

No. Screw that. She was mad, and she wasn't cooking. They'd order pizza.

Chapter 13

ADMITTEDLY, REID WAS nervous about stopping by Sam's place that night. He had no idea what he'd done to piss her off. Sam had always been laid-back and friendly, but ever since that night at the ranch, she'd avoided him.

He needed to know why. He didn't know why it was important to know, but for some reason, it was.

Not My Dog jumped out of the truck and followed him to Sam's front door, then sat by his side while he rang the bell. He looked down at the dog.

"Best behavior, okay?"

The dog gave him a cocked-head look: *Dude, I'm not the one in trouble here*.

"Yeah, you're right about that."

The door opened and Sam stood there, her beautiful blond hair pulled up in a high ponytail. She wore capri pants, a gray, long-sleeved shirt, and pink tennis shoes. Damn, she looked pretty. So distractingly pretty, he wanted to pull her against him and kiss her and pretend there was no tension between them.

That wasn't likely to happen, so he settled on a smile.

"Hi, Sam."

"Hey. Come on in."

"Thanks." Not My Dog followed right behind him, and when Sam told Reid to take a seat, the dog followed, made a couple of circles, then lay down next to the sofa and rested his face on his paws.

Sam took a spot on the floor next to the dog, obviously stating her preference for companions. She rubbed the dog's ears and looked up at Reid. "How was your day?"

"There are some issues we have to deal with, but nothing unexpected."

"Nothing that'll affect your timeline, I hope?"

"No. Demo has been completed. Now it's all internal work, like plumbing, electrical, and the like."

"Good to know."

"You could come by and I could show you what we've done so far."

"We'll see."

Yeah, she was definitely upset with him, because last week she wanted nothing more than to see the inside of the mercantile. Now she seemed disinterested.

"Okay, what did I do to make you mad?"

"It's not so much mad as it is disappointed. At the dinner party you made fun of my gender."

His brows shot up. "I did? When did I do that?"

"You were talking about your mother. I made a comment about the pain you must be in. You laughed and said I must have learned that from some women's channel, where all problems are tied up in ninety-minute movies."

"Oh. Shit." He remembered that conversation, and he'd obviously hurt her. "That was an off-the-cuff remark and was insensitive as hell of me. I'm really sorry, Sam. I don't know why I said that."

"Maybe because you believe it?"

"No. That's not it at all. I tend to get defensive when the topic of my mother comes up. As you can probably imagine, it's a pretty sensitive subject for all of us McCormacks. But that doesn't excuse my bad behavior or the things I said to you. Please forgive me for being a complete asshole that night."

She cocked her head to the side. "I was prepared to stay mad at you, but as apologies go, that was a pretty good one."

He felt a flood of relief. "So I'm forgiven?"

"Mostly. As your punishment, we're having pizza for dinner and then we're watching one of those movies on the so-called women's channel."

He laughed. "I guess I deserve that."

She grabbed her phone from the coffee table. "What kind of pizza would you like?"

"Since this is my night of contrition, I'll let you choose."

"Are you sure about that? What if I like eggplant on my pizza?"

He wrinkled his nose. "Do they even offer eggplant as a topping?"

"I have no idea. Would you eat it if they did?"

"I eat pretty much anything. Go for it."

She scrolled through her contacts list and pressed the button, then waited. "Marjorie? Hey, it's Sam Reasor. I'd like a large hamburger and pepperoni with extra cheese, delivered."

His kind of woman.

When she hung up, she looked up at him.

"What? No eggplant?" he asked.

"Funny. And no eggplant."

"Good."

After patting Not My Dog again, she stood. "Would you like something to drink? I have beer, wine, soda, and water."

After that tense conversation, he needed to unwind. "I'd definitely go for a beer."

"Okay."

She went into the kitchen, and he glanced down at the dog, who looked perfectly content to be asleep on the floor. Normally the ranch dogs lived and slept outside, so this was a treat for him.

"Yeah, you're living the life right now, aren't you, bud?"

The dog responded with a loud snore.

"Here you go." She handed him the can of beer and set

down the glass of wine she'd made for herself on the table. She kicked off her tennis shoes and curled her feet up under her on the sofa.

"So, about my mom," he started.

She put up her hand. "You don't need to offer me any explanation about your mother. It's none of my business, and now it's my turn to apologize for trying to interfere in your personal life."

He got up and went to sit next to her on the sofa, then set his beer down on a coaster on the coffee table. "You weren't interfering. You were telling me you cared by offering emotional advice. And I was a complete jackass about it. Did I mention I was sorry?"

She looked at him with those beautiful, honest blue eyes—eyes he could so easily get lost in.

"Yes. Apology accepted. I know how hard it is to talk about emotional things. Especially for men. You tend to hold it all inside."

He opened his mouth, about to deny her statement, then surprised himself by saying, "You're probably right. It hurt when she left. I'll admit that. But I was being honest when I said it's not something I lose sleep over. Martha's been a fantastic mother to all of us. She always has been. So I'm not bearing any deep emotional scars. Honest."

She cocked her head to the side and studied him. "You know what? I believe that. If anyone could seriously mother a bunch of unruly boys, and give them all the love they could ever want or need, it's Martha."

He laughed. "You're right about that. I don't feel I missed out on anything."

"Good. I'm really happy about that."

He was glad they'd gotten that straightened out. "Now tell me how your day went. You looked busy when I came by earlier."

"Oh," she said. "Yes. Today was a big day for birthdays and anniversaries. I delivered a lot of flowers to several very happy people."

"Which must give you a lot of joy."

She gave him a look. "Why, yes, actually, it does. My job is very fulfilling."

"I wasn't making fun of you, Sam. I imagine your work is extremely rewarding. You get to see surprise and happiness and often comfort on the faces of the people you deliver to. Not many people get that in their line of work."

"Thank you. And yes, I love what I do. Grammy Claire brought me into the flower shop when I was a little girl, and used to take me out with her on deliveries. I loved to see the looks of happiness on people's faces when she brought them flowers. It's such a simple gesture, but it means so much to people. Flowers signify life and love and a future. Even in death it brings comfort and a sense of ease to such a sad occasion. And when a future bride comes in to plan her wedding, helping her choose just the right flowers, seeing her eyes light up when we put her bouquet together, means everything—both to her and to me."

"I guess you don't really have a bad day at work, do you?"

She laughed. "Not really. Occasionally I can have an overwhelming day, but not a bad one."

"You're very lucky."

She took a sip of her wine. "You have some bad days."

"Here and there."

"But you love what you do as well."

"I do. There's nothing like designing a building, to see something you've created in your head built from the ground up."

"Or, in the case of the mercantile, refurbished?"

"Yeah. Just the thought of the town tearing that building down didn't sit right with me."

She nodded. "Me, neither. I'm a big proponent of progress. If our town grows, my business will as well. But the old mercantile has been around as long as I've been alive, and as long as my grandmother has as well. She has told me so many stories of all the businesses that operated out of that building. I couldn't imagine it not being there every time I walk through town."

"The building has great bones, and its structure is still

intact. There's no reason it can't still sustain businesses, which is my intent for it."

"I'm so glad you and your brothers convinced the town to sell you the building. You'll lease out the spaces and bring in new clients. So instead of leveling it to the ground to put in a pharmacy or whatever the town's idea was, you'll bring in several new businesses, which I assume is your plan."

"Yes. Retail space on the ground floor, office space on the second and third."

"Awesome. I can't wait to see what it will look like." She took another swallow of wine, then set her glass on the coffee table. "Care to tell me a little bit about what you have planned?"

"In what way?"

"Like, do you have tenants yet?"

"We've had some interest."

"So in other words, you're keeping some secrets."

"Not really. We just don't have anything firm from anyone yet, so I don't want to say anything in case people back out."

"I can accept that. But that doesn't mean I'll stop asking."

He smiled. "You can ask all you want. Doesn't mean I'll tell you anything."

She studied him, and he liked the intelligence he saw in those beautiful eyes of hers. "Keeping those cards close to the vest, aren't you, McCormack?"

"Don't ever play poker with me, Sam."

"There's a challenge if I ever heard one. How do you know I wouldn't kick your butt in poker?"

"I don't know. I'm pretty good at it."

She gave him a wicked grin. "So am I."

The doorbell rang.

"I've got this," Reid said, getting up.

Sam stood, too. "No. I invited you for dinner."

He already had his wallet out. "You fed me last time. This one's on me."

"Okay."

He paid for the pizza while she went into the kitchen and laid out plates on the counter.

"I don't know about you," he said when he opened the pizza box, "but I'm starving."

"I am, too."

They took their filled plates and napkins into the living room and settled in, and Sam turned on the television, scrolling through until she found the channel she wanted.

"Oh, good. Just in time for the start of the movie."

He looked, then grimaced. "You really were serious about making me suffer through one of these movies."

"Absolutely."

The movie was about a guy who had a secret, and a woman who knew nothing about it and fell in love with him. The heroine of the movie was sweet and had a child, and the hero ended up falling in love with her. But the hero was actually undercover DEA, and the heroine's ex-husband was an ex-con involved with a huge drug cartel. They knew the ex wanted to see his kid, and he'd probably pass through this way before he made his next delivery. They thought this was the best way to capture him.

When the ex showed up, the hero would be there to bring him down. Except by then he was in love with the heroine, and the last thing he wanted was to blow his cover with her.

"This would never happen in real life," Reid said.

"Shh." She'd made popcorn, and they'd both switched to iced tea. At a commercial break he'd taken Not My Dog out back and Sam had set a bowl of water on the floor in the kitchen. The dog lapped it up, then looked at Reid like he wanted to jump up on the sofa and cuddle with them.

"Not happening."

With a deep sigh, Not My Dog settled in on the floor in front of the sofa.

The action continued. The heroine's son was in danger once the ex went on the run, taking the kid as a hostage.

"That's some terrible parenting right there," Reid said, grabbing another handful of popcorn.

Sam shook her head.

The hero had gone after the bad guy, promising the heroine he'd get her child back. And, of course, he did. The bad guy was arrested, and the hero brought the child back to the heroine, who was rightly pissed off that he'd lied to her about everything and told the guy to take a hike.

"Bet by the end of the movie they end up back together again," he said, taking a sip of his iced tea.

"Shh," Sam said. "Of course they will. But it's how they get there that counts."

He was right. The woman and her child went back to her old life, but she was miserable without the hero. He went back to duty, but he wasn't happy, either. They ended up reunited, and the hero told the heroine he was sorry for deceiving her, that in the beginning it had been just a job, but he hadn't expected to fall in love with her and her kid.

The heroine fell into his arms and they kissed. The movie ended with them embracing, with the kid in between them.

"See?" he said. "It all ends up with a happily-ever-after."

Sam laid her glass down, crossed her legs, and faced him. "And you have some issue with happily-ever-after?"

"No. I just don't think it's realistic that every relationship that has problems can be neatly resolved in fifteen minutes, and everyone ends up happy."

"In real life, no. But you do realize this is just a movie, Reid."

He shrugged. "I guess."

"But I see your concern. You think we women watch these movies and search for perfect men who are going to ride up on that white steed and save us from our mundane or, God forbid, heinous lives, when in reality no such man exists."

He frowned. "Now you're messing with me."

She grinned back at him. "Maybe a little. But come on, Reid. It's entertainment and nothing more. I can assure you I have no illusions about men of the real or TV variety. A man is flawed just like any woman. We all make mistakes and likely screw up relationships. Did the last relationship you had make you wary about that elusive happily-ever-after?"

Is that what he was doing? Was he still holding tight to that fantasy of Britt, to what he'd thought their relationship was and what it had really ended up being? He didn't spend a lot of time thinking about her, so likely not.

"I don't know. Maybe. I haven't had a lot of luck with women."

"Really. And what does that mean? That you don't get lucky very often, or that your relationships tend to end badly?"

He laughed. "Oh, I can get lucky all right. I just don't stay lucky."

"So you have no problem getting laid. It's keeping them afterward that's a problem."

He shot her a look. "Now you're making it sound like I'm bad in bed."

She gave him a quizzical look. "Are you?"

"Hell no."

She got up and grabbed the empty popcorn bowl and headed into the kitchen. "Of course, I have no firsthand knowledge of your sexual prowess, so I can't attest to the truthfulness of that statement."

Now she really was messing with him, but he wasn't about to take it just sitting there. He got up and followed her into the kitchen. "I'll be happy to give proof of my . . . prowess, if you'd like."

After placing the bowl in the sink, she turned around to face him. "Sure. I guess it's time to put up or shut up, McCormack."

He cocked a brow. "You're serious."

"Why not? You're clearly bored with TV, and unless you have to be in bed by nine p.m., there's not much else to do. I'm game if you are."

He reached for her hand, hauling her up and against him. The scent of something sweet filled the air around him.

"Say no right now if you don't mean what you just said."

Her gaze was direct, and he saw nothing but the truth—and desire—there. "I don't say what I don't mean, Reid."

"Good enough." He slid his hand into her hair to hold her head right where he wanted it, then kissed her.

Chapter 14

WHOA. SAMANTHA HAD thrown out the dare, sure. But she hadn't expected this all-consuming takeover of her body. She was hot—all over. And Reid had lit the flame.

She'd laid down the challenge, and she'd been truthful with Reid when she told him she never said things she didn't mean. But she hadn't intended to invite him into her bed tonight—certainly hadn't intended it when she'd asked him over for dinner. The conversation had just naturally gravitated in that direction.

But—why not? They were two healthy, single, consenting adults. Plus, he was gorgeous, and right now his mouth was doing deliciously sensual things to hers, igniting her entire body into a giant, turned-on bonfire.

He had a firm grip on her head, his fingertips massaging her scalp in a way she could only define as Oh-God-keep-doing-that. His other hand roamed her back, inching ever lower until he reached her butt.

The man was definitely not shy. He grabbed hold of her butt and drew her close against every rock-hard part of him. And some parts of him were definitely harder than others, a fact her body definitely noticed and reacted to by firing up even hotter.

She was afraid she was going to self-combust. She pressed the palms of her hands against his chest, needing some air. He pulled away, igniting her with the desire she read in his eyes.

"You okay?" he asked.

His voice had dropped an octave. Who knew that was such a turn-on?

"I'm hot."

His lips ticked up. "Yeah. I noticed. I'm hard."

She reached between them, unable to resist testing him out for size. He was . . . very impressive. "I know."

"So . . . you're hot and I'm hard. Should we do something about that?"

She looped her arms around his neck. "Most definitely. If I can manage to breathe through it without dying."

He frowned. "Asthma attack? Do you need a breather or some meds?"

"Uh, no. You just steal my breath."

He splayed his hands over her back, then lifted her shirt, his fingers playing over her skin. His hands seemed to be everywhere.

Reid had always struck her as so laid-back. Suddenly he seemed so . . . urgent. And she had to admit, the fact he wanted her rather . . . urgently . . . was firing up her own need in a rather urgent way as well.

Was there anything hotter than a man who desperately wanted you?

"Take a couple of deep breaths."

She did, shuddering. "You touching me like that isn't helping."

"Like what? Like this?" He teased the top of her pants with the tips of his fingers, dipping just inside the back of them to toy with the top of her underwear.

Yeah, there went that breathing thing again. "Yes. Like that."

"If I took your clothes off, maybe you could breathe better." His fingers snaked along her rib cage, coming to rest just below her breasts.

Clothes off. Definitely. "That might help."

"Lead the way to your bedroom and let me take care of that for you."

She took his hand and started toward the hallway.

Then her landline phone rang.

Crap. Only one person called her landline these days.

"That's Grammy Claire," she said. "I have to answer it."

He let go of her hand. "Go ahead."

She dashed into the kitchen and grabbed the phone. "Hello?"

"Samantha? Is that you?"

"Of course it is, Grammy Claire. Are you home?"

"No. I'm . . . I have a question."

Something wasn't right. Sam could tell from her grandmother's voice. "Okay. What's your question?"

"How do I get home from the grocery store? I don't quite remember what street to turn on out of the parking lot."

Sam closed her eyes and leaned against the kitchen counter for support. "I'll be right there to get you."

"No need, dear. I just need a few directions."

"I was about to go out anyway, Grammy Claire," she said, giving Reid a look. "So I'll just meet you at the store and guide you home, okay?"

"Okay."

"You stay right there in your car and I'll be there in about five minutes. Promise me you won't leave the parking lot at the store?"

"Of course. I'll be right here."

"I'm leaving the house now. I'll see you soon."

She hung up. Reid had his keys in his hands. "Something's wrong with your grandmother."

Sam had her shoes in her hands. "I should drive. She won't recognize your truck."

He put his hands over hers. "Your hands are shaking. If you want to take your car, that's fine. But how about you let me drive?"

She hesitated for only a second, but realized he was right. "Of course. Keys are on the hook in the kitchen."

He grabbed them while she slipped into her shoes. Then they were out the door.

When they pulled into the grocery store lot, she directed Reid to Grammy Claire's car. Her grandmother was still sitting in the car, looking out the windshield.

Claire breathed a slight sigh of relief, pushing the major concern to the back of her mind—for now. She slid out of the car and went over to the driver's side, letting her grandmother notice her rather than knocking on the window. She didn't want to scare her.

Her grandmother smiled at her and rolled down the window.

"Hello, Samantha."

"Hi, Grammy Claire. Are you ready to go home now?"

"Yes." She looked over at Sam's car. "I see you have Reid McCormack with you. Did you two have a date?"

"We just shared a pizza together. How about if I drive?"

"That's totally not necessary."

"Of course it's not, but you mentioned you had that engine problem the other day and I wanted to listen to your car, so how about you let me drive it?"

"All right."

Her grandmother got out and moved to the passenger side and Sam got in, deciding to wait for later to have a discussion with her grandmother. Right now it was important to get her safely home.

Sam pulled into her grandmother's garage, and Grammy Claire got out of the car. Sam popped the trunk, then went to the back of the car, only to find no groceries. She looked in the backseat and didn't see anything there, either.

"Did you stop at the store for something, Grammy Claire?"

"Um . . . I thought so. Did I forget to buy the groceries?"

Yet another concern about her grandmother.

"I'll be inside in just a second, okay?"

"Sure, sure." Her grandmother waved her hand, then went inside. Sam walked down the driveway to her car, where Reid had stepped out, waiting for her.

"I need to spend some time with my grandmother. Something is definitely not right. She has never not been able to find her way home. Or forgotten to get groceries."

She tried her best to tamp down the swell of panic in her chest.

Breathe, Sam. Breathe.

"Do you need me to stay with you?" Reid asked.

She saw the sympathy in his eyes, and she was damn glad he'd been here with her tonight. But she had to deal with this by herself.

She shook her head. "No, but thanks for being so nice about this."

"Hey, it's family, Sam, and family always comes first." He brushed his lips across hers, then laid her keys in her hands. "Take care of your grandmother. I'm going to go grab the dog and head out."

She nodded. "Front door's unlocked. Just hit the button to lock it when you close it."

He nodded. "Will do. Let me know if there's anything you need, okay?"

"I will. Talk to you later."

He walked away and down the street. She watched him for a minute, then turned on her heel and went inside to talk to her grandmother.

Chapter 15

SAMANTHA SAT WITH Megan inside Megan's bakery and coffee shop, which had closed for the day. Megan shoved a latte and a cranberry muffin in front of her. She wasn't hungry, but she had to admit, a strong cup of coffee and a sweet treat was something she really needed right now.

Megan pulled up a chair and sat next to her. "Okay, talk to me. How did the doctor's appointment go?"

Sam sighed. "About like I thought. First, Grammy Claire didn't want to go, but I explained to her about not remembering how to get home, and then no groceries when she'd specifically gone to the store to get some, meant something was up. I told her I was concerned for her well-being. You know how stubborn she is. She said that it had been a momentary lapse and she was fine."

Megan had taken a sip of her coffee. She set the cup down. "But then you insisted, right?"

"I did." She picked at the muffin, unable to resist a taste of the cranberry. One didn't just turn down something Megan had baked. After she swallowed and took a sip of the latte, she said, "Grammy Claire finally relented, so we went to see her doctor. When I told him about her memory, he was definitely concerned. He ran some blood work and did a simple neurological exam, and he said she seemed fine. But depending on the results of the blood and urine tests, he wants to send her to a neurologist for a further workup."

Megan grasped her hand. "I know you're worried about her."

"I am. And other than routine health issues for someone her age, she's been fine. Until now."

"Here's hoping it's nothing too serious. She was just confused. Older folks get confused sometimes."

She knew Megan was trying to be positive and pump her up, but they both knew there was something wrong. Something serious.

"She's the only family I have left."

"Not true. You have me."

Tears pricked her eyes and she squeezed Megan's hand. "Thanks. And thank you for always being here to listen."

Megan smiled at her. "Always. And if you need any help with Grammy Claire, you let me know."

"Thank you. Now, anything going on with you and the hot body guy?"

Megan frowned, then her eyes widened. "Oh, Brady Conners?"

"Yes. You two looked fantastic together at Des's party."

"He is a hottie. And super nice. But very quiet. He took me home and walked me to my door, told me he had a very nice time, and waited for me to let myself in. I invited him in for coffee and he politely declined. He didn't even try to kiss me. Not once. Dammit."

"Oh, that's too bad. He doesn't have a girlfriend, does he?"

"I would think if he had a girlfriend he would have brought her to the dinner instead of me."

"That's true."

"I think he's still troubled over what happened with his brother."

Sam sighed. "I'm sorry about that."

"Me, too. I think I'll bake him some muffins and bring

those to him. That man needs to smile more. He has a gorgeous smile."

If anyone could make someone smile, it was Megan. And
her baking. "Good idea."

"In the meantime, how about we ditch these coffees and
go get something a little more . . . substantial?"

"Now you're talking."

"I need to finish cleaning up here. Meet you at Bash's bar
in an hour?"

Sam nodded. "It's a date."

It would give her just enough time to dash home, check
on Grammy Claire, then get ready.

For the past few days she'd been overwhelmed with
thoughts of her grandmother. A night out was just what she
needed right now.

Chapter 16

IT HAD BEEN a grueling day. Reid had butted heads with the engineer, disagreeing over structural walls, even though he'd already had his design approved once.

But no. Just like in most of the projects he worked on, it was a constant argument about design versus engineering. And a giant pain in his ass. He and Deacon had met with the engineer and discussed a twelve-foot beam that needed to be replaced on the main floor before they could remove any more walls.

It was already in the plan, he'd gone over it with the original engineer, and he knew every load-bearing wall in the building. But this engineer was being tough on them and wouldn't approve the next stage until they replaced that beam. So despite a header not being in the plan, he was going to have to go back to the drawing board and come up with a revised drawing for the main floor—one that would have to include either posts or a header. Which meant delays he didn't have time for.

He was so irritated by the end of their afternoon meeting that Deacon had insisted they stop at a bar so Reid could unwind.

What he really needed to do was spend the evening reworking his drawings, so those could be approved.

"You can take an hour for a few beers. Then you can go home and work," Deacon said.

Reid finally relented, and he followed Deacon to the No Hope at All bar. Deacon parked next to him, and they both got out of their trucks.

"You know Bash lets his dog have the run of the bar. I don't think it'll be a problem for you to bring Not My Dog inside, especially considering how well-behaved he is."

With a shrug, Reid hooked the leash to Not My Dog's collar and led him through the doors. He was immediately greeted by Bash's dog, Lou, a tiny-sized terror of a Chihuahua, who dashed up to them and started sizing up Not My Dog, who wagged his tail and sniffed the little dog.

"Hey, you two," Bash said, coming around the bar to shake their hands. "Glad to see you back here, Reid."

"Thanks."

"I fenced an area out back for Lou to run around in if you want to let your dog roam out there with her. There's water and plenty of chew toys, plus they can bark at traffic."

"Sounds good." He followed Bash out the back door to a fenced-in yard area. He let Not My Dog off the leash, then gave him a stern look. "Behave yourself."

The dog didn't even look back at him as he ran off to play with Lou.

"Heard you got yourself a dog," Bash said as they came back inside.

"The dog kind of claimed me. I didn't have much of a choice."

Bash laughed. "Yeah, I know how that is. What are you going to do with him when you head back to Boston?"

Reid shrugged. "No idea. I guess I'll worry about that when it's time for me to leave." Reid looked around at the construction area tented off from the main building. "How's it going?"

Bash crossed his arms. "Right now it's messy. And noisy. Fortunately, the bar is loud at night, and by the time the place really gets going they're done for the day, and they don't work weekends, so there's been no complaints."

"Great. Can I take a look?"

"Not much to see yet, but the foundation is poured and they have framing up, so sure."

They stepped through the white tarp. Bash was right in that there wasn't much to see from his standpoint, but from an architect's viewpoint, Reid could see the vision that he and Bash had talked through several months ago. The foundation was down, and it would offer space for the kitchen and the outdoor eating area off the side of the bar. Walls would separate the bar from the kitchen, and there'd be a doorway leading outside, perfect to enjoy outdoor eating in the summer. Plus Bash had an eating space carved out separate from the bar, a spot that would be less noisy.

"It's looking good so far," Reid said as they wandered around.

Bash nodded. "It's still pretty bare-bones, but now that the framing is up, at least I have a vision where everything's going to be."

Reid smiled. "Excited?"

"I'll be excited when it's all done. My chef is breathing down my neck to get started. He's already pushing for the new restaurant and he hasn't even started here yet."

Reid patted him on the back. "Progress is always a good thing."

"Speaking of the restaurant, I might want to . . . accelerate things on that end. Since you're here, and I hate to ask . . ."

Reid had actually hoped he would. "I'd love to sit down with you and sketch out your restaurant plans."

Bash looked relieved. "You would? That'd be great. I know you're busy as hell with the mercantile, so I didn't want to presume."

"I don't know how official we can make it, and we had only spoken in general terms when I was here last time, but if you've got a vision, then yeah, let's talk."

"Thanks, man. You did such a fantastic job helping me refine the drawings for this expansion. I know you'll be able to help me figure out what I want for the restaurant."

"I'm happy to help. Why don't you text me what you've got in mind in terms of time for next week? We'll schedule something at the bar and you can give me free beers while we talk."

Bash laughed. "You're on."

They headed inside. Bash went back behind the bar, and Reid took a seat at the bar next to Deacon.

"I stopped in and looked at the expansion the other day when I was in here," Deacon said. "Bash is pretty stoked about it."

"He should be. It'll be good for business."

"Beers?" Bash asked as he came back to where they were sitting.

"Two," Deacon said.

"Okay, and what is Reid having?"

"Funny," Deacon said. "Though considering the day we had, maybe four beers is about right."

Bash pulled two beers, popped the tops off and handed the bottles across the bar to them. "One of those kind of days, huh?"

"Yeah." Reid took two very deep swallows of beer, then, as the cold brew sailed its way down, realized Deacon was right. This was just what he needed. He was already relaxing.

Bash laid his palms on the bar. "So which one of you is going to tell me about your shit day?"

Deacon grabbed his bottle of beer. "I'll let Reid tell you."

Reid explained to Bash about the meeting with the engineer.

"It never goes smoothly, does it?"

"No, but I was hoping we had everything on this building lined out in advance. I guess I was wrong."

"Hopefully this will be the last of it," Deacon said.

"I'll drink to that." Reid raised his bottle and tipped it in Deacon's direction. "We can't afford any more delays, or bullshit additional costs. The way I drew it up the first time was suitable. It's just this engineer's idea to cost us more money and time so he can justify his damn job."

"Well, God forbid he say we did it right the first time," Deacon said, signaling to Bash for two more beers.

Reid's lips curved. "Yeah, the world might come to an end if an engineer agrees with the architect or the contractor."

Deacon took the fresh beer Bash had given him and raised it. "To engineers—the assholes."

Reid laughed. "I'll drink to that."

They talked about their day for a while, then Reid went out to check on Not My Dog. He and Lou were barking furiously at a cat that was calmly strolling by the fence, ignoring them. More like taunting them, really.

At least they were active. Satisfied the dogs were okay, he went back inside and was surprised to see Sam and Megan Lee sitting next to Deacon.

He hadn't talked to Sam since that night with her grandmother other than a few texts where she said everything was "okay" and she was "busy." He hadn't wanted to pry, so he'd let things sit. He was glad to see her now. He took his seat at the bar, and Sam smiled.

"Deacon was just telling us about your day," Sam said. "Engineer, huh?"

Reid grabbed his beer. "Yeah. And that's about all I want to talk about relating to engineers."

"Okay, then."

She had a glass of wine in her hand, and it looked like she'd already downed half of it.

"Bad day yourself?" he asked.

She took in a deep breath, then let it out. "I've had better."

"Which is why we're here," Megan said. "We're drowning out the day with a cocktail."

Deacon raised his bottle. "Same reason I dragged Reid in here. Nothing like a little alcohol to blow off a shitty day."

"Or a supremely decadent cranberry muffin," Megan added with a sly grin.

Sam nodded. "This is true. But your cranberry muffins just don't go with wine."

"Have you tried them with a glass of merlot?" Megan asked. "Because I have, and trust me, they're a perfect complement to each other."

"Maybe you should start offering wine as a menu item," Reid said. "Wine and muffins."

"I could probably bring in a lot more customers that way. I'm going to apply for that liquor license right away."

"Woman." Bash tapped his fingers on the bar, offering a

mock glare at Megan. "I can't compete with your baked goods, and I don't need you putting me out of business."

Megan laughed. "Fine. I'll stick to coffee."

"You do that."

Chelsea, Bash's girlfriend, showed up. "Hey, no one told me there was a party going on here tonight."

"It was unplanned," Sam said. "We just got here. How was your day?"

"Uneventful." Chelsea slid her purse across the bar. She walked around behind it to give Bash a kiss, ordered a drink, then came back around.

"We should get a table," Megan said. "Easier to talk that way."

"Sounds good to me," Sam said, then grabbed her purse and slid off the barstool.

They moved to one of the large, round tables near the bar. It wasn't too crowded in there, so hopefully Bash would get a free minute and could sit with them if he had some time.

In the meantime, Reid really wanted some alone time with Sam, so he could ask about her grandmother. But not now in the middle of this group. He wasn't sure who she'd talked to about Claire, and the last thing he wanted to do was bring it up in the middle of a group of people. He'd wait 'til later.

They ordered more drinks, grabbed a couple of bowls of pretzels, and talked about life and work.

"How's the house-hunting going, Chelsea?" Sam asked.

"Naturally, Bash and I disagree on everything. So it's going well." She finished her statement with a teasing smile.

"So you haven't found anything either of you like?"

Right at that moment, Bash came over and laid his hands on Chelsea's shoulders. "She's lying. We've narrowed it down to two houses we both like. It's just a matter of deciding. I think they'll both do fine. Chelsea's the one who can't make up her mind."

Chelsea tilted her head back to stare up at Bash. "Oh, sure. Make me the bad guy."

Bash leaned down and kissed her. "No, you're the bad girl."

A chorus of *ooh*s followed their kiss.

"You two should get a room," Deacon said. "Or at least a new house."

Bash grinned and wandered off. "That's one of our dilemmas," Chelsea said. "Or, my dilemma, according to Bash. One of the houses is a charming older home near the high school. The other is a new build that's farther on the outskirts of town."

"What do you like—and dislike—about both of them?" Megan asked.

"The benefits of a brand-new house are obvious," Chelsea said. "Everything is new, from the flooring to the appliances, and the square footage is outstanding. The closets are amazing, and you know I like my closet space. But it's also pricier. And the yard is a bit small, which I don't care for as much. I mean, we want a place we're going to stay long-term, which means marriage and kids and maybe another dog, so I want a big yard."

"Okay, and what about the other house?" Sam asked.

"It's amazing. It has four bedrooms, and a huge living room that's open to the kitchen and dining area. They've remodeled the entire house recently so everything has been painted, new floors have been laid down, and bathrooms have been redone, too. But it still has that touch of charm an older home represents. And it has a huge backyard."

"Sounds like a winner," Reid said. "So what's the issue?"

Chelsea wrinkled her nose. "Tiny closets in every bedroom. You can renovate a lot and put in new floors and paint, but you can't make a closet bigger."

Reid leaned back in his chair. "I could." He looked over at Deacon. "Deacon could as well. It's all about changing your square footage. And if you ask me, it sounds like that's the house you really want, Chelsea. You just need someone to tweak the design so you end up with more closet space. How does it work for you price-wise?"

"It's well under our budget, so there's room for more renovations if we wanted to go that route."

Reid shrugged. "I'm not trying to get you to lean one way or the other, but if you want me to, I'd be happy to take a look at the place with you and Bash and see if there's a way to work out the closet issue."

"I'd go along, too," Deacon said. "You know, just to make sure Reid's pie-in-the-sky architectural ideas are really doable."

Reid shot Deacon a glare. "Hey."

Deacon laughed.

"I do have a contractor's license in addition to being an architect, asshole."

"Maybe," Deacon said, grabbing a handful of pretzels. "But you're not as good as I am."

"Now I definitely want both of you to look at the house," Chelsea said. "If you're serious."

"I wouldn't have offered if I wasn't serious," Reid said. "We have the job during the day, but I could go by the house after work. And if Deacon wants to tag along and offer useless advice, I guess he can do that."

Chelsea grinned. "Great. Tomorrow's Bash's day off. Would that work for you?"

Reid nodded. "Fine with me."

"Me, too," Deacon said.

Sam laughed. "I almost want to come along just to be a fly on the wall. Plus, I'd love to see the house."

"I definitely want you to come," Chelsea said. "I'd love your opinion, Sam. You, too, Megan."

"I wish I could," Megan said, "but I have a meeting with one of my suppliers tomorrow afternoon. But someone take pictures."

They set a time to meet, and Chelsea gave them the address to the house.

Eventually Megan left, then Deacon took off as well. Chelsea moved up to the bar to sit by Bash, leaving Reid alone with Sam. He moved his seat to sit next to her.

"Hungry?" he asked.

"Starving, actually."

"Then let's ditch the alcohol and go grab something to eat. Oh, wait, I have Not My Dog with me."

"That's okay. We can go to my place. I need to check on Grammy Claire anyway. And Not My Dog can hang out at my house."

"You sure you don't mind?"

"Not at all."

"How about I pick up something for us to eat and meet you there? That'll give you time to check on your grandma."

She smiled at him. "That sounds really good. Thanks. I wasn't really in the mood to cook."

"I'll be there in a little while."

"I'll leave the door unlocked in case I'm not back from Grammy Claire's when you get there."

"Okay."

He went outside to grab Not My Dog, then said good-bye to Bash and Chelsea. He headed over to Bert's diner and ordered a couple of fried chicken dinners, complete with Bert's famous mashed potatoes and gravy, along with biscuits. While he waited, he chatted up a couple of Hope's old-timers, who told him they were glad he was renovating the mercantile. He sat and listened to them tell stories of what the mercantile was like when they were younger, which made him happy he was doing this project.

When the waitress handed him his bag, he climbed into his truck, and Not My Dog sniffed at the food.

"Not a chance, bud," he said. "This is people food."

Not My Dog gave him a mournful look. Reid shook his head. "Does that work for you at the ranch?"

The dog cocked his head and gave him a look that said, *You bet your ass, it does.*

Not My Dog's tongue hung out the side of his mouth.

"Surely Martha doesn't fall for that. She's way too smart for it. And I know Logan doesn't. I think you're lying to me."

The dog gave him that weird smile. This time it said, *Martha loves me. Even Logan is a sucker for this face.*

"You do have a cute face. Don't tell anyone I told you that."

And once again, he was talking to the dog.

He put the truck in reverse and headed over to Sam's house.

Chapter 17

_____

AFTER MAKING SURE Grammy Claire had eaten and was settled in front of the TV for the evening, Sam dashed home to take a record-breaking fast shower. She didn't know how long Reid would take to arrive, but she didn't want to be naked when he got there.

Though maybe being naked when Reid arrived was exactly what she wanted to be.

Until her stomach growled—fiercely, in fact—reminding her she'd had such a busy day she hadn't stopped to have lunch.

Okay, so dinner first.

She slid into a pair of yoga pants and a T-shirt and had her hair combed out just before the doorbell rang. She ran to answer it, then smiled at Reid.

"You're my favorite person right now," she said.

He held up the bag from Bert's. "It's because of the food, isn't it?"

"Of course. What other reason could there be? Come on in."

She closed the door behind him and the dog, then led him into the kitchen.

"Something smells great." She got out plates and utensils.

"Chicken. I hope you like chicken."

"Right now I'm so hungry I'd eat the bag. I forgot to eat lunch today. So yes, I love chicken." While Reid unpacked the bag, she set the table. "What would you like to drink?"

"Whatever you're fixing for yourself is fine."

She made two glasses of iced tea and put a bowl of water on the floor for Not My Dog, who sauntered in and took several licks, then sat. She brought the glasses of iced tea over, then slid into her chair. She wanted to be polite and make small talk, but she was too hungry. It looked like Reid was, too, so they both dove into the food.

Once she'd had a few bites of chicken, along with the amazing mashed potatoes with gravy, she felt like she could manage conversation.

"This is so good." Of course, it was about the food.

Reid looked up from his plate. "It is."

Then she laughed. "I'm sorry. I was just so hungry and food was all I could think about."

"I had a coffee and muffin from Megan's bakery for a late breakfast, and then I was busy all day."

"So no lunch for you, either, huh?"

"No."

"Then let's eat. We'll talk later."

They finished dinner, and when Sam laid her fork on her plate, she was well satisfied. "Thank you for dragging me out of the bar and bringing dinner over. Otherwise, not only would I have gotten drunk, I might have eaten all of Bash's pretzels."

Reid leaned back and laid his napkin on the table. "I might have liked to see you drunk. And I would have fought you for the pretzels."

"You'd have lost. I mentioned I was hungry, right?"

"Yeah, but you're slight. I could have taken you."

She pushed back from the table and grabbed their plates. "You'd like to think so, but I'm vicious when I want food."

He stood to help her. "I'll keep that in mind in case the zombie apocalypse hits. I'll want you on my team."

She laughed as they stood side by side at the sink. "Right.

You can shoot the zombies while I throw bouquets of flowers at them."

"Come on. You at least have scissor skills. We can turn those into mad machete abilities."

She paused, half turning to face him. "I think you have to get pretty close to them to whack them with a machete. I'd rather learn to use a gun. Preferably one of those long-range ones with a scope. That way I can stay far away."

He shook his head. "Not gonna work. Zombies always sneak up on you. You have to learn hand-to-hand combat."

She rolled her eyes, washed a dish, and slid it into the drying rack. "And you obviously play video games or watch those zombie shows on TV."

"Exactly. I'm preparing myself to face the apocalypse. Plus, it's a great way to wind down after a tense day at work."

She turned off the faucet and dried her hands while Reid wiped off the table. "I think those types of games and shows would *make* me tense, not relax me."

He tossed the paper towel in the trash. "Don't knock it 'til you've tried it. The games are fun. Next time you're at the ranch we'll go head-to-head in the apocalypse. I'll show you a few of my moves."

She'd like to see a few of his moves, but not in a video game. "We'll see."

"Speaking of the ranch, Martha told me there's a barbecue this weekend. You're coming, aren't you?"

"Of course."

"Then we'll play a game."

"Sure. You can teach me how to kill zombies."

He leaned against the counter and folded his arms across his chest. "I sense a lack of enthusiasm, Samantha."

"Really. And I was trying so hard to mask it." She gave him a teasing smile, then reached into the refrigerator and grabbed the iced tea to refill their glasses. She led him into the living room, where they both sat on the sofa. Not My Dog followed, turned around in a circle several times, then laid his head on his paws and went to sleep.

What a great dog.

Reid placed his glass on a coaster and turned to face her. "Now tell me what's going on with your grandmother. Is she doing all right after her confusion the other night?"

"I took her to see the doctor. He ran some tests. He's concerned and might want to send her to a neurologist for further workup."

He reached over and grabbed her hand. "Which only made you more of a wreck than you were the other night."

"It shows, huh?"

"A little. So what will you do if the neurological tests come up with something?"

She took in a deep breath and held it for a second or two before letting it out. "I don't know. Honestly, I don't even want to think about all this, even though I know I have to be the responsible adult and start planning ahead for my grandmother's future—no matter what that entails."

He brushed his hand over her hair. "Sometimes being the responsible adult sucks."

"It can. But I'll do what I need to do to make sure Grammy Claire is safe. Which might mean I have to take her car keys away from her."

"We had to do that with my granddad. He wasn't happy. Losing independence is so hard on folks when they get older."

She sighed—again. She'd been doing that a lot the past several days. "I don't want to do it to her. She prides herself on being independent. She loves being able to pick up and go wherever she wants, whenever she wants to. It'll kill her to lose that."

Sam felt the burden like never before—not only the responsibility of caring for her grandmother but also the potential to hurt her, which she never in a million years wanted to do. But Grammy Claire's safety was the most important thing, and she'd hurt her grandmother's feelings before she would allow her to drive off somewhere and either get in an accident or get lost.

She fought back the tears that pricked her eyes. She didn't want her grandmother to get sick. She refused to think about losing the last person who was family to her. She didn't want to be alone.

Reid moved in closer and put his arm around her. "If it helps any, my granddad got used to the idea of not having a car. Then he started making all of us chauffeur him around. I wasn't driving back then, but Logan loved it, because he got to drive all the time, and he'd just gotten his license."

She sniffed back the tears that threatened to fall. Now wasn't the time. Instead, she tilted her head back and smiled. "I'll bet Logan enjoyed that. What teenager wouldn't? Grammy Claire used to ask me to bring items to the flower shop for her after I got my license. I don't think she really needed any of the items she asked me to get for her. It was just an excuse for me to practice driving. I was a little tentative behind the wheel."

Reid smiled. "Whereas growing up on the ranch, we were driving the big trucks and tractors as soon as our legs were long enough that our feet could reach the pedals. As long as we were on ranch property, anyway. So driving was second nature to all of us."

"That must have been fun."

"It was. And, hey, if you do have to suspend your grandmother's driving privileges, you can always bring her out to the ranch. We'll put her behind the wheel of one of the trucks or tractors and she can drive anywhere she likes out there."

Sam laughed. "I can just picture her now, mowing down a herd of cattle."

"You'd be surprised how fast those cattle can haul ass when an eight-thousand-pound monster of a truck is bearing down on them."

She pulled her legs up and crossed them, facing Reid. "I can't even imagine my tiny little grandmother behind the wheel of one of those trucks."

His lips curved. "Makes you want to bring her out to the ranch and let her try, though, doesn't it? You know she'd have a great time rolling around the back roads of the property. All the freedom in the world, and nothing to worry about."

"That does sound lovely. Maybe *I* need a day at the ranch to drive around and let myself get lost."

"I could arrange that."

"You could, huh? Would you come get lost with me?"

His eyes darkened, and what she saw there was very . . . compelling. Interest mixed with definite desire.

"I know all the great places to get lost on the ranch, Sam. Places where no one would come looking for us, and no one would find us. Maybe I can kidnap you this weekend when you're out for the barbecue, and we'll get lost together."

"I like the sound of this. Des has told me the ranch has some beautiful lakes. And cabins. Very secluded."

He drew circles around one of her knees with his fingers, then pulled her legs out and draped them over his lap. The temperature in the room suddenly soared as their bodies touched. Even fully clothed, she felt the searing heat of Reid's body and wanted nothing more than to touch him. That kiss the other night, the one before they'd been interrupted by the phone call from her grandmother, still burned hot in her memories.

They had just begun to explore each other, to see where this explosive chemistry between them could go.

She wanted to do a lot more exploring with him.

When he shifted their bodies and she suddenly found herself on his lap, she was about three seconds short of an explosion.

"You know," he said, "if we go find some of those hidden places at the ranch this weekend, we might get so lost we'd be gone all night."

Her heart beat so rapidly she could barely think straight. It wasn't often she found herself so wrapped up in a man that she lost all sense of coherent thought, but Reid had amazing eyes, and an incredible mouth. She traced his lips with her fingertip.

"I don't think we'll have to go very far, Reid. I'm feeling a little lost right now."

He tilted her back onto the sofa, then covered her body with his. "Are you?"

He rubbed his erection against her, and she instinctually arched against him. "Oh. Definitely."

His lips curved. "Good."

And then he kissed her.

Chapter 18

SAM HAD NEVER experienced the kind of kiss that took her breath away.

Until now.

There was something so exponentially hot about a man who knew how to kiss, who wasn't tentative about it and kissed with authority. Reid was that kind of man. He had one hand on her hip and the other on her neck, and his mouth moved over hers with an eager passion that told her he was as much into this as she was.

A definitely heady feeling.

Sam lifted into him, her lips and tongue doing a desperate dance with his. As he pressed into her, his body all hard planes and angles, she tried to memorize this moment, to feel every moving part of him, from his mouth to where his hands were. Her senses went haywire, like electrical zings pulsing through her, her body crying out for more, more, more.

And when he moved his hand underneath her to cup her butt, she moaned against his mouth, arching toward him. It was almost embarrassing how close she was to an orgasm already. It had been sort of a dry spell for her in the sex department, and Reid was supremely hot and sexy, and the way he rubbed against her hit all those hot, delicious parts that hadn't been . . . serviced lately.

He lifted his head. "You're shaking. Everything okay?"

She managed a smile. "Everything is definitely okay. More than okay. Like, I could come really soon if you keep moving that way kind of okay."

His lips curved. "So what you're saying is you'd like to stay in this position?"

He surged against her, and she gasped as tingles of pleasure shivered through her.

She wrapped her legs around his hips. "Yes, this could definitely work for me. Or, we could get naked."

"I like the naked idea a lot. Hold on."

He pushed off the sofa and stood, his hands cradling her behind.

"Can I just say I like your hands on my butt?"

He grinned. "I'm making a mental note of that."

He held her so easily as he headed toward the hallway, as if she weighed nothing.

"Which door?" he asked.

"Last one on the right."

He shifted her, holding her with one hand while he turned the knob on her bedroom door.

So. Impressive.

He pushed the door open, walked in, and flipped the light switch on, and at that moment she really hoped she hadn't flung her bra and underwear on the floor before her shower earlier.

Not that he would notice her underwear on the floor, since his gaze was most definitely fixed on her, which only heated her insides more. He laid her on the bed, then leaned over her.

"Now. How about we take some clothes off?"

If it were possible to go up in flames spontaneously, this would be the time. The man just oozed sex appeal with his bedroom eyes and the way his voice lowered when he suggested they get naked. And they hadn't even gotten to all the actual sex stuff yet.

She could well imagine just how good he was at the

actual sex stuff, and she couldn't wait to get there. She pulled off her shirt and wriggled out of her yoga pants, watching intently as Reid kicked off his boots and undid the buckle of his jeans. When he drew his shirt over his head, she had to pause, because, oh, his chest and those abs. *Rockhard* didn't even begin to describe him.

Wow.

This was about to get really interesting, and she didn't want to miss a thing.

He held his shirt in his hand. "You stopped."

She got up on her knees and moved to the edge of the bed so she could touch all that beautiful, sculpted skin. She laid her hands on his shoulders, then skimmed her fingers down his arms. "You took your shirt off. I got distracted."

He grinned, then dropped his jeans to the floor, making her shudder with anticipation.

He wrapped his arm around her waist, then dropped them both to the mattress. "And you're wearing pink underwear."

"I am."

"I have a thing for pink."

She looked down at him. "You do? Because your boxer briefs are black."

He laughed. "I don't mean I wear pink."

"Good to know. Because my sex buzz might have died a little if you did."

He smoothed his hand over her stomach, his fingers teasing the top of her panties. "I meant I have a thing about women who wear pink underwear. And you look very sexy in yours. Hot pink especially is my favorite."

"That's very good to know, because I happen to own a lot of pink underwear."

He rolled her onto her back and toured the curves of her breasts with his fingertips. "Then I might just have to see them all."

"I guess you might."

"But for now, let's take these off." He reached for the clasp in front of her bra and, with one expert flick of his fingers, unhooked it. He pulled the cups away, then swept his hands over her breasts, brushing his thumb over her nipples.

He met her gaze.

"These are pink, too. And hot."

Her senses went haywire as he leaned over and put his mouth on one of her nipples, while his fingers teased the other. She tunneled her fingers into his hair, holding tight while tingling pulses shot south, making her sex quiver in anticipation.

She wanted his hands on her everywhere. She wanted to explore his body with her hands and her mouth. She wanted everything. Right now.

She lifted his head and looked down at him. "Panties."

He smiled up at her. "Yes. Did I mention those were hot?"

"Off. Take them off."

"I can definitely do that."

He pressed kisses down her body, which only prolonged the torment as his mouth moved over her hip bone. When he dragged one edge of her underwear over her hip with his teeth, she shuddered.

"Reid."

He lifted his head. "I like the way you say my name, Sam." He drew up on his knees and dragged her underwear over her hips and down her legs, then spread her thighs and nestled between them. "Let's see if I can make you scream it out."

She sucked in a deep breath as he put his mouth on her sex.

He swept his hot, wet tongue across her and she lifted up, craving more of the delicious sensation. She was already spiraling so fast it made her dizzy. She grabbed the sheets to hold on, to suspend the moment, because the things he was making her feel were just so good she wanted to delay the inevitable fall.

But it had been too long, and Reid must have some kind of sorcerer's tongue, because she was out of breath, hit by lightning and losing it fast.

She did cry out his name when she hit her climax. And she had absolutely no regrets about it, because it had been glorious.

When he climbed up her body and hovered above her, she framed his face with her hands.

"Well. That was a very good start."

He grinned. "I'm glad you thought so. You seemed kind of into it."

"Kind of? I nearly passed out."

"Hey, don't pass out. I'm not finished with you yet."

She brushed his hair away from his face. "If this gets any better, you might need to bring in an oxygen tank for me."

"You sure know how to feed a guy's ego." He rolled to his side, then swept his hands over her breasts.

There went those tingles again. She shifted to face him. "You sure know how to give a woman a great orgasm. Just stating the facts."

"How about we try that orgasm thing again? The first one seemed to go well." He shifted his trajectory, moving his hand over her stomach. He was slow with his movements, which she appreciated, since he seemed to enjoy touching her. And she sure liked the feel of his fingers exploring her body, especially when he went lower, cupping her sex, using those exceptional skills he possessed to make her breath catch.

"Keep doing that," she said.

He moved over her so his face was aligned with hers. She saw the heat in his eyes, making desire coil deep in her belly.

He increased his movements. "That?"

She gasped. "Definitely a lot more of that."

His erection lay hot and hard against her hip. She knew what she needed, what she wanted more than anything right now.

"I need you inside me. How about right now?"

"You sure you don't want more screaming?"

She managed a laugh. "I have a suspicion there'll be more of that."

He rolled over and shrugged out of his boxer briefs, then grabbed a condom from his jeans pocket.

After he put it on, he rolled on top of her.

"Were you thinking of me when you slipped that condom into your pocket?"

He entered her. "Every fucking day and night, Samantha."

His words inflamed her. And when he took her mouth in a deep, passionate kiss and began to move inside her, her world turned upside down. She wrapped her legs around Reid's hips and lifted against him, needing him to give her all he had.

She'd never felt so fused to a man before, so deeply connected. Maybe it was nothing more than his finesse, the way he so thoroughly captured her with every touch, every kiss. But for her, it felt like so much more. She was in deep here, and if Reid hadn't been kissing her, holding so tight to her, grounding her, she'd drown in it all.

But he held her and kissed her and she felt every movement, every thrust, and it was perfect as he ground against her, taking her right where she wanted to go.

She had no words to give him, only her touch as she smoothed her hands down his arms, only moans and whimpers to voice her approval, only her body as she rose against him to meet him halfway.

He grabbed a handful of her hair and tugged. Sensation shot right to her core.

She came with a wild cry, her body tightening around his cock. He shoved in deep, only increasing her pleasure as waves of orgasm tunneled through her. He kissed her, a deep, thorough kiss that rocketed her further into those waves.

And then he went with her, his entire body shuddering as he came. She held on, reveling in every body-shocking sensation.

After they both came down from that incredible high, she smoothed her hands over his shoulders. His body was slick with sweat, his heart beating in fast time against her chest, matching her own hard-driving rhythm.

He ran his tongue against her bottom lip, then lifted his head, looking down at her with a satisfied smile and those sexy eyes of his.

"Need oxygen yet?"

She smiled up at him. "Maybe."

He got up and disappeared into the bathroom for a minute, then came back and climbed into bed with her, pulling her against his chest. It felt good to lie there with him, to feel the warmth of his body. She wrapped her leg around him and just . . . settled.

This had been good. Really good, especially now when they were quiet. There was nothing awkward about it, and Reid didn't seem in any hurry to take off. He rubbed her back, his fingers occasionally gliding into her hair.

She hadn't felt this peaceful and relaxed in a very long time.

She closed her eyes and let the calm wash over her.

REID JERKED HIS eyes open as something wet slid along his hand.

Disorientation took over for a few seconds before he got his bearings. There was a warm, naked body next to him.

Samantha.

And a dog with a wet tongue licking his hand.

Not My Dog.

Okay, check. Bearings realigned.

He slid out of bed and got dressed—at least half dressed, anyway.

He took Not My Dog out back and let him do his thing.

"Sorry, bud," he said as he led the dog back inside. "I kind of passed out."

The dog went into the kitchen for a drink, then sat and looked up at him.

"Yeah. I agree. Time to go."

He had no idea what time it was. He found his phone on the chair in the bedroom, grabbed it, and checked the time.

Four a.m.

Shit. He hadn't meant to fall asleep. Sex was fun and all, but he didn't want Sam to think—

A warm, naked body—with breasts—pressed against his back.

Damn, that felt good.

"What time is it?" she asked.

"Four. The dog needed to go out."

"Oh. Are you coming back to bed?"

He turned around, and damn if the sight of her—naked, her hair tousled from sleep—wasn't tempting as hell.

"Actually, no. I have an early meeting tomorrow—today. I need to get back to the ranch so I can shower and change clothes."

"Okay."

No argument. No whining or pouting. She sure made this hard on him.

Hell, she made everything hard on him. Including his dick. Which made him want to pull her back in bed and slide inside her warm, wet heat until at least dawn.

But, no.

Instead, he kissed her—briefly, because she was too tempting for him to linger. Then he grabbed his shirt and his keys while she put on a robe and walked him to the front door.

"Thanks for bringing me dinner tonight," she said. "Though, I suppose that was last night."

"You're welcome." He grabbed the lapels of her robe and brought her close. "Thanks for dessert."

She laughed and twined her hand around his neck to bring him down for a kiss. "Anytime."

If he kissed her for any longer he was going to pick her up and carry her to the bed. If they even made it to the bed.

"I gotta go."

She nodded. "See you later, Reid."

He walked out with the dog and climbed into his truck. The air was chilly, and he turned the heater on, wishing he were still in bed with Sam.

But that would be a really bad idea. The last thing he wanted was to get close to Sam. To get close to anyone while he was here.

He put the truck in reverse and backed out.

Chapter 19

SAM PUT THE finishing touches on a funeral spray, constantly checking the clock on the wall. The delivery was time sensitive.

It was a rush order, and for funerals, she did what needed to be done.

She knew the family of Mr. Tyrone, and had known him personally. He'd bought flowers for his wife for many years before she'd died. She'd stopped hearing from Mr. Tyrone after he'd gone into the nursing home many years ago.

And now she was making beautiful flowers for his casket.

Samantha took a step back and surveyed the red, white, and blue flower spray his family had decided on for their family tribute, signifying his military service. It would stand upright next to his casket, next to the flag that would be draped over it.

Perfect.

His grandchildren and great-grandchildren had already stopped by and selected the flowers they wanted. Several people had called to order wreaths, sprays, bouquets, and baskets as well. Edgar Tyrone had been popular and well-loved in Hope. And though he'd spent the last six years in a nursing home, people hadn't forgotten him.

Sam intended to make sure gorgeous bouquets to celebrate his life abounded at his funeral service.

It took her the entire day to make all the flowers, which she delivered to the funeral home before they were due. She helped the funeral director set everything up, then lingered in front of Mr. Tyrone's casket. She wasn't a personal friend—she had only known him from his trips into the flower shop—so she wouldn't be attending the funeral. But she said a few words and wished him well on his journey, then thanked the director and let him know to call her if there was anything else he needed.

Feeling a little melancholy, she stopped in at Megan's bakery after she got back.

It was late and the bakery was closed, so she rang the bell. It took Megan a few minutes to come to the front of the shop.

"Sorry," she said after she opened the door. "I was baking. Come on in."

Sam stepped in and inhaled the fresh smell of something amazing. Then again, it always smelled amazing in the bakery.

"What are you fixing?"

"Pies for tomorrow." Megan locked the door behind them. "Do you want something to drink? I just made raspberry iced tea. It's hot back there and I wanted something cool to drink."

"That sounds so good. And yes, thank you."

Sam grabbed a seat at one of the tables in front, trying to ignore the grumbling in her stomach. She'd been busy today—again. And had forgotten to eat lunch—again. Busy was good for business, but bad in that she wasn't eating lunch.

Megan came out bearing a tray with glasses of tea and muffins.

"You must have heard my stomach all the way in the back."

Megan smiled. "I didn't. Why, are you hungry? I'm hungry. I've been busy back there and needed a snack. Did you forget to eat lunch today?"

"I was doing the funeral flowers for Mr. Tyrone."

Megan's smile disappeared. "I had heard he passed. He was always so nice."

"He was. He used to stop in the store at least a few times a year to pick up flowers for his wife."

"He'd come in for baked goods, too, when Mrs. T was still alive. She was fond of cheesecake, and he liked to surprise her."

Sam sighed. "He must have really missed her after she died. He never came into the flower shop after."

"He didn't stop in here, either."

They both looked at each other. Sam wondered if Megan was thinking the same thing, about what it must be like to lose that one person you love more than anything.

"Did you get a lot of floral orders for his funeral?" Megan asked.

"I did."

"That's good to hear. I like knowing people loved him."

"They did. I think he'll have a lot of attendance." She grabbed a muffin and looked it over. "What are these? Chocolate with white macadamia nut?"

"Yes. Also, white chocolate chips."

"I love you, Megan."

Megan grinned. "I know."

Sam bit into the muffin, letting its sweet and nutty goodness melt in her mouth. "Mmm, these are fantastic."

"Thank you."

They downed their muffins, sipped tea, and caught up on the day's events.

"I saw a lot of work going on over at the mercantile today," Megan said.

"You did? I was so busy I didn't have time to check it out. What was going on?"

"Trades and such. Electrical and plumbing and HVAC stuff. I don't really know other than it was super busy. I didn't see Reid much, though."

"He said he had an early meeting this morning, so maybe that was off-site."

"Oh, he said that, did he? And when did he tell you that?"

Damn. She hadn't meant to spill that information. "Oh, uh, when we talked last night."

"When you talked last night. While you were at the bar, or was this after?"

She could lie—but she would never lie to her best friend. "No. We had dinner together."

"You had dinner, huh? At a restaurant?"

Megan was very good at this game. "No, at my place. I needed to check on Grammy Claire, so while I did that, he went and got chicken dinners from Bert's."

"Sounds cozy. Was it cozy?"

She sipped her tea and looked over the rim of her glass at Megan, who stared at her expectantly. "It was cozy. The chicken was very good."

"You know I'm not at all interested in your chicken dinner, right?"

"I'm aware."

"Which means you're being coy, and you're never coy. Which means you and Reid had sex."

Sam leaned back in her chair. "You're like some super sleuth, aren't you?"

"Not really. You're just transparent." Megan popped the last piece of muffin in her mouth, following it up with a swallow of iced tea. "So how was it? And if you tell me how good the chicken was, I'm going to deny you muffins for a week."

Sam gasped. "That's a pretty brutal threat, Megan."

Megan shrugged. "Hey, I'm trying to live vicariously through someone who actually has a sex life, so I have to use all the weapons in my arsenal. Now spill."

"It was . . . I don't know if I have the words."

"Try to find some. With adjectives."

"It was wonderful. He's a very inventive lover. And he has exceptional hands. Not to mention an incredible mouth."

Megan sighed. "I don't know whether to be supremely happy for you or to hate you."

"Oh, please don't hate me. You're my best friend. I need you. And your baked goods. Not to mention your coffee."

"I'm going to assume it's my friendship you cherish more than my baked goods and coffee."

Sam held up her right hand. "Hand to heart, I swear if you closed your bakery tomorrow, I'd still love you forever."

"Good enough. And I am happy for you. It sounds like your night went very well."

"Mostly."

"Uh-oh. What part didn't go well?"

"He didn't stay the night."

"Oh. He didn't get up right after and leave, did he?"

She shook her head. "We fell asleep together. But he got up in the wee hours and said he had to head back to the ranch to shower and change clothes."

"Okay, that's not too bad, is it?"

She shrugged. "I guess not. I mean, it's a reasonable excuse for not spending the night."

"But . . ."

"But I could tell he was uncomfortable about having slept in my bed. You know how it is with guys."

Megan shrugged. "I have a vague recollection."

She laughed. "You can tell the ones who genuinely want to be there with you and the ones who are slightly uncomfortable. I mean, when you're naked and having sex, they're of course all in. But it's the after part where they start second-guessing everything."

Megan studied her. "And you think Reid was second-guessing the sex part."

"Maybe. I don't know. It was four a.m. and things were a little hazy. So it's possible I'm overthinking it."

"Are you going to the barbecue this weekend at the ranch?"

Sam nodded. "Are you?"

"Of course. I'm providing baked goods. And I wouldn't miss ranch barbecue."

"Will the hot mechanic be there?"

Megan lifted her chin. "Brady? I have no idea. Just because we were paired up for one dinner at Des and Logan's place means absolutely nothing. I haven't even seen him since then."

"Maybe you should pursue it. Or him, I should say."

Megan let out a huff. "And maybe if he was interested he'd have pursued me. Which he didn't."

"Some men need a push. Like a car with a dead battery. Or some such vehicular analogy."

"I'm not much for pushing men around who don't want a push."

"Oh, please, Megan. It's the twenty-first century. If you're interested in him, you should go for it. Maybe he's shy."

"Brady Conners is hot and definitely as sexy as any man I've ever known. Shy? I don't think so. He's just . . . quiet."

"So unquiet him. Then seduce him with baked goods."

Megan laughed. "I'll think about it."

After Sam left Megan's place, she went back to clean up the shop. Once everything was in order, she locked the door and headed to her car. She took a passing glance over at the mercantile. It was after six and Reid's truck was there. She thought about walking over there to see what was up, but then changed her mind.

He hadn't called or texted her today. Maybe he'd been busy all day, or maybe his late-night flight out of her house had been his subtle way of telling her he'd like to keep things light and easy between them.

They were all supposed to meet over at the house Chelsea and Bash were interested in tonight. So she'd check him out then and see how he felt about . . . things. And if he wanted to do light and easy, she could do that.

After all, she knew whatever they had was only temporary.

First she needed to go home and check on her grandmother. Then she'd go check out Chelsea's dream house.

And Reid.

IT HAD BEEN a long day with electrical and plumbing and HVAC, and, much as Reid had suspected, it was going to be one expensive fix after another. He'd barely had time to run out and grab a sandwich to choke down for lunch today. They'd been working nonstop. But at least he knew that everything would be modernized and up to code in the building once they were finished.

When everyone was done for the day he checked his phone. Just enough time to meet Bash and Chelsea at the house they were interested in buying.

He knew Sam was going to be there, and he hadn't even had a second to call or text her since he'd left her house early this morning, which made him feel shitty, but it had just been that kind of day.

He'd talk to her after they looked at the house.

He plotted directions into the GPS on his phone and made his way to the house. It was on a quiet street with mature trees. Looked like a great neighborhood. Lots of kids outside playing. He parked at the curb and got out. Bash and Chelsea were already there. Deacon was going to meet him there after he gassed up his truck.

Reid stood on the sidewalk and surveyed the front of the house. He could see the appeal. It was a one-story brick with a good-sized front yard and an awesome porch with enough room for several chairs and a table. He could already envision Bash and Chelsea sitting out there to watch the sun set at night.

There was great landscaping, with a lot of tall trees to provide shade to the house, and close enough to have neighbors to chat with, but not so close they could see into your windows.

He walked up the long driveway and headed to the front door, noting the nice-sized bay window that was probably either in the living room or the kitchen. From typical layouts for the time period, he'd wager it was the living area.

He knocked on the door, which was answered by an attractive woman with short, dark hair and a friendly smile.

"Hello, I'm Layla Appleton of Hope Realtors. You must be Reid McCormack?"

"I am."

They shook hands.

"I'm going to step outside and make some calls. Chelsea and Bash are in the main bathroom arguing about something," Layla said with a smile.

Reid laughed. "That sounds normal for them. Thanks."

He wandered into the living area. It was spacious, with a modern fireplace and spectacular wood floors.

Chelsea was right about these rooms having been updated. The kitchen was modern, with new appliances and a good-sized island, and it was open to the dining and living area. It was a great entertainment space.

He walked down the hall, following the sound of Chelsea's and Bash's voices, and ended up in what had to be the master bedroom.

"We are not painting the walls purple," Bash said.

Chelsea heaved a sigh. "It's not purple. It's eggplant. And just one wall."

Reid grinned. "Sounds like you two have already made up your minds about this place."

"That all depends on what you can do with the closet in the master bedroom," Chelsea said.

His phone buzzed, so he answered it. When he finished the call, he tucked the phone in his pocket. "Deacon got sidetracked on another one of his company's jobs, so he won't be able to make it. He said to tell you he trusts me completely to handle this."

"Is that what he really said?" Bash asked.

"No. He told me not to screw this up."

Bash grinned. "That sounds more like Deacon."

Reid laughed. "Come on, let's go take a look at the closet."

Chelsea led the way. "Sam called me right before you got here. She's not going to be able to make it, either. She said her grandmother isn't feeling well."

"Oh," Reid said. "I hope she's okay."

"Me, too," Chelsea said. "Anyway, as far as the closet, it's over here, in a hallway between the master bedroom and master bath."

Reid tucked away his disappointment at not being able to talk to Sam. He followed Chelsea, deciding he needed to concentrate on this task and get Sam out of his head for now.

The hallway had good space leading into the master bath, but the two closets on either side of the hallway were super small.

"You need a bigger master closet."

"Yes."

"She has a lot of shoes," Bash said.

Chelsea nodded. "This is true."

"What are the closets in the other bedrooms like?"

"Not very big."

"Okay. Let me do a walk-through of the entire house."

He went into the master bath, noting the size, then got out his tape measure and jotted down dimensions, including the hallway. Then he walked out of the bedroom and into the hall, following it to the other three bedrooms, as well as another full-sized bathroom, making notes along the way. When he finished, he met up with Bash and Chelsea in the kitchen.

"Great house."

Bash smiled. "You haven't even seen the backyard yet."

Bash opened the sliding glass door and led them out into a very spacious yard.

"Now, granted, we have a small dog, but Lou will still enjoy all this space."

Reid laughed. "Yeah, I could see a Chihuahua thinking this was like having her own private oasis."

The yard was super spacious, with more mature trees and great landscaping. There was a deck covered by a wood arbor and lots of greenery, which would provide shade in the hot summer months. Flowering bushes surrounded the deck, and there was still plenty of grassy area for Lou to play in, and even add more dogs—or kids.

"Great yard."

"Isn't it?" Chelsea said. "We're already planning parties back here."

They headed back inside, and Reid laid his notebook on the counter. "So the only holdout is the closet space. Actually, the ones in the other bedrooms aren't too bad. You have a walk-in in one of the bedrooms. Not a huge one, but it's workable."

"True," Bash said. "They're not bad, just not acceptable to the closet queen here."

Chelsea elbowed Bash. "Hey. I like closet space."

Reid took out his pencil and started drawing. "This is

going to be rough, but here's what I think is your best option. You can lose the hallway and redo the master bath." He drew a rudimentary sketch, showing how to make best use of the space. "This will not only expand your bathroom area, but also your closet space."

He handed the drawing to Chelsea and Bash. Chelsea's eyes widened. "This is perfect. The size of the closet is just what I'm looking for."

Bash nodded. "It would definitely work, without sacrificing the square footage in the master bedroom."

"Right," Reid said. "All I did was eliminate the hallway between the bedroom and bath. Now as far as the other bedrooms, since they're all good-sized, I could add closet space, but you'll lose room square footage."

Chelsea stared at the drawing, waving her hand at Reid. "This is all I need." She looked up at Bash. "All *we* need. Don't you think?"

"I agree," Bash said. "Expanding the bath and closet in the master makes this the perfect house for us."

"Yay," Chelsea said, grinning. "I think we've found our house."

Chelsea and Bash embraced and kissed.

"That's my cue to get out of here," Reid said.

"No." Chelsea grabbed his arm. "Thank you. I knew what I wanted, but without your vision, this would never have happened. So now what?"

"I'll draw up something that looks a lot better than this. Once you buy the house, you can hire Deacon, or whatever contractor you want, to make it a reality for you."

"Fantastic." Chelsea hugged him. "Thank you, Reid."

"You're welcome."

Bash shook his hand. "Thanks, man. You helped me out again. You should consider sticking around Hope."

Reid smiled. "Well, you know I have a business in Boston."

"You could have a lot of business here, too."

"Yeah, I'll think about it. In the meantime, I'm sure your agent is outside waiting to hear what you've decided."

"Oh, right," Chelsea said, then looked at Bash. "We should tell her we're ready to make an offer."

"And then we have to sell my house."

Chelsea was nearly vibrating. "I'm *so* excited right now."

Reid said his good-byes and headed out. He left a message for Deacon and told him about the house, just in case he wanted to touch base with Bash and Chelsea. He figured Deacon would be perfect for the renovation.

All in all, not a bad end to the day. He'd like to see how that renovation turned out, but it wouldn't happen while he was still in Hope.

Too bad.

As he drove away, he thought about calling Sam. Or maybe dropping by. But in the end, he decided she likely had her hands full dealing with her grandmother, so he'd let things settle. For now.

Or maybe not, because he thought about her for the entire drive back to the ranch, so after he got home and had dinner, he pulled out his phone and texted her.

Sorry you couldn't make it earlier.

It took her about five minutes to reply.

I'm sorry, too! Grammy Claire was a bit under the weather.

He texted back: Is she okay?

She replied with: She's fine. An upset stomach, but I figured I should stay with her tonight.

He sent back: I'm glad it's nothing serious.

She replied: Me, too.

He should have let it go at that, but he couldn't, so he sent back: I missed seeing you tonight.

Within a minute, she replied: I missed you, too. Can't wait for the barbecue Saturday.

He smiled and felt a lot better.

Chapter 20

REID HAD BEEN working nonstop all week. Between meetings with the engineer and the city inspectors, not to mention having to tiptoe around the stiff requirements laid down by the historical society as far as what they could and could not do to the building, he'd been up to his eyeballs in paperwork and red tape—the parts of his job he hated the most. He had a multipage list from the society of what couldn't be changed, and unless it was a code violation, certain standards had to be maintained to keep the building as close to its original condition as possible. Fortunately, that was his plan all along, so he and the historical society were in agreement on that. It was just getting there that was going to be a headache, and having bureaucrats breathing down his neck wasn't going to be fun. He knew what he was doing and so did Deacon, and having people who didn't have the first clue about renovating a building monitoring every step in the process would only put them behind.

He'd put in long days that had somehow fallen into early evenings. By the time he'd gotten back to the ranch, he'd managed to stuff dinner into his mouth, carried on mostly one-syllable conversations with Ben, Martha, Logan, and Des, and then had dragged himself off to bed to face-plant into an exhausted oblivion.

Today, though, was Saturday. He could have gone in to work to catch up, but that wasn't going to happen today. He planned to drink a lot of beer and eat a metric ton of barbecued ribs.

And not think about work. At least not anything associated with the mercantile. Martha, on the other hand, had put them all to work early that morning getting the ranch ready for the barbecue. He, Logan, and the ranch hands had pulled the picnic tables from storage, scrubbed them clean, and made sure there was plenty of seating for everyone. Because when the McCormacks hosted their annual barbecue, hundreds of people attended.

Not My Dog followed him around all morning as he washed down driveways and furniture and prepped the multiple grills they were going to use for the ribs. Wherever he went, the dog was right next to him.

Like always. He was getting used to Not My Dog being an extra appendage.

When Luke and Emma arrived, Emma dashed into the house, and Luke found Reid. They'd brought their three dogs: Boomer, Luke's German shepherd; Annie, the pit bull; and Daisy, the lab. Not that he blamed them. There was nothing better than letting your dogs run wild and free on ranch property. There was so much land, those dogs could roam for hours and miles and be exhausted by the time Luke and Emma brought them home tonight. Plus, they'd play with all the ranch dogs, which would further wear them out.

The dogs all sniffed and huddled around Not My Dog, who wagged his tail and played.

"Got yourself a dog, I see," Luke said.

"Not My Dog."

Luke laughed. "Yeah, I heard about his name."

"I tried to disown him, but he seems to have attached himself to me."

"Apparently he's pretty popular in town."

Reid rolled his eyes. "Yeah. I don't know what's more popular—the dog or the mercantile. But a lot of folks have stopped by the mercantile to visit the dog. And ask about the building. So maybe both of them."

Luke walked in step with Reid as he headed toward the barn to grab a side table to put in between the two grills.

"How's the reno going, by the way?" Luke asked.

"This week was a lot of red tape and paperwork, so a pain in my ass. Otherwise, it's going okay."

They carried the table out and set it between the grills. Luke started up the grills just as Logan came out carrying pans of ribs.

"More of these inside," Logan said.

Reid nodded, and he and Luke went inside to grab the pans.

"Are you as hungry as I am for these?" Luke asked as they walked back outside.

Reid juggled multiple pans loaded with ribs. "Like you would not believe. I'm amazed I'm actually in town for this. It's been years since I've been here for the barbecue. I actually have dreams about it."

Luke laughed. "Hey, you know where the ranch is. You could come home more often."

"Not as easy as it seems."

"It's as easy as you want to make it. All you have to do is buy a plane ticket."

He waved his hand to dismiss his brother. "Yeah, yeah."

Logan looked up from where he was placing ribs on the grill. "Why would you even want him to come back here for the barbecue, Luke? You've seen how much he eats. That's just fewer ribs for you and me."

"You make a good point, Logan." Luke turned to Reid. "Never mind. Stay in Boston."

Reid laughed. "You're both assholes."

"Like that's a revelation," Logan said. "Now grab some tongs and help me get these spread out on the grills. And someone needs to drag a cooler of beer out here."

"I'll get the beer," Luke said.

Reid took charge of one of the grills. It felt good to be

home again, to be cooking ribs with his brothers at his side. This had been a McCormack family tradition every year, going back to when his dad was still alive. His father and his grandfather had stood at the grills cooking together when Reid had been just a kid. He could still remember knocking around in the front yard with his brothers, the smell of those ribs cooking for hours while they threw the football around or played in the dirt.

As the day progressed, people would show up at the house bringing food. By late afternoon, Reid's stomach would be growling from smelling the meat cook.

He was certain today would be a lot like that. Except for wrestling his brothers in the dirt.

"You must be thinking deep thoughts over there," Logan said, "because you haven't said a word."

He slanted a look at his brother. "I was thinking about how long this annual barbecue has been going on, and how you and me and Luke used to play in the front yard all day, just smelling the ribs cooking and getting hungrier every hour."

Logan's lips ticked up. "And Dad and Grandpa would sit in their chairs, drink beer, and occasionally yell at us to break up a fight."

Reid smiled at the memories. "Yeah."

"And when Mom was around, she'd be pissed that we got dirty."

Logan's lips curved. "She was always pissed about something."

"Don't miss that."

"Me, neither."

That was one thing the brothers all had in common. They had loved their father, and had always stuck together when their mother had gotten riled up about something trivial— like young boys getting dirty.

Their mother hadn't been happy being a ranch wife and mother. Fortunately, their dad had taken up the slack and loved them enough for two people.

And so had Martha and Ben. They'd had plenty of love and parental influence, so once their mother had divorced

Dad and taken off, Reid figured they were all better off without her.

Which had suited him just fine. He sometimes wondered where she was, but he didn't wonder enough to look her up. She'd remarried some guy and was apparently living her happily-ever-after city life somewhere on the east coast. That's all he knew and he didn't care to know more.

Some people just weren't cut out to live life on a ranch. Or to be a parent. And that's just how it was.

A car drove up, and Reid thought for a minute it might be Sam.

It wasn't. It was Megan, who pulled up to the front drive-way. Emma, Des, and Martha came out and helped her bring boxes into the house.

He saw Luke come out carrying a large cooler. Reid and Logan went and grabbed several chairs, then set them up while Luke and Logan flipped the ribs. They opened their beers and took seats.

Another car pulled up. Reid took a look, but it was one of Martha's church friends.

"Waiting for someone?" Logan asked.

"No. Just . . . watching."

"Uh-huh."

Reid ignored his brother and they spent time talking ranch stuff.

More cars pulled in. Several people from town arrived. Some of them wandered over to grab beers and talk ranch life, or anything in general.

"Mercantile's coming along, Reid," Walter Louis said.

"Yeah, it is."

"Daisy and I are anxious to take a peek. We figure it's going to be good business for our sandwich shop once you finish it and get tenants in there."

"I figure it will be, too."

"Speaking of our sandwich shop, Daisy and I have been thinkin' of expanding, opening up another place on the north side of town."

"Is that right? Business is that good, huh?"

Walter offered up a sly smile. "It's decent enough. I was wondering if you had any pointers on where we might situate, and maybe you could think about drawing up some plans. Health food's a big deal nowadays, and we have to compete with the chains as well. The current place is good for the downtown crowd, but we'd like to capture some highway business."

Before Reid knew what was happening, he and Walter had pulled up chairs and Reid was talking architectural plans for a new sandwich shop. Walter had told him they had looked at some existing spaces, but didn't really see anything they liked. But there was a vacant plot of land near one of the ice-cream stores they were interested in buying, and maybe Reid could draw up plans for the shop.

Walter had big ideas and just needed a boost. Reid had to admit it would be easy enough to provide sketches for him. He told him he'd try to work that in sometime next week.

After Walter wandered off, he took over grill duty while Logan went inside to refill the beer cooler.

"You know, if you lived here, you'd probably have a lot of business," Luke said. "Especially since you're both an architect and a contractor."

Reid studied his brother. "I've got plenty of work to keep me busy in Boston."

Luke shrugged. "Just sayin'."

Reid knew exactly what Luke was saying. And he intended to ignore it.

"What did I miss?" Logan asked, setting the rolling cooler down.

"Luke's trying to tell me that I'd have plenty of work if I moved back here."

"He's right. You're good at what you do, and there's a lot of growth in Hope right now. Plus you have a contractor's license as well. You could stay busy."

"Yeah. I'm ignoring both of you."

"He doesn't like us enough to want to move back here," Luke said.

"That's not what I meant," Reid said, glaring at Luke.

"No problem, kid," Logan said. "We don't like you, either."

Reid rolled his eyes. It was a familiar tune, and he knew both of his brothers were giving him a hard time.

He refused to entertain the idea, to think it might be appealing, because it wasn't. He was settled in Boston. He'd built a stake there with his business. He had a great condo downtown. He had friends. He made damn good money.

He was content there.

Samantha pulled up, drawing his attention away from his brothers. He couldn't help watching as she got out of the car. She wore jeans, those cute pink tennis shoes, and a long-sleeved shirt, wisps of her hair flowing in the slight breeze.

She went around to the passenger side, and he was happy to see that she'd brought her grandmother with her. Martha and Ben came outside and helped Claire into the house. Sam came back out a short while later and grabbed a bag out of the car. She looked their way as she made her way to the porch, then smiled and waved before she disappeared inside.

She might have waved to all of them, but he saw the way her eyes lit up when she made eye contact with him.

Just with him.

Everything in him tightened.

"Naw, he wasn't waiting for just one person, was he, Luke?" Logan asked.

"Not at all." Luke slanted a smirk in Reid's direction and took a long swallow of beer.

"Which means he was totally waiting for Sam to show up," Logan said.

Sometimes he wished he didn't have any siblings, especially the kind that noticed every damn thing. "I wasn't waiting for her."

Logan and Luke exchanged knowing looks.

"What?" Reid asked.

"We've been there," Luke said.

"Really. And where is that?"

"At the intersection of Love and Denial."

Reid shot Luke a glare. "Definitely not in love. Not in denial, either."

"Yup. He's made the turn onto Denial Street," Logan said, getting up to flip the lid open on one of the grills.

"I think you're both full of shit. You know nothing about what's going on with Sam and me."

"You like her, don't you?" Logan asked, his back still turned to him.

"Sure. But we're just having some fun together."

Luke got up to check the other grill. "I've played out this scenario before."

"Me, too. It's like déjà vu." Logan turned to Reid, waving his tongs in the air. "'It's nothing serious. I'm just in it for the sex. I'm not looking for a relationship.'"

"'I don't want a commitment right now,'" Luke added. "'Or ever. She's not the right one for me. No woman will ever be the right one for me.'"

Reid crossed his arms. "You two are hilarious, really."

"Not trying to be funny, just honest," Logan said. "It's obvious you were watching out for her. And when she showed up you nearly fell out of your chair trying to get a glimpse of her. That means something, whether you want to admit it or not."

Reid shrugged. "It can't mean anything. I'm not staying here once the project is over."

"Yeah, and I wasn't ever going to get married again," Luke said. "Look at me now."

"And I wasn't ever going to get married, period," Logan said. "So never say never, brother."

Reid decided to ignore his brothers. Their stories were different. They'd found women who made them break their rules.

Reid had a long-term life and career plan, and nothing—and no one—was going to change that.

Not even Samantha Reasor.

SAM GOT GRAMMY Claire settled in next to a few of her friends who'd shown up early. The ladies had decided on the kitchen because, as Grammy Claire explained, everyone eventually made their way into the kitchen, and all the good gossip happened in there. Her grandmother had also said all the food and drink was in there as well, so they never had far to walk.

It made sense to Sam, and Martha said she'd spend most of the day in there and that someone would be constantly in there, so they'd keep an eye on her.

Sam intended to check on her grandmother frequently, but she'd felt a great sense of relief when Grammy Claire had told her she intended to accompany her to the barbecue today, which meant she was feeling a lot better.

Now that she didn't have to worry about her grandmother, she fixed herself a glass of iced tea and wandered outside. She found Emma, Des, and Megan sitting at one of the picnic tables, so she wandered over to join them.

"Don't you look cute today," Emma said with a smile.

"Thanks. So do you. That maxi skirt and top are adorable, Emma. And I need to know where you got that cardigan. It looks so soft, and the color peach is gorgeous on you."

"Thanks. I'm going for comfort today. Early fall means our weather is ever-changing."

"Which is why I'm in pants and a hoodie today," Des said. "Of course, that's kind of my standard uniform on the ranch."

Sam's gaze switched to Des. "You could wear a potato sack and still be gorgeous, Des. Whether you're all glammed up for a movie premiere or dressed like you are today, you're still beautiful."

Des smiled. "Thank you. The check is in the mail."

Megan laughed.

"You're looking pretty hot today, too, Megan," Des said. "Meeting a date here?"

"I wish. And thank you. I just bought a new shirt and decided to show it off."

"Red is definitely your color," Emma said.

"Thanks. Now I just have to hope I don't get barbecue sauce all over it, because I intend to eat plenty of ribs today."

"Don't we all," Des said. "I do love the big party the ranch throws on the Fourth of July with all the fireworks, but I have to admit that the annual barbecue is my favorite event."

"I think we all love it," Sam said. "Not only for the chance to catch up with everyone before the weather turns cold, but because the ribs are always fantastic."

"And now I'm hungry," Megan said. "Think we could throw rocks at the guys and make them cook faster?"

Des grinned. "I don't know if it would make them cook faster, but throwing rocks at boys sounds fun. And juvenile."

"The problem is, they're a lot bigger than us, they run faster than we do, and I'm afraid of repercussions," Emma said.

"I don't think you have anything to be concerned about with your husbands," Sam said to Des and Emma. "They adore you both."

Emma looked at Des. "This is true. So we should throw rocks at them."

Des laughed. "You go ahead. Logan has unique ways of getting back at me when I pull pranks on him."

"I'm not even going to ask," Megan said.

Samantha nodded. "Me, neither."

"Speaking of us getting lucky with hot guys," Des said, "I heard you've been spending a lot of time with Reid, Sam. How's that going?"

Sam shrugged. "We haven't been spending all that much time together. Just a little here and there."

"What does that mean exactly?" Emma asked. "Are you not dating him?"

"I don't know if *dating* is what you'd call it."

"What she means is she's just having sex with him."

They all looked up to see their friend Chelsea take a seat. Chelsea was the outspoken, gorgeous bombshell of the group. And leave it to her to say what they were all thinking.

But Sam still shot her a look.

Chelsea just shrugged. "What? It's the truth. You are sleeping with him, aren't you?"

"Once."

"So far," Megan said.

"Which means you intend for there to be more than just once, right?" Des asked, leaning forward.

She looked at all her friends, not sure if she really wanted to get into this with them or not. She wasn't even sure where things stood with Reid, so it was difficult to talk about. Still, some advice couldn't hurt.

"I don't know. I mean, yes, I'd like to see him again. But the way we left things the other night—I don't know. We haven't managed to get together again. I had an issue with Grammy Claire and he's got work that's sort of all-consuming for him at the moment. We've both been busy, so that could be why . . ."

Chelsea frowned. "Sounds confusing as hell, if you ask me. A man either likes you or he doesn't. And once he's gotten into your pants, if there's no follow-up after, then maybe he doesn't intend to get into them again."

"Chelsea," Emma said, frowning.

Sam held up her hand. "No, it's okay, Em. Chelsea's right. I think it was just a one-time thing that neither of us expected to happen. We're definitely attracted to each other. Or we were. And maybe now that the itch has been scratched, it could be Reid isn't interested in scratching it again."

"Oh, please," Megan said. "Men are always itchy. All they ever think about is getting scratched."

Des laughed. "I have to agree with Megan. He was probably busy, but I still think he should have called or texted you."

"Oh, he did text the other night. That night he went to see the house you and Bash were interested in buying," she said to Chelsea. "I had to cancel because Grammy Claire had gotten sick."

"And was the texting hot?" Chelsea asked, waggling her brows.

"Well . . . not exactly. He texted to check on how Grammy Claire was feeling."

"Oh," Chelsea said. "That's disappointing. I mean, yes, that's nice he did that, but you didn't talk about anything hot or sexy or romantic?"

"Not really. He said he missed me."

"Well, that's something, right?" Megan asked.

"Not enough, if you ask me," Chelsea said.

"Wow, you're tough, Chelse," Des said.

Chelsea shrugged. "Hey, a woman needs to feel pursued, especially after sex. There has to be some substance beyond just the sex, and it should never be a one-time thing. And if you're not interested in just being his booty call when he's itchy, then tell him to kiss off," Chelsea said.

Now Sam was more confused than ever. But her friends were right. She was interested in Reid, but maybe not in the way he was interested in her.

"Thanks, all of you. You've given me a lot to think about."

Now she just had to talk to Reid.

About his itchiness and when and how or if he wanted to scratch it.

Or something like that.

Chapter 21

"WHAT DO YOU think they're all talking about?" Reid asked as he finished off a beer and loaded up another set of ribs into a pan, then piled up another set onto the grill.

"I think they're talking about how all men are assholes, how lousy we are in bed, and how our communication skills suck."

Reid arched his brow and looked over at Bash. "Or is that just what Chelsea says about you?"

Bash grinned. "I can guarantee you that Chelsea is lording it over the other women, saying her man is a stud in bed, always listens to her, and is the greatest guy she's ever met."

Carter Richards pulled his beer away from his mouth and laughed so hard he went into a coughing fit. "Goddammit, Bash. I nearly choked to death."

"While Molly is likely telling her sad story about how her fiancé, Carter, has a tiny dick."

"Fuck off, Bash," Carter said.

Bash laughed. So did Reid and the rest of the guys, who for some reason had ended up gathered around the grills—and the beer.

No surprise there.

He enjoyed catching up with the guys. Before he'd left town, many of these men had been his friends. Some of them were friends of his brothers, but he'd known a lot of them most of his life. They were as much his brothers as his own brothers were. He trusted them as much as his family.

With Luke and Logan in charge of the grills, he carried a pan of fully cooked ribs into the house. Martha took them from him and laid them in the ovens to stay warm.

"How's it going in here?" he asked, taking a moment to slide into a spot next to Sam's grandmother, Claire, as well as a few other women close to Claire's age. They had several decks of cards laid out across the kitchen table.

"We're playing rummy," Claire said. "Care to join us?"

Reid grinned and rolled up his sleeves. "I'd love to."

Three games later, he'd had his butt soundly kicked, once by Claire and twice by Faith.

He got up. "You ladies are too good for me."

Claire smiled up at him. "You need to play more often."

"I do. I haven't played that game in years."

"Which is why you were so bad at it."

He laughed. "You're right about that."

He wandered off, intending to head back to the barbecue, but literally ran into Sam as he rounded the corner of the kitchen.

She was juggling a few empty pitchers, and they all went tumbling in the air when they collided. Sam grabbed one, and he lunged for the other two before they hit the floor.

"Sorry," he said. "I didn't see you coming around the corner."

"It's my fault," she said, rubbing at a wet spot on her shirt, which just so happened to be on her left breast.

Not that he had been staring at her breasts or anything.

"Need me to help you with that?"

She lifted her gaze to his, and he was instantly lost in the blue depths of her eyes. She gave him an easy smile.

"I need to refill these pitchers, and now I need to borrow a shirt from Des."

Wow. That was a quick shutdown.

"Okay."

"I'll see you around, Reid."

Before he had a chance to say anything else, she was gone.

Huh. A definite brush-off. He thought about going outside, but then changed his mind, turned around, and went into the kitchen.

Sam was in there talking to Martha.

"I, uh, need to go find Ben," Martha said after she saw Reid.

"Last I saw him he was out with the guys by the grills."

"Thank you, Reid. I'll be back shortly."

Martha left the kitchen. Sam was refilling pitchers with iced tea and lemonade.

"Need some help?"

"No, I've got this, but thanks."

He shifted his gaze to the women at the kitchen table. They were talking loudly and laughing, totally engrossed in their card game and ignoring Sam and him.

He leaned in closer. "So what's with the brush-off?"

Sam frowned. "Brush-off? I don't know what you're talking about."

"Just now, in the entryway."

She straightened and leaned a hip against the kitchen island. "Reid. I have two more pitchers to refill and I dumped some of the tea and lemonade on my shirt. Which reminds me, I need to go find Des and have her loan me a shirt."

Just as he was about to think she was going to run out on him again, she grasped his shirtsleeve. "Oh, but I do want to talk to you later, if you have a minute."

"Sure."

"Great." She gave him a bright smile. "See you around."

She grabbed the pitchers and walked out. He heaved in a deep breath and let it out, then made his way back to the grills, deciding it was best if he didn't try to figure out the mind of a woman. It would only give him a headache.

Chapter 22

DES HAD GIVEN Sam one of her T-shirts. After she had changed, she was much happier not having a giant wet spot on her breasts. Not that she minded attention of the male variety, but she preferred it not be because of boob stains.

She checked in on her grandmother, whom she'd seen yawning. Martha suggested the ladies move into the living room, so they settled in there with their glasses of iced tea and were now watching television. Sam had clicked to a classic movie channel, but Grammy Claire wanted to watch a new show about vampires. When she explained the premise about the hot vampire and how he was torn between two women, one a vampire and the other a human, all the women decided they wanted to watch that show as well.

Sam shook her head. Her grandmother was nothing if not unpredictable.

Satisfied her grandmother was settled for a while, she made her way back outside. She found her friends clustered at the same table as before. Some had gone and others had showed up. It would likely be that way for the remainder of the day now that they'd claimed their spot.

Right now it was Chelsea, Molly, and Megan.

"Where did Emma and Des disappear to?"

Chelsea shrugged. "Somewhere in the house. And Emma said something about Will and Jane and the kids being late because of Will's schedule."

Sam poured herself a glass of lemonade and they all started a conversation about Molly's wedding, which then brought up a conversation with Molly about wedding flowers—again. Once she assured Molly everything was under control, the wedding convo moved on.

"Are you excited about the wedding, Molly?" Chelsea asked.

Molly grinned. "Beyond. Thank you all for being so supportive and for putting up with my neuroses."

"You? Neurotic? No way," Megan said with a smile.

"Okay, so I might have checked and double-checked and triple-checked venue and flowers and cake and I've looked at my dress sitting in the closet about a thousand times. And I'm certain I'm driving Carter crazy asking him to make sure he's taken care of the tux rentals and that the hotel reservations have been made for family members and friends coming in from out of town. And poor Emma, she's probably going to regret ever agreeing to be my matron of honor. She's probably rethinking being my sister right now."

Megan squeezed her hand. "You sound like a normal bride to me, honey."

Molly sighed. "Thankfully, my mother has lists. Lots and lots of lists. And she loves being in charge of nearly everything. When Carter and I set the date and selected the venue, I was so happy to shove it all off on Mom. I thought I'd never have to think or worry about the wedding again."

"But it's your wedding," Chelsea said. "So inevitably you're going to obsess about every minor detail."

Molly nodded. "That's an understatement. I intended to be all laid-back about this whole wedding thing. Carter and I love each other. It took us a lot of years to make our way back to each other. We just want to get married and be official and all that nonsense."

"And then the wedding bug hit," Samantha said. She'd

seen it countless times from brides-to-be who came to order their flowers, all nonchalant about how their weddings were going to be no big deal. Until they became a really big deal.

Because that's what weddings were to a bride—a big deal.

"Oh my God, yes," Molly said. "That's exactly what it is—the wedding bug. Anyway, I'll be glad when it's over."

"And you're sure you don't want a bachelorette party?" Chelsea asked. "Because we can throw one hell of a party for you. It's a great time of year for Vegas."

Molly laughed. "Thanks, Chelsea, but Carter and I are having enough issues just dealing with work at the auto repair shop plus wedding planning. We'll party plenty on the honeymoon."

"Okay, but if you change your mind, I know people who can make us a great group deal at the last minute."

"I think Chelsea wants to go to Vegas," Megan said.

Chelsea slid a smirk Megan's way. "Maybe."

"Get your hot boyfriend to take you," Sam said.

"My hot boyfriend is busy with the bar. And the expansion to the bar. And we're house-hunting."

"And there's school for you," Molly said.

"Yes. Why aren't we millionaires who don't have to work?"

"You'd hate that, Chelsea," Sam said. "You love teaching."

"I do. But I wouldn't mind the millionaire part."

Sam laughed. Then Bash came over and pulled Chelsea away, and Molly got a phone call from her mother, Georgia, so she stepped away, leaving just Sam and Megan, whose attention was somewhere off in the distance.

Sam followed Megan's gaze and caught sight of a very hot guy riding up the driveway on a gorgeous motorcycle. He parked and got off, then removed his helmet.

Oh. Brady Conners.

Megan sighed.

"That man is so damn hot," Megan whispered.

Sam couldn't deny the truth of that statement. He was tall, with dark hair and amazing green eyes. As he strode toward the men, his worn jeans showed off one great butt, and his tight T-shirt showcased well-muscled arms and some rather amazing tattoos.

Sam leaned into her. "You should do something about that drool problem, Megan."

Megan looked over at her. "I'd like to butter him up like my best batch of cinnamon raisin bread and lick him all over."

Sam burst out laughing. "Well. That was nicely descriptive. I can tell you've given this—or should I say Brady—a great deal of thought."

"You have no idea."

Since they were currently ogling the group of guys, her gaze settled on Reid. "Oh, I think I have a fairly good idea."

"And what have you done about Reid? Anything yet?"

"No. We haven't really had a chance to talk yet. Hopefully at some point today."

But that some point never came around. She hung out with the women until dinner was served. Which, by the way, was amazing. The ribs were sweet and tender and probably the most amazing food she'd ever had. Everyone had brought side dishes, so she had her fill of various types of salad, along with corn on the cob and beans and rolls, and she was so stuffed she didn't think she could eat dessert.

Until she spotted the dessert table filled with her favorites. Not only the things Megan had brought, which she knew would be melt-in-your-mouth incredible, but old-time favorites like hummingbird cake and chocolate sheet cake. Of course she had to have small pieces of each of those. And then Megan had made chocolate chip mini muffins that Sam could swear were made of butterflies, unicorns, and angels. They melted in her mouth and were so good she wanted to weep with joy.

When she finally got up to help clear plates and put dishes back into the refrigerator, she was so full she wanted to die.

But she was happy to see her grandmother in there covering dishes with foil. Grammy Claire liked to stay active and feel like she served a purpose. Sam sent a very grateful smile over to Martha for allowing her grandmother to help out in the kitchen.

Martha came over to hug her. "How was dinner?"

"I don't think I'll be able to eat for a week."

Martha laughed. "I feel the same way. Those boys know how to grill ribs, that's for sure."

"Not just the ribs, but everything else, too." Sam gave Martha a squeeze. "Thanks for looking out for Grammy Claire."

"It was my pleasure. She's told us all a lot of stories today about the early days in Hope. Did you know my great-grandmother was her high school music teacher?"

"I didn't know that."

"Yes. We've had fun talking about that."

"How was she today?—you know." Sam wasn't sure how to reference her grandmother's possible illness, but she had mentioned her grandmother's medical issues to Martha, and she knew Martha understood.

"She was fine. I didn't notice any memory lapses. She seemed sharp as a tack to me today, honey."

Sam breathed a sigh of relief. "Thank you."

"Hey, y'all," Reid said, popping his head in. "Logan wants everyone outside. They're going to start the bonfire."

"We'll be right out."

Grammy Claire and some of her friends decided it was too chilly to go outside for the bonfire, so Sam made sure they were settled in the living room with their card games and the television.

"Are you doing okay?" she asked her grandmother. "If you're tired, we can go home."

Her grandmother waved a hand at her. "Go have fun with the other young people, Samantha. Quit fussing over me. We're all fine here."

"Okay." She kissed her grandmother's cheek and headed outside.

There was a giant woodpile in the dirt, and several of the guys had started the fire. It had already gotten dark and Sam was glad she'd grabbed her hooded sweatshirt. Though the day had been warm, fall in Oklahoma meant cooler nights.

Perfect time for a bonfire.

Sam mingled with the crowd, finding Megan standing

among Molly and Chelsea and Jane, who'd finally shown up with Will and their kids.

She snuggled in next to Megan. "I'm cold."

"Me, too," Megan said.

"You both need hot man bodies to keep you warm," Jane said, leaning against Will.

"Oh sure, rub it in, why don't you?" Megan said.

"And yet my hot man is at the edge of the bonfire playing caveman with the other boys," Chelsea said.

"You can come snuggle with us."

"Thanks, Sam." Chelsea inched over to Sam's open side. Now Sam was definitely a lot warmer.

The fire licked higher and higher, consuming the giant woodpile. Soon the chill left the air and everyone settled into the chairs they'd dragged near the fire.

Logan and Luke brought out more coolers, a couple of the ranch hands following with boxes of glasses. The coolers were filled with . . .

Champagne?

"What's that all about?" Megan asked.

"I have no idea," Sam said.

Logan stood on one of the picnic tables. "Hey, everyone, if I could have your attention for a minute. I have an announcement to make."

The crowd hushed.

Logan looked down at Des. "I'm not a big speech maker, but those of you who know Des and me know that love and family means everything to us. That being said, I wanted to announce to all of you that my beautiful wife, Des, and I are going to have a baby."

"Oh, wow," Sam said, grinning widely and standing and clapping with everyone else.

Cheers went out, and everyone started to move forward.

But Logan put his hand up. "Hang on, hang on. I appreciate the congrats, but my brother has something he wants to say."

Logan jumped off the table, dragged Des into his arms, and planted a kiss on her that made Sam's stomach tumble.

So. Sweet.

Then Luke hopped up on the table.

"Like my brother, I'm not into speeches, and I sure didn't want to steal his and Des's thunder tonight, but timing being what it is, well . . ."

Luke looked down at Emma, who smiled up at him.

"Just say it, Luke," Des said, grinning.

"Well, it looks like there's going to be more than one McCormack baby coming. Emma and I are pregnant. Well, she's pregnant."

"Oh. My. God," Megan said, turning her wide-eyed gaze to Sam.

"I know," Sam said, unable to believe two of her good friends were both pregnant. At the same time. Tears of joy welled in her eyes and she fought them back.

The crowd went crazy with cheers and applause. Luke jumped down off the table and kissed Emma, and everyone made their way to the couple to congratulate them, including Sam and Megan.

Sam waited patiently, not wanting to crowd them. She caught a glimpse of Reid grinning and hugging both of his brothers, and then Des and Emma. Martha was out there crying, and even Ben had tears in his eyes.

Sam finally made her way to Des and Emma and pulled them both into a hug.

"You didn't tell me. You didn't tell any of us."

Emma shook her head. "We didn't."

"I could have sworn I saw you drinking wine the night of the dinner party, Emma."

"It was sparkling cider," Emma said.

Sam laughed. "You keep good secrets."

"I do."

"So did you two plan this?"

"No," Emma said. "I'm three months. I wanted to wait to get past my first trimester before I told anyone. Well, Molly and Mom knew, and, of course, Luke, but no one else. And then I noticed Des wasn't drinking wine the night of her party, so I suspected . . ."

Des nodded. "And she came out and asked me. And I

was a little nauseous, so I told her I was. And then she told me she was, too. We're due like two weeks apart."

"That is amazing. I am so happy for both of you. We have so much to talk about, but I know so many people want to talk to you right now." She squeezed their hands, then eased out of the way so Megan could hug them.

Sam had never been more excited. Two McCormack babies.

She turned around and saw Reid standing off to the side. He looked just as shocked as the rest of them, so it was obvious he hadn't known ahead of time.

And then she saw him take a deep breath and let it out.

Was that a sigh of relief, or a deep breath of disappointment?

Sam intended to find out.

She walked over to him, slid her hand in his.

"How about a walk away from all these people?"

He looked down where their hands were joined, then back up at her. "Sure."

Chapter 23

REID WAS STUNNED. Floored. Shocked. Pretty goddamned stupefied. And all those other words he could add in, but just couldn't come up with any more at the moment.

Both his brothers were going to be fathers. He was going to be an uncle—times two. That was . . .

"So I saw that deep breath you took," Sam said as they walked down the dark path toward the back of the house.

He hadn't even had time to process this yet. "Yeah."

She stopped and turned to him. "Are you upset? About the babies?"

He frowned. "Upset? Hell no. Why would I be?"

"I don't know. I just thought maybe because both of your brothers having babies at the same time . . ."

"Oh, you thought I'd feel like I was being left behind?"

"Maybe something like that."

One of the things he liked most about Sam was that she was very perceptive. Out of all that chaos tonight, she'd noticed him, when he should have been the last person she was paying attention to. He knew both Emma and Des were good friends of hers, so she should have flung herself into that melee of joy and congratulations. Instead, she'd noticed him breathing.

"No, that wasn't at all what I was feeling."

She cocked her head to the side, her ponytail swaying with the motion. "So maybe a little . . . relief?"

Huh. Nailed it. "Maybe."

Instead of recriminations, she put her arm in his and continued walking. "Takes a little pressure off you to produce little McCormacks and continue the family line, huh?"

She read him well. Maybe a little too well. "I think Logan and Luke have the little McCormacks handled for a while."

Or maybe forever.

She stopped again. "Do you want kids?"

"I don't know. Never thought about it."

She gave him a don't-bullshit-me look. "And yet there was that sigh of relief, Reid."

"Okay, maybe I've thought more about not having them than having them. Not that I don't like kids. I do."

"You just like other people's kids?"

He laughed. "Something like that."

They walked again, and got farther away from the party. It was quieter out here, where you could hear the wind whistle through the trees.

"What about you?" he asked.

"What about me?"

"Do you want kids?"

She didn't hesitate, just shrugged. "I've never been one to worry about my biological clock ticking, or have a timeline to get married or whatever it is that some women do in order to have a child. I can't say I've ever had a burning desire to be a parent. But, like you, I really love kids."

Now it was his turn to stop their forward motion. "That was incredibly honest."

"No reason not to be, is there? I don't think my desire to have or not have kids is some deep dark secret I need to hold on to."

"I guess not. Though you'd be surprised how many women have asked me on a first date how many kids I want to have."

She laughed. "No, I wouldn't be surprised. I've known a few women who, instead of being happy to find a man to have deep conversations with, a man who can make them laugh and make their toes curl and whose kisses set their hair on fire, search out someone they think will make the best babies. As if that's the criteria to find the love of your life."

He stared at her.

She laughed. "What?"

"That's pretty deep, Sam."

She shoved at him. "It is not. It's simply logic. Sort of. You either want children or you don't, and I hardly think that's anyone's business on the first date anyway. And if a guy asks me, I give him an honest answer—I don't know. Because right now I don't. Maybe someday. But right now? I don't know."

A gust of wind blew up, and scattered pieces of her hair pulled loose from her ponytail, whipping across her face. He tucked those hairs behind her ears, then left his hands there, framing her face. It felt right touching her like this, as if this was something he should have been doing for the past few days.

He realized now that he'd missed touching her. "It's a good answer."

"Well, thanks." She grasped hold of his wrists, and his pulse rate shot up.

Which made him want to kiss her.

So he did. His mouth lashed across hers, her kiss grabbing him in a fierce hold that flew through him as furious as the wind whipping around them. She clung to him, and he tugged her against him, his arms coming around her to bring his body closer, to feel the heat that seemed to come off of her in waves as he deepened the kiss.

He wished they were alone so he could peel off her clothes and kiss her neck, her collarbone, her breasts. But they were standing outside in his backyard, and he was getting hard as he kissed her, and out front were over a hundred people.

Time to back this up.

He licked her bottom lip and pulled back. "Remember when I told you that I could take you someplace remote here on the ranch?"

She looked at him, her eyes glazed over with passion he wanted desperately to tap into. "Yes."

"Let's go."

She shook her head. "I can't. I have Grammy Claire here with me and I need to take her home."

"Okay. Let's take Grammy Claire home. Then I'll bring you back here."

"Really. You'd drive all the way home with me and back."

He rubbed his hands up and down her arms. "Yes."

"Is this just to scratch an itch?"

He frowned. "What?"

"You and me. Is it just sex?"

"I don't know what you're talking about, Sam." Sex and scratching itches? What the hell was this all about?

"I think you do."

Whatever it was that had fueled up hotter and higher than the bonfire abruptly fizzled out and confusion took over. "No, I don't. But maybe you can explain it to me."

"Well, we had a really great time that night we spent together. Then . . . nothing. And now here we are again. So I want to know if I'm just an itch you're scratching."

Maybe it was the beers he'd had, but he didn't think so, because he'd stopped drinking beer hours ago, and maybe it was just him being obtuse, but he liked having a clear head, especially as it related to women and sex. He didn't want any misunderstandings between Sam and him.

"I'm going to be honest with you here and tell you I have no idea what the hell you're talking about."

"Sex, Reid. I'm talking about sex. And you and me."

"Okay. I like the topic of you and me and sex. I can get behind that. Isn't that what we're talking about doing?"

"Yes. I guess I want to know if there's more than that between us."

He took in a deep breath. "I can't offer you more."

He saw the disappointment on her face, and it sent a deep shot right to his gut.

"I need to go take my grandmother home. Good night, Reid."

She turned to walk away, but he grasped her wrist. "Sam, wait. Let's talk about this."

"Some other time, okay? I'm tired."

He let her hand slip through his fingers and he watched

her walk away, desire evaporating in the wind and confusion taking its place.

What the hell had just happened? He'd hurt her. He had seen that, but he wasn't sure how or why. Had she wanted more than just sex? He wished he could offer her more, but right now it was all he could give her.

Dammit, he hated seeing that hurt look on Sam's face, hated even more knowing he'd been the one to put it there.

But he needed to give her some space right now. And maybe give himself some as well.

Then he'd talk to her again.

SAM WOUND HER way around the side of the house. The bonfire was still going strong, and several people were still sitting there, partying hard. But most of the folks had packed up to go home.

She went into the house and found her grandmother sitting with two other women watching television.

"I'm ready to go home, Grammy Claire. How about you?"

Her grandmother looked up at her. "Of course. Whenever you're ready."

"I'll come get you in a few minutes. Let me go say my good-byes."

She went outside and found Des and Emma and hugged them, congratulating them again, as well as Logan and Luke, and thanked them for the barbecue. She didn't see Reid, so she made her way into the house, grabbed the things she'd brought and bagged those up and put them in her car, then helped her grandmother out and put her in her seat.

She climbed in and backed out onto the road.

"Did you have a good time tonight?" Grammy Claire asked.

"I did. How about you?"

"I had a wonderful time. I can't wait to go home and tell Bob all about it."

Bob. Grammy Claire's husband, who had died two years ago. Oh, damn.

Chapter 24

SWIPING THE SWEAT from his face with his shirtsleeve, Reid wished for that cold front the weather forecasters kept promising. He was working on the third floor today, and it was so hot up there it felt like he'd stepped into hell.

"You don't have to be up here," Deacon said as he and his team laid the tile in the upstairs bathrooms. "We've got this handled."

Reid shot him a glare. "I told you when we started this project that I was going to be hands-on. This is me, with my hands on the goddamn floor."

Deacon grinned at him. "I can tell you need to get laid. You're grouchy as hell, man."

"Screw you, Deacon."

Deacon straightened. "I don't think I'm the one you need to be screwing."

Reid couldn't help but laugh. "We need a break. How about a cold drink?"

"Sounds good."

Deacon told the crew to take a break as well. They walked

down the stairs, and Reid and Deacon took up a spot on the front porch, where Not My Dog was snoozing.

"That dog is going to end up taking up permanent residence on this front porch. He's become a fixture here."

Reid nodded and unscrewed the cap on the jug of water he'd brought, quickly downing half the contents. After a satisfied sigh, he said, "People bring him bones and toys, too. He's even got a favorite blanket now. They're spoiling him. Which is why he likes the porch. He knows a good thing when he's got one."

Deacon rubbed Not My Dog's ears. "Smart dog."

The dog snorted, then rolled over on his back for Deacon to rub his belly.

"He's a master manipulator," Reid said. "He's even got you trained."

"Hey, he's cute. It works."

Reid rolled his eyes and took another couple swallows of water. "Third floor's coming along."

"Yeah. Framing is finished. Bathrooms up there should be done by the end of the week. Then we should be able to start laying flooring."

"The tiles look good," Reid said. "Sinks and fixtures should be in this afternoon."

"Okay."

One of the laborers came over to ask Deacon a question, so he wandered inside, leaving Reid sitting on the stairs with the dog. He decided to take another couple minutes to enjoy the slight breeze.

His gaze wandered across the street to the flower shop. It was shut down tight, which was unusual for this time of day. He wondered where Sam was. He knew she wasn't making a flower delivery, because her van was parked next to the building.

He could call her, but after the other night, he was still confused about where they stood.

Then again, he was a friend and he was concerned about her. Maybe she was sick or something. He pulled out his phone and clicked on her number, then punched the call button.

It rang several times, then he got her voice mail.

"Hey, Sam, it's Reid. I saw your shop was closed so I thought I'd check to make sure you were all right. Uh . . . let me know, okay?"

He hung up, stared at the flower shop again, then got up and went back inside.

At the end of the workday he was the last one out the door. He locked up, put all of Not My Dog's toys and his blanket into the truck, and headed toward the other side to climb in. As he headed off, he did a slow roll past Sam's shop and noticed there was still no activity there. He'd been outside several times today, had taken the dog for a walk a few times, and hadn't seen Sam once.

She hadn't called him back, either.

His foot on the brake, he looked down at the dog.

"What do you think?"

The dog looked up at him, his tongue hanging out the side of his mouth.

"I know what you're thinking," he said to the dog.

Not My Dog looked up at him as if to say, *Yeah, we need to check and make sure she's okay.*

"That's what I think, too." He put his foot on the gas and drove toward Sam's house.

Her car was in the driveway, so maybe she was sick and just hadn't answered her phone today. He parked in the street and got out, Not My Dog following next to him.

He rang the bell and waited.

It only took a minute for Sam to answer the door.

"Oh. Hi, Reid. What's up?"

"You weren't at work today. And I thought maybe you were sick. I called you."

"You did? My phone . . . I don't know. It might be in my purse. I'm sorry. It's been kind of a day."

She looked rattled or tired or upset or something. "I should go. Sorry."

"No. Actually, I could use the company. Please, come in."

She held the door open, so he and the dog went inside.

"Would you like something to drink?"

"I'm fine, thanks. I really just wanted to stop by to see if you were all right."

"I'm okay. I spent the day at the hospital."

Dread dropped like a lead balloon in his stomach. "The hospital? So you're not all right."

"No, it wasn't for me. It was Grammy Claire."

He frowned. "Is this about the issues she had before, or is she sick or hurt?"

She sighed. "Have a seat."

He grabbed a spot on the sofa and Sam sat next to him. As if he could sense her distress, Not My Dog curled up next to Sam's feet.

"The other night on the way home from the barbecue, she mentioned she couldn't wait to get home and tell my grandfather all about what a great time she'd had."

Worry compounded that dread in his stomach. "But your grandfather passed away a couple of years ago."

"Yes. When we got home, she went looking for him. I had to tell her he wasn't there. And why. It actually took her a few minutes to get right with that, to come back to the present."

He picked up her hand. "I'm really sorry. That couldn't have been easy."

"It wasn't. The problem was, she was fine all day long. She'd been fine for a few days before that. Then suddenly— this. And after that, she was fine again. But I called her doctor Monday morning and he made a referral to the neurologist, so that's where we were today, having a battery of tests run. We'll get the results in a day or two."

"This situation is so hard on you. I'm sorry you have to go through it. How's your grandmother dealing with all of it?"

"She a little confused about all the tests and says she feels fine. I explained to her what happened, that she was asking after Grandpa Bob. She doesn't remember any of it."

"Which makes it more difficult for you." He squeezed her hand.

"I can deal with it. I feel bad for putting her through all of the tests."

"It's necessary though, right? You have to find out."

"Yes. I do. If there's a treatment for what's happening to her, then we need to know so we can get medications or . . . whatever."

He knew what she wasn't saying. Or if there was no help for her, and there'd be a gradual decline, she needed to prepare herself—and her grandmother—for that as well.

"Is she at home right now?"

Sam nodded. "Tucked in front of the television. One of her friends is over and there's some dancing show on they like to watch, so they're going to cook together, curl up in front of the TV, and critique ballroom dance moves. I'll check on her later tonight. I may even stay there."

Reid smiled. "Sounds fun."

"I'm glad she has company. And Faith promised to call me if there were any issues."

"Good. So you can relax tonight. How about some dinner?"

"I'm not really hungry."

"When was the last time you ate a decent meal?"

She didn't answer, and since he figured she'd been worrying about her grandmother, she probably wasn't eating or sleeping well. He stood. "Come on. We'll go eat something."

"I should really stay close to home."

"You said your grandmother had a friend over, right? And that she'd call if there was anything to worry about?"

"Yes."

"Then we won't be far if she needs you." He got up and called Not My Dog. "I'm going to put him out in your backyard."

"Okay. There's a bowl out back. You can fill it with water for him."

He grabbed some of the dog's toys and his favorite bone out of the truck, then settled him in the yard. By the time he came back inside, Sam was standing by the door with her purse in her hand.

"Ready?"

She nodded. "I called Faith and let her know I was going out. She has my cell phone number."

She looked sad. Worried. Tired. God, all he wanted to

do was fold her in his arms and give her a big hug. She looked like she was going to crumble at any minute.

But first, food.

He led her outside to his truck and held the door for her while she climbed in, careful to keep his libido in check when her sweetly curved butt slid into the seat.

This wasn't about sex right now. It was about giving comfort to someone who really needed it.

After he got in, he looked over at her. "What are you hungry for?"

She shrugged. "Nothing, really."

That meant comfort food, and he knew just the place—an old hometown restaurant that served some of the best food in town.

When he pulled up, he saw the corners of Sam's mouth tip up. "I haven't eaten here in a long time. They make the best chocolate cream pie."

"And serve up the most amazing chicken fried steak."

They went inside and were seated right away. Their waitress came over and took their drink orders while they perused the menus.

"Grammy Claire and Grandpa Bob used to love to eat at this place. They'd bring me here all the time when I was little. I think she still eats here on luncheon days with her friends."

Sam glanced at the menu, then set it aside.

"Decided already?"

"Definitely. I'm having the meat loaf."

"Sounds great."

She looked down at his menu, which had remained unopened. "You didn't even look at the menu."

"I don't need to. I already told you what I'm having."

Their waitress came over with their drinks.

"The chicken fried steak does sound good," Sam said, pursing her lips. "I'm totally changing my mind. I'll have that, with mashed potatoes and gravy."

"Same for me," Reid said, handing their menus back to the waitress.

"And chocolate pie for dessert," Sam added.

"Make mine coconut cream pie."

Their waitress went off to put in their orders.

"How's work?" she asked.

"Moving along, finally." He told her about his day, figuring if he could get her mind off her grandmother, it would be a good thing.

"I'd like to come see the progress," she said.

"You're welcome to drop by anytime."

"Would you put me to work? I can wield a hammer."

He laughed. "I could use you. Do you know how to refinish an old floor?"

She laughed. "No, but it sounds fun."

"It's definitely not fun."

"I don't know, it sounds thrilling. I'd love to be a part of making something old look new again."

"Like I said, come on over. Bring your work boots."

Her lips quirked. "I'll do that. In my spare time."

They talked about the mercantile for a while and he filled her in on every step of the process. Her cheeks brightened and, God, he liked seeing her smile and laugh again.

After their waitress brought their food, Sam seemed to relish every bite. She might have claimed she wasn't hungry, but she finished almost all of her chicken fried steak, and all of her pie.

He was glad he'd dragged her out to eat.

As they were drinking coffee, her phone buzzed. She hurriedly answered, concern on her face as she spoke.

He saw her relax and breathe a sigh of relief, then listened to her part of the conversation.

"Of course. Sure, that'll be fine, Faith. Thanks for staying with her. I'll talk to you in the morning."

She hung up.

"Everything okay?"

She nodded. "They're having such a good time that Faith decided to stay over. They're watching some movie that's going to finish late, and Grammy Claire doesn't want Faith driving on the streets that late."

He smiled. "I know that gives you a sense of relief."

"It does."

"Now you can relax."

"At least for tonight."

After he paid for dinner, he took her home and let Not My Dog inside. The dog sniffed him and let Reid pet him, but he went over and sat next to Sam again. She bent over to pet him.

"He seems to like me tonight."

"He senses you're upset. For some reason he's good at tuning in to people's moods."

Sam leaned her nose into the dog's neck. "You're a sweetheart."

"Don't do that. You'll ruin his tough exterior."

"You're not tough, are you, baby boy? You're actually a marshmallow, aren't you, Notty?"

Reid rolled his eyes. "Notty?"

She lifted her head. "Come on. He needs a nickname. Notty is cute."

"Whatever. He should be named Brutus or something."

She got up and went into the kitchen to pour them both glasses of iced tea. "You're the one who started calling him Not My Dog. You have no one but yourself to blame that it stuck."

He accepted the tea she handed to him. "Thanks. And he's Not My Dog."

She nodded. "Exactly. That's his name now. And he's totally yours." She looked down at the dog. "Aren't you, Notty?"

Reid had a feeling that nickname would stick as well.

He also knew he should probably leave, but for some reason he wanted to stay. He didn't think Sam should be alone.

"Are you busy at work?" he asked.

"Fortunately, no. At least I wasn't today, which worked out well for Grammy Claire's doctor appointment. I pushed a couple projects that didn't need to be delivered today off until tomorrow."

"Good. That had to be a relief for you."

"It was." She shifted on the sofa to face him. "Would it be all right it I came by tomorrow to see the mercantile?"

"Of course."

"Great. I haven't seen it since demolition day and I've been dying to get inside. I have some morning deliveries to make, but I could come by in the afternoon."

"I'll be around all day."

"Good."

He figured she was waiting for him to leave. He still didn't want to. "I hear there's a great movie on tonight."

"Really?" She grabbed the remote and clicked on the television, then handed it to him. "I hadn't heard anything."

"Yeah, uh, Deacon was talking about it."

"Oh, then no doubt some blood-and-guts horror film or action movie."

He laughed. "Not your thing, huh?" He scrolled through the listings. "How about this one?"

She shot him a look. "It's a war movie."

"So no, huh?"

"No."

He kept scrolling. "This one looks good."

She watched it for a few seconds, then gave him another hopeless look. "Vampire zombies? You have got to be kidding me."

"Fine." He handed her the remote. "You find one."

She scrolled for a few seconds, then grinned and clicked on a channel. "This one."

His eyes widened and he slanted a dismayed look at her. "It's a Disney movie."

"Of course it is."

"And you would sit through one of those?"

"Wouldn't anyone?"

"Not necessarily."

"You don't have to if you don't want to." She lifted the remote to change the channel, but he stopped her.

"No, this is fine. We'll watch it."

"You sure?"

He nodded.

"Okay. Let's do it."

He wouldn't admit to her that he liked these kinds of

movies. He settled back against the sofa, and eventually she cuddled close against him.

This was actually one of his favorites, and he was happy she'd chosen it. They laughed during some of the funny scenes, and he heard her hum during the songs. When he felt her body relax against his, he smiled.

By the end of the movie, she was asleep, her head resting against his shoulder. He stayed like that with her through another movie, then got up, led her to the bedroom and put her into bed. He took the dog out one last time, locked the doors, turned out the lights and undressed, climbing into bed next to her.

She snuggled up next to him and flung her leg across him.

Yeah, this was what he wanted—and hopefully what Sam needed.

He closed his eyes.

Chapter 25

SAM FINISHED HER last delivery for the day and headed back to the shop, feeling a lot more relaxed today than she had in the last several days.

When she woke this morning, Reid was already gone. But he left her a note on her kitchen table telling her she snored. And that he'd see her later at the mercantile. He finished it off with a smiley face at the bottom.

That was crap. She totally did not snore.

But she'd smiled at his note anyway.

They'd discuss the snoring thing when she saw him.

She'd gone over to her grandmother's house to check on her. She and Faith were having breakfast, and everything had seemed okay. Faith had told her Grammy Claire had been fine all night and so far this morning, and they were headed out to an art show at the museum today. With a whispered thanks to Faith, Sam showered, dressed, and went into work.

She'd been swamped with yesterday's orders, plus several more that had come in, so it ended up being later in the afternoon before she had a chance to make her way over to the mercantile.

When she got there, she saw that they were working on the outside as well, cleaning up the brick, and replacing windows—and there were even people on the roof.

So much progress it gave her chills. She didn't see Not My Dog in his usual place on the front porch, but Deacon was out there on his phone. He hung up just as she reached the porch and gave her a smile.

"Hey, Sam, how's it going?"

"It's pretty good, Deacon. Looks like you are all staying busy here."

"Full-time job right now. I saw you with your van filled with flowers this morning, so you're obviously staying busy, too."

"I am. Is Reid around?"

"He's on the third floor. Go on inside. I'd show you up, but I'm waiting on a supplier phone call, and I think I'll take it out here since there might be some cussing involved."

She laughed. "Nothing I haven't heard before, but I'm sure I can find my way. Thanks, Deacon."

She walked inside, shocked at the changes that had occurred. The piles of wood and debris had disappeared from the first floor. The former ceiling had been ripped out, and the old tin ceiling was visible. There was so much light in the room now, and even though there were no walls yet, and nothing but electrical and plumbing fixtures, she could see how spacious it was.

She could see potential. Reid must be thrilled with how it was coming along.

She made her way up the stairs, pausing only momentarily at the second floor. A lot more had been done there than on the first. Progress.

She wound her way up to the third floor, where it looked similar to the second floor. Walls had been framed in and drywall was going up. Wood floors had been put in, and there was defined space up here. She wanted to linger, to walk into every room, but first she had to find Reid, because she had questions. She heard banging and talking, so she followed the sound.

She found him talking to one of the workers in one of the bathrooms.

"The wrong color sinks were delivered for up here," the guy said, causing Reid to rub the side of his temple. "And the window people sent the wrong sizes for the second floor, so those don't fit."

"Shit. And how long until we get replacements for the sinks?"

"They said tomorrow for the sinks. I think Deacon's on the phone with them right now. He wasn't happy."

"Neither am I." With a sigh, Reid said, "Okay, go ahead and finish up the sinks and fixtures on the second floor, since we know those are right. We'll drop in sinks up here tomorrow—provided the supplier gets it right this time. What about windows?"

"Deacon's talking to them, too. That could be a few days," he said.

"Fine. Thanks, Chris. I'll get an update on the rest of it from Deacon."

The guy nodded, brushed past Sam with a nod and a smile, and left the room.

She stepped inside. "Problems?"

Reid finally noticed her and looked up with a smile. "It's always something. In this case, one's minor, the other not so much. All of it's a setback to the project timeline."

"I'm sorry." She looked around. "It looks amazing so far. This is one of the main bathrooms for the floor?"

"Yeah. Such as it is. It would have looked a lot better if we'd been able to drop in the sinks today."

"It looks pretty incredible even without the sinks." There were six stalls, with wide porcelain plank tiles on the floor, beautiful tile on the walls, four sinks—or places where the sinks would go, anyway, lots of mirror space, and . . .

"Is that a lounge area out front here?"

"Yeah."

"This is amazing, Reid. And very luxurious for a bathroom."

"This is the ladies' room, obviously."

"Obviously. As a woman, I highly approve."

"There are also private bathrooms in some of the office spaces."

Her brow arched. "Really? Show me."

He led her out of the bathroom and to an office space in the corner. "This one's my favorite because of all the light and space. The walls will be gray, and there will be chair rail here, a reception area out front, and two offices. The main office is in the back."

She could tell from the animated way he spoke that he was excited about this. When they got to the room she could see why. The entire space was windows, and since it was a sunny day, her jaw dropped.

"Wow. You can see the entire town from these windows."

He grinned. "Yeah. Isn't it great?"

She walked to one of the windows and looked out. "I'm pretty sure I can see my house from here." She pointed to the south. "There's Hope High, too."

He moved over to the northern windows. "If I got a telescope in here we might be able to see the ranch."

"No way." She moved over to where he was standing. "That far away?"

He laughed. "I have no idea. But the view is pretty outstanding."

"No kidding. I'm so impressed. Someone is going to have an amazing office in here."

"Yeah."

She turned to face the office. The walls weren't painted yet, but the office would be spacious. "I can already picture a desk in here, pictures on the walls, a large clock over there. The space is so large you could put a sofa over in the corner, or a couple of trendy chairs and a table."

"There's an amazing desk in storage at the ranch," Reid said, leaning against the windowsill. "My grandfather made it himself from a tree that had fallen in a storm. It would be perfect in this office. It's supersized, so it would sit well in this space."

"Why don't you have that in your office in Boston?"

He shrugged. "I don't know. My office there isn't large. It wouldn't match the modern furnishings there anyway."

"But it would go well here."

"It would."

"It's interesting how you visualize something, see how it would work in one place but not another. Is it the same way with your designs?"

"Sort of. When I design a space I visualize it first before I ever draw it out. It's more a feeling, a sense I get about a place." He paused, looking at her. "It's hard to describe."

"No, you're doing a fine job. I understand what you're saying. It's like when I create a bouquet. It's not just random flowers thrown together. It's an emotional connection. Who are these flowers for? What is the occasion? Who are the people? What are they celebrating? Is it joy or sorrow? I tap into those emotions and try to make every bouquet suit the people I'm creating for. I'm sure for you it's the same thing. You're not just drawing lines for a building—you're emotionally connecting to a place, a sense of time. I imagine doing the mercantile has been especially emotional for you, because you have a connection to it."

He stared out the window. "I don't know about that. It's just a building, Sam."

"Is it?" She rubbed her hand up and down his back. "Or is it something more? You're already placing your dad's desk in this office. Can you see yourself in here, too?"

"No, I don't see myself here."

Her hand slipped away. "Okay. Just thought I'd throw that out there to give you something to think about."

He turned to face her. "Trying to entice me to stay in town?"

She shrugged. "It's not the worst idea ever, you know."

"Sure it is. I have a business in Boston. A life."

"So you keep saying. But you have family here. People who love you." She pivoted, facing the window. "And this amazing office space that seems to just . . . fit."

He stepped up behind her and wrapped his arms around her. "I created this office space for someone else."

She turned around in his arms, her gaze direct. "Did you?"

"Yeah. I did. Just like I create buildings and spaces for other people all the time. Don't make this emotional, Sam. Because it isn't for me."

"If you say so." And maybe it was her being emotional about it, because the space was so beautiful and she could see him sitting there with his computer and his drawings, making new spaces for people here in Hope and Tulsa and the surrounding areas.

Maybe it was she who thought he belonged here, when quite obviously he knew exactly where his life was.

And it wasn't in Hope. She needed to shake loose of the emotional connection she had to Reid, because there was nothing in it for her but heartbreak.

"So are you done for the day, work-wise?" he asked.

She shook her head. "Not quite. How about you?"

"Same. I have a few hours left. I was just wondering if you were free tonight."

"I might be. I need to go home and check on Grammy Claire."

"How's she doing?"

"She was fine this morning. She's spending the day with Faith."

"That's good. I know you're worried about her being by herself."

"Yeah. But I'll check on her. If everything's okay, I could be free."

"Want to come out to the ranch with me tonight?"

"I could maybe be coaxed." She didn't really want to be that far away from her grandmother, but she'd make arrangements so Grammy Claire wasn't alone.

"Good. How about you come out after you see to your grandmother's comfort. Say around six?"

"Sounds perfect. I'll see you then."

"Okay."

She started to leave, but Reid grasped her hand and pulled her against him. He wanted a taste of her, to feel her body pressed up against his. She came into his arms willingly, and he slid his hand into her hair to hold her in place while he tasted her.

She must have popped a peppermint in her mouth before she came in here, because that's what he tasted. Then again, she always tasted hot and sweet to him. He explored her mouth, teased her tongue with his, and ran his hands down her back, cupping her butt and pulling her in tighter.

When he heard Deacon's voice downstairs, he pulled back, lingering for a few seconds on the barely banked desire he saw in her eyes.

"Yeah. Not the right time or place," he said.

She pushed against him, rubbing her body against his erection. "Too bad, because it feels really right."

He let out a laugh. "Unless you want to put on a show for everyone who works here, I think we need to shelve that thought for later."

With a sigh, she took a step back, but gave him a lingering look, letting her gaze travel south. "That'll be on my mind the rest of the day."

"You're killing me, Sam."

Her lips curved. "You won't be the only one suffering. I'll see you tonight."

She turned and walked out, giving him a glimpse of her very fine ass in her tight jeans.

Damn. He raked his fingers through his hair, grabbed his notebook, and went over plans, hoping like hell that immersing himself in architectural drawings would cool down his libido in a hurry.

By the time Deacon found him, he'd managed to cool down.

"Sam told me she was in love with this office."

Reid nodded. "It's a great office space."

"Do you have interest in it yet?"

Yeah. He wanted it. But he'd never say that to Deacon— or to Sam. And it was never going to happen. "I've had several people show interest in several of the spaces so far."

"How about the main space downstairs?"

"That, too. As a matter of fact, someone you know came by recently and asked about it."

"Yeah? Who?"

"Loretta Simmons."

He saw the smile disappear from Deacon's face. "Loretta. I didn't know she was back in town."

"Apparently she's moved back. Recently divorced, from what she told me."

"Huh. Interesting."

Reid imagined it was a lot more than just interesting to Deacon, considering he and Loretta had been nearly inseparable in high school. Until she and Deacon had broken up and Loretta had married someone else and left Hope. Reid knew their breakup had crushed Deacon.

"Is that a problem?"

"You can rent out space to whoever the hell you want to. Makes no difference to me. I don't own the mercantile. Besides, Loretta and I were a long time ago."

Judging from his tone of voice, probably not long enough. "I just thought you might want to know."

Deacon shrugged. "What Loretta does or doesn't do isn't my business anymore, and hasn't been for a lot of years."

"I know her marrying someone else was painful for you."

"I was the one who broke up with her, remember?"

"I remember. So maybe now that she's back in town—"

Deacon shot a sharp glare in his direction. "No. Not gonna happen."

Reid lifted his hands, palms up, toward Deacon. "Okay. I just thought—"

"You thought wrong. Loretta and I are history, and that history is never going to repeat itself."

"Got it. Never gonna happen."

But Reid didn't much believe in *never* where Deacon and Loretta were concerned. He'd had a front-row seat back in high school to that love story, and he'd never seen two people more in love. It had mystified him why Deacon had broken up with Loretta a couple of years after high school. Reid had been in college then, so he hadn't been in town to witness what happened, but he'd been certain Deacon and Loretta were headed for the altar. All Deacon had told him back then was that they had drifted apart and it had become clear to him they weren't suited for each other.

He hadn't bought that story then any more than he bought the bullshit Deacon was trying to shovel at him now. Reid didn't believe Deacon had ever gotten over Loretta.

But he knew better than to get in the middle of it, which was why he'd brought up the fact that Loretta had contacted him the other day about the bottom-floor space.

All he wanted Deacon to know was that Loretta was back in town.

What happened after that was between the two of them.

Right now he wanted to concentrate on finishing up his work for the day.

Because tonight, he was seeing Samantha.

Chapter 26

SURPRISINGLY, FAITH HAD spent the entire day with Grammy Claire, then invited her to spend the night at her place tonight.

Sam didn't know if Faith was doing that to keep a close eye on her grandmother or if the two of them just had a lot of social events going on. Either way, Sam was relieved and happy. She had known Faith a long time. She had Faith's phone number and Faith had hers, so she told her she'd be out tonight and to call her if there were any issues. Faith assured her everything should be fine and told her to go out and have a good time.

Sam took a shower and changed into jeans and a long-sleeved shirt, then slid into her canvas shoes. She packed an extra set of clothes and her toothbrush—just in case—in her backpack.

Not that she was expecting to spend the night with Reid, but she wanted to be prepared. After kissing him today at the mercantile, she was fired up, and she'd had so much stress lately that there was nothing wrong with thinking that maybe she and Reid could enjoy a nice evening of . . .

Stress relief.

That's what she intended to think of it. Some enjoyable

time together, and maybe a little stress relief for both of them. After all, he'd looked a little wound up today, too.

Or maybe she was just projecting.

She drove out to the ranch and parked in front of the house. Reid's truck was there, and when she got out of her car, she was greeted by all the ranch dogs, Not My Dog included. She stopped for a few minutes to pet the dogs. They were all so sweet and friendly, and her heart ached for one of her own.

Someday.

The front door was open, but she rang the bell.

"Door's open. Come on in."

Reid's voice. She opened the screen door and walked inside. Reid was in the kitchen.

"Where is everyone else?"

"Martha and Ben have a dinner with friends tonight and Des and Logan are doing some baby thing in Tulsa with Emma and Luke."

"A baby thing?"

"Yeah. I dunno. I was only half listening. Some informational meeting at the hospital. And then they were going out to dinner. Or something like that."

She laughed. "Okay. So we're alone."

He leaned against the counter and crossed his arms. "We are."

"That means we could . . . jump on the furniture if we wanted to." She moved closer to him, breathing in his freshly showered scent. She wound her fingers into his hair, which was still damp.

"We could, but I have other ideas."

"You do, huh?"

"I do. Remember when I told you there were places on the ranch where we could get lost?"

"Yes."

"Tonight we're going to go get lost on the ranch."

It felt good to be nestled against his body. She wouldn't mind getting lost in him right here in the kitchen. But whatever he had in mind, she was game. "Sounds fun."

"I've got some grilled chicken and potato salad in the

cooler, along with a bottle of wine and some beer, water, and soda. Oh, and brownies, too."

She arched a brow. "Brownies? Really?"

"Well, yeah. Gotta have dessert, right?"

She liked the way his mind worked. Though in her mind, he was dessert. She'd have to file that thought away for later. "I'm already hungry just thinking about it."

He smiled and tucked her hair behind her ear. "Let's get this party started, then."

He carried the cooler out to his truck while she went to her car to grab her backpack. She climbed into the truck, and Reid did, too, shaking his head when Not My Dog tried to hop inside with them.

"Not this time, buddy."

"Aww, he looks so sad," Sam said.

"He can hang with his dog pals. Tonight, it's just you and me."

Not My Dog finally got the hint and ran off with the other dogs. Reid backed out, heading down the main gravel road.

She'd always loved being on the McCormack ranch, had always enjoyed how expansive the property was. You could drive for miles and see nothing but land. Scrub and trees and cattle. It was beautiful out here.

"Do you miss living here?" she asked.

"Sometimes. It's a little cramped in my condo in Boston. Plus the traffic. I miss the space out here. Even in Hope there's no congestion."

"I can imagine the difference. I've traveled here and there and have been to bigger cities. Small-town life is definitely more my speed."

He took a glance over at her. "Did you like traveling?"

"I love it. I've been to San Francisco and Los Angeles, Dallas, Chicago, and Philadelphia. I try to get to florist conventions and flower shows as often as I can. It gives me the chance to not only meet other florists from around the country, but to improve my craft."

"Good for you. Plus, you can't beat travel."

"I agree. I'd love to go more, but being the sole owner and operator of the shop, I can't get out as much as I'd like to."

Reid made a left turn, heading them down a dirt road. "You could always hire help, someone you trust enough that you could train to run the shop while you're gone."

"This is true. I guess because Grammy Claire ran the shop herself, and then it was me, I've never thought about anyone outside the family doing it."

"When I first started my business, I felt the same way. I didn't want anyone handling it but me. It was my baby and I was very protective of it. Until I figured out I couldn't handle it alone. Then I brought in another architect, and he's fantastic. I trust him with the business and with my staff."

"He's handling things right now?"

Reid nodded. "Yeah. He's not only a great employee, but he's become a good friend. So I know he'll make all the right decisions. He and I have built a fantastic staff at the firm."

"I'm glad to hear things are going so well for you in Boston. You must be very proud of the company you've built."

"I've done okay. You could do the same thing, Sam. Find someone you trust, and give yourself some breathing room so you can have a life."

She thought about it and nodded. "You're right about that. There are times when I just can't be there, and I can't allow the business to suffer. Being a one-person owner can have its advantages, but also drawbacks."

"Yeah it can. I speak from experience on that. And if you need help finding personnel, I'm happy to help you with that."

A warm feeling settled in her stomach. The one thing she hadn't had in her life in quite a few years was backup. "Thanks. I appreciate it. And I might just take you up on that offer."

"Anytime."

He pulled down a road that wasn't even a road, the truck bumping over ruts until he stopped.

"Where are we?" she asked.

"We're here. Come on, let's get out and I'll show you."

All she saw were trees and bushes and a whole lot of nothing. She came around to the front of the truck, and Reid took her hand.

"It's this way. Watch your step."

"This way" was through a small hole in between two hedges.

"Seriously?" she asked him.

He grinned. "Yeah. Trust me."

He led her through the hedge, and it was like she'd arrived in heaven. The setting sun hit the cabin and adjacent stream perfectly, and Sam had never seen anything like it. Green grass surrounded the cabin, while perfectly trimmed bushes adorned the walkway.

"Wow. Does someone live here?"

"No. But it's well maintained in case someone needs to get away."

"It's amazing. And the stream is gorgeous."

"Yeah, it's kind of a cool hideaway. I used to love to come here to fish or just hang out near the water."

Large river rocks stood tall at the edge of the stream, allowing for a waterfall. Sam could happily prop up a chair at the edge of the stream and just watch the water for hours.

Reid led her to the cabin, used his set of keys to open the door, and held it while she walked inside.

The inside of the cabin was as perfectly manicured as the outside. Knotted pine floors were spread throughout. It was small, but again, perfectly maintained, with a couple of chairs, a sofa, a fireplace, and a kitchen. There was a second-floor loft with a bed.

It was cozy and utterly charming.

She turned around to face him. "I love this place, Reid."

"Thanks. I do, too. I'm going to go grab our stuff."

"I'll help."

She followed him back to the truck and toted her backpack and his while he carried the cooler inside. She helped him unpack the food and drinks into the refrigerator, then she climbed the stairs to the loft and dropped their bags onto the bed.

It was lovely up here, with tall windows overlooking the woods and the water. There was an attached bathroom as well, with a very roomy tub, along with a shower.

She already had ideas for later.

She went downstairs to find Reid in the kitchen. He was pulling plates out of the cabinet.

"Are you hungry?" he asked.

"Yes."

"Good. Me, too. Let's eat."

There was a microwave on the counter, so she heated the chicken while Reid scooped out potato salad and poured sodas for them. They pulled up seats at the small round table just off the kitchen and dug in.

"Martha made this?" she asked

"Yeah. She always has extra food in the fridge for whenever she's not around. Though Des has been doing some cooking as well. She's getting really good at it."

"I imagine she is. And this is exceptional chicken. I've had her potato salad before. It's very good."

"Yeah. Makes me miss home."

She took a scoop of potato salad and let the flavors melt in her mouth. There was something about Martha's potato salad that was simply unparalleled. She waved her fork at Reid. "Chalk up something else to things you can't get in Boston."

"They do have potato salad in Boston, ya know."

"Not Martha's."

"That's true." He gave her a look. "Are you making some kind of list?"

She frowned. "What list?"

"A list of reasons why I should live here."

"No. Why would I make a list? I already know why I live here and not somewhere else. As far as you . . . Well, I think that list would be self-explanatory."

He had taken a bite of chicken, chewed and swallowed, and followed it up with several sips of soda. "Really. And what would those things be?"

"Your brothers. Your awesome sisters-in-law. Future nieces and nephews now. This amazing ranch. The town of Hope and the potential business you could have there. That incredible office space on the third floor of the mercantile. Not My Dog."

He laughed. "Those are quite a few things."

She pointed her fork at him. "None of which you can find in Boston."

"You forgot one thing."

"I did? What?"

"You."

Her entire body heated. "That's true. And I'm pretty exceptional all by myself."

He took his napkin and swiped it along one corner of her mouth. "Yeah, you are."

She wanted to get up and sit on his lap, to feel all that hard muscle pressed against her. But she was still eating, and she wanted to exercise some restraint.

Still, his compliment lingered all through their meal and after, while they stood side by side at the sink and washed dishes.

"This feels familiar," he said, looking down at her with a sexy smile that made her toes curl.

"That first night you came over and I cooked you dinner."

"Only tonight I cooked you dinner."

She turned sideways to face him. "You are not taking credit for Martha's chicken and potato salad."

"Oh, did I say Martha fixed it? I meant me."

She laughed. "Too late now. No credit for you."

"You're very tough, Ms. Reasor."

"Next time fix your own chicken, Mr. McCormack."

After they dried the dishes and put them away, Reid suggested they go outside and walk by the stream before it got dark.

They went outside, and Sam breathed in the crisp, cool fall air.

"It's perfect out here."

"Are you cold?" he asked, pulling her next to him.

"Not right now." She had her long-sleeved shirt to keep her warm, though the sun had set behind all the trees. And clouds were gathering.

They climbed their way to the top of the rocks, where the water sifted underneath. Reid sat and pulled Sam down next to him.

"This is a perfect spot," she said. "I could sit here—especially when the sun is shining—for hours, just listening to and watching the water."

"It's a great spot. When I was a kid I'd come out here a lot. Sometimes with my dad, sometimes by myself. It's a good place to think."

"I'm pretty sure it's the sound of the rushing water. It helps relax the mind."

His lips curved. "Is that what it is?"

"Of course. Close your eyes and just listen to it."

He gave her a look. "I don't think so."

"Oh, come on. You're a creative type. Tap into it with me." She grabbed his hand in hers. "Now close your eyes."

He did, so she did as well, her mind drifting as she tapped into the sound of the water.

"Doesn't it make your creative juices flow just listening to the sound of the water?"

"Totally."

"Are you imagining building designs in your head?"

"No, I'm picturing getting you naked on the top of this rock."

She opened her eyes and laughed. "Okay, well, I can't exactly complain about where your mind is going with that one, but maybe not tonight. The wind is picking up and the clouds are starting to look a little angry. Not exactly conducive to getting naked."

"Too bad, because I was having some very creative visions."

She shifted, drawing her feet behind her. "Were you? Care to elaborate?"

"How about I just show you instead?" He tugged her against him, and his lips fused to hers in a kiss that instantly made her forget all about creative vision and sent her reeling into passionate territory.

And when he pulled her onto his lap, all she could think about were his muscular thighs and the way it felt to be close to his body heat. To be wrapped in his arms as the wind whipped around them was the best kind of feeling, especially when he deepened the kiss.

She was always so lost in him when he kissed her, as if nothing else in the world existed.

Until a cold, fat raindrop slapped her cheek. Then another, and another, and the angry wind got really pissed off as the clouds opened and they were suddenly sitting in the middle of a downpour.

Thunder boomed loudly, and a crack of lightning snapped off in the distance.

Reid rose, helping her up, and held her hand as they raced to the house, a deluge of rain blinding them along the way.

By the time they reached the front door, Sam was soaked. She toed off her tennis shoes at the door and held them in her hand as they made their way inside. Reid shut and locked the door, and the two of them stood there, shaking.

"Well. That was fun," she said.

"Not really. But if I haven't mentioned before that you look sexy as hell all wet, let me say it now."

She laughed. "I probably look a lot like wet dog."

He wound his arms around her. "Trust me, Sam. You don't look anything like a wet dog. You look hot. So hot, in fact, that we should get these wet clothes off right here."

Before she knew what was happening, he'd pulled off her top, and then his own. Her bra followed, and his mouth was on her cold, puckering nipples, instantly warming her.

They were a tangle of shivering limbs as they worked themselves out of their clinging wet jeans, socks, and underwear.

But when Reid put his arms around her and pulled her against his body, she heated up in a hurry.

"I think a hot shower would warm things up."

She looked up at him, at the water droplets clinging to his hair. "I don't know about you, but I'm already hot."

"Then we'll get even hotter."

He took her hand, and they dashed up the stairs. Sam grabbed towels while Reid turned on the shower. As soon as the water was warm, he tugged her inside.

It wasn't a huge shower, but it was perfect, because it kept them close and under the water together. And when Reid's hands splayed across her back and he pulled her against him, his mouth covering hers, Sam couldn't think of anything more perfect.

His rock-hard body pressed against hers, his erection sliding between her thighs as he kissed her until the warm water and his mouth made her dizzy with heat and desire. She slid her fingers into his hair, her fingers gliding into the silky wetness to massage his scalp. When he groaned and his cock lurched up against her sex, she responded with a moan.

He backed her up against the wall of the shower and palmed her breast, using his thumb to brush against her nipple until sensation exploded and made her sex throb with anticipation. And when he moved his hand lower, snaking down over her rib cage and stomach, her breath caught.

He cupped her sex, sliding his hand back and forth over her slick, sensitized flesh. He pulled his mouth from hers, his gaze fixed on hers as his hand glided over her. He seemingly knew exactly where to touch her, the perfect pressure to give her to take her right to the edge of orgasm—then over.

It was a heady sensation, to be that intimately connected to someone as she came. And then he kissed her again, his body moving over hers in a way that told her they were just getting started.

Reid turned the water off, his thumb brushing over her lower lip.

"Warm now?" he asked.

"Oh, yeah."

He stepped out and grabbed a towel, wrapping it around her body, then grabbed one for himself. They hurriedly dried off, and Sam towel-dried her hair, then ran a comb through it. That was good enough, because by then Reid was in the bedroom. She was anxious to join him.

She turned out the light in the bathroom and headed into the bedroom, and the room was instantly bathed with light as a strike of lightning hit.

"Wow," she said. "That was close."

"If you're scared, come on over here and I'll take care of you."

Reid pulled down the comforter on the empty side of the bed.

She wasn't afraid. She loved storms. But the idea of making love with Reid as one raged outside appealed. She climbed onto the bed, drew the covers back, and straddled him.

Lightning flashed again outside, giving Reid a perfect view of Samantha's gorgeous body sitting on top of him. He hadn't expected the storm when he'd brought her out here, but he sure as hell wasn't going to complain about it. Her body was creamy perfection as she leaned over to kiss him, her breasts rubbing against his chest, making him ache to be inside her.

He smoothed his hands down her back and grasped her hips.

"You ready for me?" she murmured against his lips.

"More than ready." He arched against her, letting her know just how ready he was.

She lifted up and gave him a sexy smile that made his balls clench. "So you are."

He grabbed the condom he'd laid on the nightstand. She took it from him, tore open the package, and slowly slid it down over his cock. He'd never once thought putting a condom on was hot—until now.

She slid down on him, giving him one incredible view of her sex, of the perfect way the two of them fit together, as she lowered herself fully onto him. He reached up to touch her breasts, to rub his thumbs over her nipples.

"Have I told you how much I enjoy you touching me?" she asked.

"No, but I get a pretty good idea from the sounds you make." He put his hands behind her back and drew her forward, fitting one of her nipples into his mouth, and was rewarded with her sweet moans.

She tightened around him, squeezing him as he sucked and licked her nipple. God, that was good. He could come right now, but the way she writhed against him was the best damn thing he'd ever felt and he could last all night long if he could keep this going.

But when she ground against him and he felt her tight

vise quivering around him, he knew she was going to go off soon. He drove hard into her and she rose up, tilted her head back, and cried out.

"That's it," he said, then thrust and went with her, holding on to her hips as he shuddered with his climax.

He held tight to her as she trembled against him with her orgasm. It was a wild ride, both of them shaking with the aftereffects.

He swept his hand along her back, listening to the sound of rumbling thunder.

"Mmm," she said against his neck.

"Yeah."

She rolled off of him, and he got up to dispose of the condom, then went downstairs and poured them both a glass of wine. He came back up to find her propped up against the head of the bed.

"Ooh, wine. That sounds good." She smiled at him when he handed her a glass.

"I thought you might be thirsty after all that screaming you did."

She laughed. "Well, it was a lot of work."

He climbed on the bed next to her. "Next round, I'll do all the work."

She tipped her glass against his, then took a sip.

"Next round, huh?" she asked.

"Well, yeah. We've got all night together. Unless you're tired."

"Oh, I'm absolutely not tired. And, you know, there are some amazing views out of the downstairs window. And all that privacy. We could do it standing up and watch the storm."

He set his wineglass on the table and got out of bed, then held his hand out for her.

"Let's go."

She laughed. "I have a feeling it's going to be a very long, sleepless night."

He hauled her out of bed. "It's your own fault for having such creative ideas."

They both laughed as they ran downstairs.

Chapter 27

THE STORM OF the night before had given way to a beautiful morning. Reid was up early making coffee, and Sam came downstairs about twenty minutes after he did. She only wore one of his T-shirts.

He leaned against the kitchen counter. "You know, if I could see that every morning I could die a happy man."

She came over and accepted the cup he handed to her. "See what?"

"You, wearing one of my shirts and nothing else."

She leaned against him and pressed her lips to his. "Come over to my house and make me coffee every morning and we could probably work something out."

"A tempting offer, Ms. Reasor. Unfortunately, if I saw you like this every morning, it's possible I'd never go to work. Then I'd end up unemployed and destitute, a shell of my former self." Then he lifted up her shirt and teased the band of her underwear. "Screw it. You're worth it."

He took her mouth in a kiss that made him instantly hard. He heard her coffee cup hit the counter with a loud bang, and then her nails dug into his shirt. After that, his mind kind of went blank, and all he could think about was her sweet scent and the way she wriggled her body against his erection.

He laid her back against the kitchen table, lifted the shirt and put his mouth on her breasts, needing to taste her, to touch her, furious passion overtaking him until all he wanted to do was sink inside her.

He went to grab a condom and put it on, then shoved into her with a hard thrust that pushed her halfway up the table. Her eyes were heavy-lidded with passion as she wrapped her legs around his hips and held on to his arms while he drove into her.

This wasn't slow, heady lovemaking like they'd done last night. It was fast, furious, need-filled desire for each other that fueled them both. He couldn't get enough of her, needing to fill her, taste her, breathe her in as he pumped hard into her. Her cries of pleasure only spurred him on to thrust harder.

And when she came apart for him, he drove deeper, shuddering as his climax rocked him.

He closed his eyes and settled, his arms shaking as he lifted his torso off of Sam's body. He stayed like that, trying to catch his breath.

"You're dripping sweat all over me."

He opened his eyes and smiled down on her. "You made me work for it."

She arched against him. "You complaining?"

"No."

He bent, wrapped his arms around her back, and lifted her, walking up the stairs to the loft and depositing both of them in the shower.

"Hmm," she said as she drew him under the hot spray with her. "This feels familiar."

He kissed her. "It does, doesn't it?"

"Yes. And as much as I'd love round two—or maybe six, depending on how we're counting—I'm hungry."

"Me, too." They washed, rinsed, and got out, then dried off and dressed.

He'd like to stay here with her longer. It was nice out here. Quiet. He could make love to her over and over again.

Unfortunately, he hadn't brought enough food. They packed up and loaded the truck.

Reid drove them back to the ranch. "Stay for breakfast?" he asked.

"Sure. I called my grandmother when I first got up. She and Faith are in town having breakfast at Bert's. Then they are going to hit up the yard sales."

"Sounds like Faith is a good friend to Grammy Claire."

Sam smiled. "She is."

After getting out of the truck and stopping to love on all the dogs, they headed into the house. Logan was seated at the table, and Des was at the island drinking a glass of juice.

"Morning," Des said, coming over to give Sam a hug. Reid headed to the coffeepot for a cup, then went to sit next to his brother.

"Good morning," Sam said. "How was your baby thing last night? Reid said he couldn't remember exactly what it was about."

"Oh." Des laughed. "It was a tour of the hospital labor and delivery area and birthing rooms, and an informational meeting discussing different types of birthing options. Fun stuff."

"I'm sure it was."

Des laid her hand over her lower belly. "A little nerve-racking, all the decisions that have to be made."

"I'm sure it is."

"I made waffles this morning," Des said. "Would you like one?"

"I'd love one."

"Good. I see Reid has already dug in."

"You know it," Reid said, his mouth full when he answered.

Des laughed. "Come on, you'd better grab one before the guys eat them all."

Sam and Des went to sit at the table with the guys. Reid had already wolfed down a waffle.

"While you're here, you can help me with some maintenance on the tractor," Logan said.

Reid stood, picking up a waffle in his hand. "Okay. Let's go."

"You ladies have a good time," Logan said, kissing Des as they walked out.

Reid gave Sam a grin and disappeared.

She poured syrup on her waffle and dug in. "These are great, Des."

"Thanks. I'm happy to be home now so I can do some cooking. And I know Martha is glad to have time off so she and Ben can spend time with each other."

"Plus, you and Logan get alone time as well. I know you've been busy with movie-making."

Des leaned back in her chair and nodded. "It's been pretty intense."

Sam took a sip of juice and swallowed. "How are you going to handle the pregnancy, time-wise, with your filming schedule?"

"I'm in postproduction right now, so I have a few scenes left to add in to a film I just finished. I won't start another until after the baby arrives. And other than a premiere where I have to do a press tour in a couple of months, I'm free and clear."

"That's great. You've been working nonstop for a lot of years now. You deserve the time off."

"I'm sure I'll drive Logan crazy, but Martha and I are excited about clearing out one of the spare rooms upstairs next to the master bedroom to decorate the nursery. And Emma and I have so much shopping to do."

Sam grinned. "I can imagine the fun the two of you are having being pregnant together."

Des laughed. "We didn't plan it, but we're delighted that it turned out this way. Plus, the cousins will grow up together, and that's kind of awesome."

"It is."

"Okay, enough about me and baby stuff. I want to know about you and Reid."

Sam really didn't know how to explain her relationship with Reid. "We're having fun together."

Des gave her a look. "And that's it?"

"I . . . guess. I mean, both our lives are kind of complicated right now. He lives in Boston. I don't think that's going to change. I have Grammy Claire to deal with. Neither of us is looking for a relationship."

"So . . . just fun times and sex and there's no emotional attachment?"

She'd like to answer yes to that question, but that wouldn't be the truth. She was becoming attached to Reid—emotionally and otherwise. "I don't know. And even if I had feelings for him, it wouldn't make any difference. His life isn't here."

Des crossed her arms. "It's not here at the moment. That could change, you know. My life wasn't here when I was filming a movie on the ranch. And then I fell in love with Logan, and we all know how that turned out."

"True. But your situation is entirely different."

Des's lips curved. "Really. How is it different?"

"I—" She didn't have a comeback.

"Exactly. So if you think you might be falling in love with Reid, don't give up just because of his geography, okay?"

She didn't necessarily believe that, but she nodded. "Okay."

Des leaned forward and grabbed her hand, giving it a squeeze. "Love has a way of making everything work out for the best."

Did it? She'd like to think so. But she didn't know if she was falling in love with Reid, or grasping at someone—anyone— solid to hold on to because her world was turning upside down.

She supposed she needed to figure that out.

In the meantime, she should head home, so she helped Des with the dishes, despite all of Des's complaints about that, then headed outside to find Reid so she could tell him she was leaving.

She found Not My Dog wandering.

"Hey, Notty. Where's Reid?"

The dog wagged his tail and wiggled his butt, so she bent and petted him, then ran off a few feet and came back with a stick.

"You want me to throw this, don't you?"

More tail-wagging, so Sam threw the stick across the front yard. Notty ran like crazy after it, then brought it back to her and dropped it at her feet. She picked it up, careful to avoid the part of the stick Notty had slobbered all over, and threw it again.

This went on for about ten throws.

"He'll do that all day long."

She looked up to find Reid walking toward her, wiping his hands on a towel.

"Yes, I was beginning to grab a clue."

"Go play with your stick, Notty."

Stick in his mouth, the dog ran off to sit under the tall oak tree and gnaw on his prize.

Sam smiled. "I see the nickname has stuck."

"Apparently."

"I was actually on my way to find you. I'm going to head home."

"Oh? I thought maybe we'd spend the day together. Do you have important things to do today?"

"Well, I was going to check on Grammy Claire and see what she and Faith are up to. Then I need to run some errands and do a little shopping."

"Okay. Let's do that."

She cocked a brow. "You want to come with me to run errands."

"Sure."

"Don't you have things of your own to do?"

"Not really."

"Reid. I might even have to go into Tulsa—to go to the mall."

He opened his mouth, paused, then said, "I'll still go."

She laughed. She couldn't believe that any man would want to go shopping with a woman.

"Fine. You want to follow me to my house?"

"Actually, I got a little greasy working with Logan, so let me go clean up. I'll meet you there?"

"Okay."

She got into her car and headed off the ranch property, still unable to believe Reid was going to shop with her today.

He must be really bored—or really want to spend time with her.

Either way, she was looking forward to spending the day with him today.

Chapter 28

REID LEARNED A lot of things about Sam after spending the day with her.

One, she liked underwear. Two, she could spend an hour in the lingerie store. He wasn't sure if she did that on purpose to see if he'd flinch and run like hell, but hey, a guy could learn a lot about a woman by hanging out with her in the lingerie store.

Plus, he could indulge in some serious fantasies about her while she browsed. Who knew these places were so sexy? Or maybe it was envisioning Sam wearing this stuff that got to him. Either way, she wandered, and his mind went crazy while she held up hot pink silk panties with flimsy little ties on either end and asked him what he thought.

"I think I can get those off of you in about two seconds."

That made her blush. And made his dick twitch. Which he learned after she did that to him the third time wasn't a good idea in a lingerie store filled with women. So he learned to keep his dirty thoughts to himself.

"You know I think you'll look sexy in every single thing here."

That made her smile. "Well, I needed some new underwear

and I've been meaning to go shopping. It's just a bonus that you're here with me today so you can help me pick them out."

Bonus? By the time she started choosing black and pink lacy and silky bras, all he could think about was getting his hands—and his mouth—on her breasts. So for him it was more torture than anything, but he hung in there.

Next up was dress shopping for Molly and Carter's wedding. Reid found a seat while Sam tried on dress after dress and modeled them for him.

He thought she looked beautiful in all the dresses, but Sam apparently didn't. One was too tight in the hips, the other was too short. She didn't like the particular green color on one dress, and with another dress something called a bodice squeezed her boobs.

Who knew that being a woman meant you had to deal with so many issues trying on dresses?

It made him glad to be a guy. He owned several suits, and he'd wear one of those for the wedding.

She finally came out wearing a red dress that nearly made him fall out of his chair. It hit her just below her thighs, and it showed off her curves in a way that made him want to put his hands all over her.

"That one," he said as she stood and looked at herself in the mirror.

She turned around to face him. "Really?"

"Yes. That one."

She turned back and stared. "It does fit well, and I like it. But you're not just saying that because you're tired of sitting there, are you?"

He got up and stepped behind her, laying his hands on her hips. "Sam, you look sexy as hell in this dress, and if we weren't in a public place right now, I would definitely show you how sexy you look."

She met his gaze in the mirror, her eyes flashing hot. "This one."

"Yeah."

She went back into the dressing room and changed, then bought the dress.

"Are we done?" he asked as he held on to the dress for her.

"Not quite. Now I need new shoes to go with the dress."

He resisted the urge to groan. Instead, he held all her bags while she sat and tried on about twenty pairs of shoes. They all looked the same to him, but to Sam they were all different. And just like the dresses, some didn't work for varying reasons. One pair was too tight in the toe area, one rubbed her ankles, on one pair the heel was too tall, and another the heel was too short.

It was like shopping with freaking Goldilocks.

She finally found a pair she loved—thank God—and they were finished in the shoe department.

"What's next?" he asked.

"Oh, we're done here."

He breathed a sigh of relief.

"Now we're off to the flower store."

A florist at the flower store? He wanted to cry.

"But I'm kind of hungry," she said. "Are you?"

He didn't know about hunger, but he sure as hell needed a beer. "Sure."

"Great. How about we stop for lunch first?"

"Sounds perfect. Where would you like to go?"

She thought about it for a few seconds, then said, "You choose."

Reid drove them far away from the mall, just in case Sam got inspired during lunch and decided she had to have socks or perfume or something else that might require two damn hours to select.

He took them to the Dirt Road Bar and Grill, one of his favorite burger places, that also doubled as a sports bar. It was off the beaten path, a place bikers liked to stop in because it was on the back roads, but he'd often come here because he liked the old building and the ambience.

"I don't think I've ever been here before," she said as they walked inside.

The place was dark and cool inside, with original brickwork walls and an old, scarred bar he'd love to pony up to and down several beers. But since Sam was with him, he found them a seat at one of the booths, choosing one that had a prime view of all the big-screen televisions.

"This is kind of like Bash's place, though on a larger scale," she said as she slid into the booth.

"Yeah, though it caters to the biker crowd."

"I noticed all the bikes when we came in. There were some awesome ones out there."

"Yeah, there were."

"What would you like to drink?"

"An iced tea if they have one."

His lips curved. "They have one. I'll be right back."

He went up to the bar, ordered their drinks, and said hello to Casey, the owner and bartender who'd been there for as long as he'd been coming here.

"Hey, Reid. Haven't seen you around here in years."

"I've been in Boston."

He and Casey caught up while Casey made their drinks.

"You staying for lunch?"

"Yeah."

Casey grabbed two menus from behind the bar.

"That your girl?" Casey asked, motioning with his head to Sam.

Reid didn't quite know how to answer that, so he went with a nod. "Yeah."

"Pretty."

"Thanks. I'll let you know when we decide on lunch."

He took their drinks and the menus back to the table.

"You know the bartender."

"That's Casey. He owns the place. I used to come in here for drinks when I was home for breaks from college."

She gave him a look. "And maybe before?"

He laughed. "Yeah. But he wouldn't serve me alcohol. Casey's a straight-up, no-bullshit kind of guy. But sometimes I'd go for long drives when I needed to get away from the ranch. I found this place on one of those drives. I liked the looks of it, I could watch sports on TV, and Casey and I became friends."

"It's always nice to have a place where you can run away from home."

"Where's yours?"

She fiddled with the edge of the menu. "I guess it's the flower shop."

"That's work, Sam. That's not a place where you can forget about your problems."

"But I like it there. It relaxes me, and I enjoy creating bouquets. It's not really a stressful environment for me."

"Still, it's work. You need a play place, somewhere you can go, either by yourself or with friends, where there's no work and no stressors."

"I don't really have a lot of stressors. Or at least I didn't until this whole issue with Grammy Claire surfaced."

"Where do you go with your friends?"

"Oh, we hang out at each others' houses. Go to the movies or to Bash's bar. Trust me, I get out plenty."

"That's good. And you're beautiful, so you obviously date a lot."

She laughed. "I can't tell you how much I appreciate that compliment. But no, I don't really date a lot. My calendar is full with work and with my grandmother. Plus, I'm kind of choosy about men."

He arched a brow. "Is that right?"

"It is."

"So I should feel complimented that you're spending time with me."

She gave him a wicked smile. "Very."

Since they were sitting on the same side of the booth, he leaned over and brushed his lips across hers. "Thanks. I feel the same way."

She brought her finger up to his lips. "You do very strange things to me, Reid McCormack."

"I do? In what way?"

"You give me very warm feelings in parts of my body."

Yeah, he was getting hot, too. "Care to be a little more descriptive about which parts?"

She laughed, then gave him a light shove. "No. What I'd care for is one of these chicken sandwiches."

He could tell she was hot and bothered, but also very

aware of their environment. The bar was crowded for a Saturday afternoon. Not exactly a romantic atmosphere—but for a few minutes it had only been the two of them.

He took their order to Casey, who ran it back into the kitchen and told Reid it would be about fifteen minutes. Casey refilled their drinks, and Reid carried them back to their seats. He and Sam settled in to watch some sports, Reid zeroing in on one of the baseball games.

"Have I ever mentioned my utter love of baseball?" Sam asked.

Reid slanted a surprised gaze to her. "You have not."

She nodded. "Grammy Claire and I share this love. My Grandpa Bob always had a baseball game on TV in the summer. We'd watch games together all the time. St. Louis is my favorite team. I've been watching since I was a kid."

"Have you ever been to a game?"

"No. We often talked about heading up for a weekend of games, but we never did. I was always a little sad about that."

"We should go to a game. Take a weekend and drive up for a game."

"Oh, I couldn't do that. It sounds fun, but I couldn't be that far away from my grandmother."

"Of course. I hadn't thought about that." He wished there were a way that he could take her, though. He knew she'd enjoy it. He'd gone to plenty of games in Boston. He loved baseball—any baseball game.

Casey finally brought their food, and they started to eat.

"Oh my God, this chicken is fantastic," Sam said after she'd taken a few bites of her sandwich. "And the fries are so good."

Reid nodded. "Yeah, this place has awesome food. I think I've eaten everything on the menu over the years. There's nothing bad on it."

They watched the baseball game, arguing over balls and strikes. If it was possible, Sam's knowledge of baseball made her even more attractive to him.

"Isn't that Brady Conners?" Reid asked as the door opened and a dark-haired guy came in.

Sam looked over. "It is. Hey, Brady." She called out his name and waved at him.

He smiled and walked over, shaking Reid's hand. "Didn't expect to see you two in here."

"I used to come here a lot when I lived here," Reid explained.

Brady nodded. "It's a great hangout."

Reid motioned to Brady's helmet. "Out riding today?"

"Yeah. Road testing one of the bikes I was working on, so I decided to stop in for a burger and a beer."

"You can join us if you'd like," Sam said.

"I don't want to interrupt you two if you're on a date."

"No interruption at all," Sam said. "We'd love the company."

Reid said, "Take a seat."

"Okay. Let me grab a beer and order a burger and I'll be right back."

He wandered off.

"I hope you don't mind that I invited him to sit with us," Sam said.

"I don't mind at all." Reid hadn't gone to the same high school as Brady, but he'd known him. They were the same age, so they'd hung out in the same circles.

He'd known Brady's brother, Kurt, and had heard about what had happened to him.

He felt bad for Brady and his family. When you suffered a loss like that, it had to be tough to get over.

Brady sat and took a long pull of his beer. "Warm day outside for fall."

"But great bike weather, isn't it?"

Brady grinned. "That's the best part."

"So it's not your bike you're riding?" Sam asked.

"No, it's a client's. I replaced the clutch and brake lines, so I'm testing them out on a long ride before I give it the all clear."

"And since you're here and unscathed, I assume it's all working well."

He smiled at Sam. "It's running perfectly now."

"Carter tells me business has been really good for you since you started working for him at his shop," Reid said.

"More than I thought it would be, actually. I estimated I'd get a small amount of bike repair along with some paint work. But I've stayed busy every day."

"There are a lot more bikers on the road than ever before," Sam said. "And with the weather staying warmer longer, it makes the bikers happy. Which means more work for you."

"Yeah."

"So your goal is to eventually open your own bike shop?" Reid asked.

"Yeah. My specialty is custom painting. That's what I really want to do. For now, repairs and things are fine. They pay the bills."

Reid understood that. "But not your dream job."

"Exactly."

"Are you planning to stay in Hope?" Sam asked. "Will you do your custom paint work at Carter's auto shop?"

Brady shook his head. "That's not my plan, no. I mean, I don't know about staying in Hope. My parents are here, so I might. But as far as setting up shop at Carter's place, I doubt it. My plan is to set up my own shop someday."

"And is that someday soon on the horizon?" Sam asked.

Brady tipped his beer to his lips and took a sip, then set the bottle down on the table. "Not yet. But soon, I hope."

"Well, I hope you decide to stay in town when you do set up your shop. A lot of people would be very happy if you stayed."

Reid saw the glimmer of a smile on his face. "Thanks. That's nice to hear."

Reid could tell Brady wasn't one of those people who shared his emotions. He understood that. Some guys held it all close to the vest, the quiet kind of guys who, when they had something important to say, said it. Otherwise, they were observers.

Reid figured Brady was an observer. But he'd had some conversations with him, and he was a decent guy and a hard worker, and he knew Sam liked him. So that made him a good guy in his eyes. He was just sorry for what Brady and his family had had to go through.

They finished up their meal and chatted with Brady for a while, watched the games and then paid their bill. Brady said he was going to move to the bar and hang out a little longer, so they said their good-byes.

They headed back to the truck and drove off. Sam told him where the flower store was, so they made a stop there. He prepared himself for several hours there, but she told him she knew exactly what she wanted.

"I need to plant some bulbs in the front garden. Some of my spring flowers aren't blooming any longer, so it's time to replace them," she said as she wandered the aisles at the nursery.

"Oh. That makes sense. So you're not looking for something for your shop."

"No. I order those online and have flowers shipped in, unless it's an emergency. Then I'll head out and shop for something I might need right away."

She filled the cart with the bulbs she wanted. Reid followed behind her as she walked up and down the aisle, selecting tulips and crocus and daffodils and hyacinths.

"You know," he said as they wandered the store, "I create drawings of homes and buildings, and often those drawings include flowers. So I know the names of the flowers and what they look like. But I've never planted a bulb before in my life. I really know nothing about flowers."

She gave him a horrified look. "We need to fix this serious gap in your floral education."

"We do?"

"Yes. We'll take these back to my house and I'll educate you in the planting of bulbs."

"How did you know it was just what I was thinking of doing today?"

She laughed. "I'm sure it was."

They checked out, and he drove her back to her place, helping her unpack her bags and carry them into the house. She took the clothing items back to her bedroom while he stored the bags of bulbs in the garage. When he came inside, she was in the kitchen.

"I need to go over to my grandmother's house to check on her. Would you like to join me?"

"Sure."

They walked across the street and down the sidewalk. Sam got out her keys, but rang the bell first.

Her grandmother answered. "Hello, Samantha. And hello to you, too, Reid. Nice to see both of you. Come on inside."

Sam kissed her grandmother's cheek. So did Reid. "How was your day today, Claire?"

"I had a wonderful day. Faith and I were busy all day." She led them inside, where she had the television on. "Now I'm tired."

Sam and Reid took a seat on the sofa. "What did you and Faith do?"

"We went to several yard sales. Faith picked up an old pitcher that she really liked. I found a garden gnome. It's out in the garage if you want to see it."

"I'll definitely go look before I leave," Sam said. "I know you love gnomes."

Her grandmother smiled. "I do. Then we went out to lunch and back to Faith's house, where we played cards for a while and watched some baseball on TV. Faith wanted to check out another sale at one of the shops downtown, so we went there. That woman can run and run. Since she's only a few years younger than me, I don't know how she does it."

Sam laughed. "She is very active, isn't she?"

"Yes. Anyway, she dropped me off just a little while ago. I'm going to fix some soup for dinner, then crawl into my pajamas and go to bed early tonight. My legs are tired. How was your day?"

"Your granddaughter ran my legs off today," Reid said, telling Grammy Claire about all the shopping they'd done.

Grammy Claire slanted a wry smile Reid's way. "You poor boy. That's Samantha, all right. She does love to shop."

"You know it," Sam said with a proud grin. "And, surprisingly, Reid held up without complaint."

"That's because he's a McCormack, and the McCormack men don't complain. Isn't that right, Reid?"

"Yes, ma'am."

"All right, you two. Out. I'm going to take a bath before I fix dinner."

Sam stood and kissed her grandmother. "I'll call you before bedtime, Grammy Claire."

"You do that."

Reid gave her a peck on the cheek, too. "You call if you need anything."

Grammy Claire grasped his wrist and pulled him down so she could whisper in his ear. "You're good for her. You make her smile."

Something tightened in his gut. "Thanks. She makes me smile, too."

Grammy Claire's eyes sparkled. "So I noticed."

Sam shut and locked the front door. "She seems fine."

"Yeah, she does."

"But I have a feeling that won't last."

He put his arm around her as they walked across the street. "Don't go worrying about things you don't have to worry about just yet, okay? It sounds to me like she and Faith had a great time today, and no issues surfaced. Your grandmother is enjoying her life right now. Can't that be enough?"

"You're right. It should be." She looked up at the sky. "It's starting to get dark, so we won't be able to plant bulbs today. You're off the hook."

"Oh, damn. And I was so looking forward to that."

"I'll bet you were. I guess you'll have to settle for hanging out with me indoors. Where we'll find other . . . activities to occupy our time."

He opened the front door for her. "I like the sound of that. Unless you mean you have some leaky faucet you'd like me to fix."

She laughed and took his hand, leading him to her bedroom. "No, my faucets are just fine, thank you. I was thinking something more personal. That requires us to get naked. I have this tension issue I'd like you to assist me with."

He followed her down the hall. When they got to the bedroom and she turned around to face him, he put his arms around her. "Tension issue, huh? I can definitely help release some of that stress you're holding in your body, Sam."

She drew her shirt off, then slid out of her shoes. "I knew you could."

He removed his shirt and tossed it on the bed. "I have an idea."

"You do? And what is that?"

"How about a bath? Together."

"I like this idea."

They finished undressing, and Sam led him to her bathroom. She turned on the faucet, grateful she had a nice soaker tub big enough to accommodate both of them. Just the thought of relaxing in the tub with Reid made her quiver with excitement.

When the water reached the appropriate level, Reid held her hand while she climbed in. Then he got in behind her. She turned the water off, letting the steam envelop her—letting Reid envelop her. He put his arms around her and pulled her back against his chest.

She settled in, sliding her legs along his.

"This is damn near perfect," he said, smoothing his hands down her arms.

"Yes." She felt the tension from the day—from the past several days—melt away as his hands moved over her body. And despite the hot water in the tub, her skin broke out in chill bumps from his touch, her nipples puckering as he cupped her breasts.

"I hope this is relaxing you," he whispered in her ear as his thumbs brushed across her aching nipples.

Her breath quickened as his erection pushed against her back.

"I don't know if I can say I'm very relaxed right now, Reid."

"That's too bad. Let me fix that."

He wrapped his arm around her and pulled her closer, his fingers inching down to cup her sex.

She gasped. In this position, she could watch the movements

of his hand just under the water, could see and feel what he did to her.

"Lean your head back against my shoulder," he said. "Close your eyes and just feel."

She did, surrendering to the sensations as his fingers worked their magic on her.

It was as if everything in her mind had melted away, and there was only Reid. Reid and his hands, coaxing her every desire to feverish proportions. She lifted against his hand, needing more and more of what he could give her.

"That's it," he said, his voice low and soft against her ear.

The water seemed so hot all of a sudden as she grew ever closer to that explosion she knew was imminent, Reid's questing fingers rolling over the throbbing bud of her clit. She cried out as she came and he held tight to her while she shuddered through her orgasm.

When she settled, his tongue razed her neck. "Now that was good."

"Definitely for me." She turned around in the water and straddled him, looping her arms around his neck. She kissed him, her body still quaking with hot, liquid passion. And since she was sitting on, and sliding against, the evidence of his passion, it only made her need for him greater.

Apparently Reid had had enough of bath time, too, because he stood, holding on to her, and stepped out of the tub, both of them dripping water all over her bathroom floor.

"Wait right here," he said, his voice gruff with passion as he hurriedly dried off his body and stalked out of the room.

She did her own drying off as fast as she could, and by the time she finished, he was back, condom in hand, his erection still gloriously prominent.

His obvious desire for her made her body flush hot. Not that she wasn't already seriously warm, from both the bath and the amazing orgasm he'd just given her.

Reid didn't speak, just put his mouth on hers in a very demanding, very delicious way.

Her hunger fed on his and she felt the tension in his upper arms as she gripped them, holding on to him while he groaned against her lips. This was no easy, laid-back kiss he gave her. It was fueled with a hard driving passion, and she felt his need when he drew his lips from hers, gave her a look of desperate desire and pushed their discarded towels against the bathroom counter. He lifted her, sat her on top of them, then put the condom on in record time.

Their mouths and tongues fused again as he slid inside of her, a fury of hot passion and tangled limbs. He cupped her butt to hold her steady as he drove into her with hard thrusts, his body aligning with hers in a way that told her he knew exactly how to take her right where she wanted to go. All she could do was hold on to the edge of the sink and just . . . feel every inch of him.

She wrapped her legs around his hips and lifted into him, rubbing herself against him as sparks shot right to her core. And when she tightened around him, he pulled back, searching her face. She reached up and rubbed her fingers against his lips, then cupped his neck and brought him forward for a kiss.

He groaned against her mouth and drove deep into her. She lost it then, her climax taking her breath and her balance. But Reid was there to steady her as she quivered around him, losing all sense of reality. And when it was his orgasm that shook them both, she held tight to him, holding them both upright as his deep kiss threatened to topple them off the counter.

Afterward, they panted against each other, both of them mingled in sweat and discarded towels.

"So," he said, pressing kisses along her neck and shoulder. "We might need to get back in the bathtub."

She smiled against his shoulder. "We might."

In the end they decided a quick dash into the shower to rinse off the sweat was the best idea. Then they dried off, got dressed, and headed into the kitchen to grab something to drink before curling up on the sofa together to watch a movie.

She didn't make it through five minutes of the movie they'd chosen before she passed out on Reid's shoulder.

Chapter 29

SAMANTHA SAT IN the doctor's office with her grandmother, continually blinking to keep the tears from falling as Dr. Westphal delivered his diagnosis.

As Sam had suspected but had done her best to deny, Grammy Claire was suffering from the early stages of Alzheimer's. Sam tried to keep her head clear as Dr. Westphal went over everything, from medication to treatment plans to long-term care.

Grammy Claire took it better than Sam did, listening and nodding and asking a lot of questions, while Sam just sat there mute and unable to process the fact that sometime in the near future she'd lose the only family member she had left, and the one person she loved more than anything in the world.

She held her grandmother's hand, and it was her grandmother who squeezed her hand in comfort, when it should have been the other way around.

She took her grandmother home, then went inside with her.

"Are you hungry?" her grandmother asked, setting her purse on its usual spot on the table next to the front door. "I could make us some grilled cheese sandwiches."

Sam's lips curved. Whenever she'd had a bad day in school, Grammy Claire had always made her grilled cheese. She started to say no, then thought better of it. "I think grilled cheese sounds great."

She wanted everything to be normal for as long as it could be, especially for her grandmother.

So she sat in the kitchen and talked flowers while she watched her grandmother take out the pan and make grilled cheese for both of them. Then, Grammy Claire sat at the kitchen table and they ate together.

And for a short while, everything was just like it used to be, the two of them chatting and laughing together. Sam was transported to her childhood, where she didn't have a worry in the world and Grammy Claire took care of everything for her and all she had to think about was her friends and how much playtime she'd get that day.

"We're going to have to talk about this, Samantha."

And then the bubble burst.

Sam inhaled, then let it out. "I know."

"I'm still lucid enough that I understand the diagnosis—and what it means. Not only for myself, but for you."

"I'm not concerned about me, Grammy Claire. I only care about your welfare."

Her grandmother pulled her chair closer and covered Sam's hands with her own. Those lovely wrinkled hands of hers. She stared down at Grammy Claire's rings. The single gold wedding band and the cluster of diamonds Grandpa Bob had gotten her for their fortieth wedding anniversary. The other one, on her right hand, that belonged to Grammy Claire's mother. Sam used to hold Grammy Claire's hand and twirl those rings around on her grandmother's fingers.

"I'm not a senile child—yet," her grandmother said. "So while I still have all my faculties, we'll need to make some decisions."

"I should probably move in with you."

Her grandmother shook her head. "No."

Sam blinked. "Why not? I'm perfectly capable of caring for you."

"Yes, you are, and no, I won't let you. You're young and single and the last thing you need to do with your life is to spend it caring for an old woman."

The tears pricked her eyes again. "Do you believe that's how I think of you, Grammy Claire? As some kind of burden? I love you. You're my family. I'd do anything for you."

Seeing the tears well up in her grandmother's eyes nearly tore her apart. "I love you, too. Which is why I would never allow you to sacrifice your life for mine. In a short period of time I won't even remember who—"

Her grandmother couldn't finish the sentence, but they both knew what she hadn't said.

At some point in the future, her grandmother wouldn't even remember who Sam was. The thought of it was like a knife to the heart. To still have her grandmother, but not be able to talk to her, not be able to reminisce with her, would be heartbreaking.

But they'd get through this—together. Because when Sam had needed her most, Grammy Claire had been there for her. And now that her grandmother needed her, Sam wouldn't abandon her.

No matter what her grandmother thought was best.

Chapter 30

REID HAD BEEN spending a lot of time on the first floor of the mercantile. The exposed brick had been cleaned and now gleamed as new—or as old-new—as it was going to be. It looked fucking fantastic along the entire west wall of the first floor. The columns had been finished; the ceiling gleamed.

It was perfect, just as he'd envisioned.

Loretta was due in this morning to look over the floor plan for the first floor. He didn't want to put walls up until she decided how she wanted the setup.

Not My Dog strolled inside the open front door and dropped a ball at his foot.

"Dude. It's work time, not playtime."

The dog just looked at him, so Reid shook his head, picked up the ball, and tossed it to the far end of the space. Not My Dog dashed after it, came loping back, and dropped it at his feet.

Obviously he'd gotten bored outside, so Reid threw the ball several more times.

"Clearly the square footage in here is large enough to throw a ball."

Reid turned to see Loretta Simmons standing in the

doorway. Tall and slim, with dark hair pulled into a high pony-tail, she pulled off her sunglasses and walked into the room.

"Yeah, sorry. Took a few minutes of dog time."

"He's very cute." She crouched down to greet Not My Dog, who had trotted over to check her out. The dog wagged his tail when Loretta scratched under his chin. "Is this your assistant, Reid?"

"He thinks he runs the place."

She laughed, then stood. "I imagine he does." She turned around, then looked up. "I love this ceiling."

"Yeah, I was jazzed about it when we uncovered it."

She walked around. "The columns are amazing. As is the brick wall. Original to the building, I assume?"

"Yes. The columns are, too, so the historical society has mandated that those stay."

She nodded. "I wouldn't want it any other way." She walked the length and width of the space—three times—and he could tell she was formulating ideas in her head.

He liked that she was thorough, and he could see her mind working as she familiarized herself with the layout of the first floor.

"If you'd like to see what the capabilities are, I can take you upstairs to the second and third floor. We've done a lot more finishing up there."

"I would like to see that. Thanks."

They headed upstairs to the second floor.

"You'll have to excuse the dust. Some things aren't finished yet."

She laughed. "I've been in a renovation zone before, so it's nothing new to me. When Tom—my ex—and I renovated one of our houses, it was like living in hell for three months. Trust me, this is nothing."

"Okay, then." He showed her around the second and third floors so she could see some of the finishes in the offices, the windows, and the bathrooms.

He took her to the third floor to show off the big office. She stared out the window.

"It's amazing up here." She turned to face him. "Do you have this space rented out yet?"

"No. Not yet."

"Someone will grab this right up. The view is extraordinary."

"Yeah, it is."

"You can see all of Hope out here, and so much farther." She looked out, crossed her arms over herself, and took a deep breath. "Definitely all of home. I've missed this. All of this."

He wondered what had brought her back here. He knew who she'd married, the amount of money she'd married into. Even after the divorce she could have lived anywhere. So why here?

It wasn't his business to ask that question.

They headed back downstairs, and she walked around again.

"It's plenty big enough for the bookstore," she said. "At first glance I was afraid it was going to be too small. I want it to be a comfortable place, a spot where people can come in and sit down. But now that I've seen it, I realize there's an abundance of room not only for the shelves, but also for sofas and tables. It has a true old-world feel to it, but has the potential for modern touches as well from what I've seen with how you've finished parts of the upstairs. You've done an amazing job with the restoration so far."

"Thanks."

The front door opened, and Deacon walked in. In an instant the tension grew so thick it was like a sudden fog had rolled in.

Deacon stopped, frowned. "Loretta."

She nodded. "Deacon, I didn't expect to—" She shot a look over at Reid. "Deacon's working this job."

"Yes, Deacon's working this job," Deacon said, drawing Loretta's attention from Reid.

Loretta looked at him. "I didn't mean to—"

Deacon held up his hand. "It's okay. Great to see you again, Loretta. I'm heading upstairs."

Deacon walked away, and Reid caught Loretta's gaze tracking him.

Yeah. That was one hell of a reunion after twelve years.

And now Reid was stuck with what looked like a very uncomfortable leftover. He was going to have to try to smooth things over.

"So . . . about the space, Loretta. Do you think it's going to work for you?"

She snapped to attention. "Oh, of course. I love it. I love absolutely everything about it."

"Great. We're about to get ready to put walls in. I showed you the drawings for the initial plans, but I can change some things up if you'd like. We can add or move electrical, lighting, outlets, and things like that. The plumbing, however, is already in place."

She nodded, seeming to have her emotions under control again. "The bathroom location is fine. Let's talk about wall and outlet placement. I'd also like to put in a coffee and tea bar."

He sat down with her, and for the next hour they drew it all out. He asked her if she was ready to commit, and she said she was. He told her he'd e-mail her a contract, and she said she'd forward it on to her attorney. They finished off with a handshake. Loretta said she was excited to be back in Hope, and she was ready to sign for the first floor.

After he finished work he saw that the flower shop was closed up. He hadn't seen much of Sam in the past few days—again. He'd tried calling her and texting her, but all he'd gotten from her was "Busy."

He understood busy, so he'd left her alone. He knew she had stuff going on with her grandmother, but he wanted to make sure she was okay. He decided to take a drive over to her place after work.

She wasn't home, so he and Not My Dog walked down the street and knocked on Claire Reasor's door.

Sam answered. "Oh, hi."

"Hey. Just checking in—on both of you."

Claire came up behind Sam. "Reid. How nice to see you. And you brought your adorable dog. Please come in, we were just fixing dinner."

"I don't want to intrude. I just stopped by to say hello."

"You're not intruding. Come on inside."

"I can put the dog out back if you'd like."

Claire's grandmother waved her hand. "Nonsense. Bob and I had dogs for years. I've missed having them around. Bring him in, too."

He stepped into the hall, and Sam shut the door. "Sorry," he said after Claire had wandered off into the kitchen. "I hadn't seen or heard from you and I was worried about you—and your grandmother."

"I know. I apologize for brushing you off. I've been . . . hanging out with her."

Claire seemed to be busy in the kitchen. "Is she okay?"

Sam just lifted a shoulder. "Right now she's fine. I'll tell you about it later. Come on in, have dinner with us."

Sam reached down to pet Not My Dog.

"Are you sure? I really don't want to intrude."

Sam clutched his arm. "You're not intruding. Grammy Claire loves company." She smiled at him. "We're making chicken fried steak and mashed potatoes for dinner."

He put his hand over his heart. "You're joking."

"I am not. And you're just in time to peel potatoes."

"I'd be happy to."

He followed her into the kitchen, sitting Not My Dog down just outside the kitchen area. The dog circled and laid down on the living room rug, watching all the action.

"Would you like some sweet tea, Reid?" Claire asked.

"Yes, ma'am. I can fix it myself."

"You go ahead then."

He fixed the tea, then washed his hands. Sam handed him the potatoes, and he stood by the sink and peeled them while Sam and Claire worked at the stove. He put the peeled potatoes in a pot, filled it with water, then set it on one of the burners, taking a long drink of the most amazing sweet tea ever as he watched Sam and Claire coat the meat and prepare it for frying.

"Would you like me to take care of that?" he asked.

Sam slanted him a look. "As if. Grammy Claire and I have

been cooking chicken fried steak together since I was old enough to stand near the stove. You can watch the potatoes."

He'd been told, hadn't he? Having been put in charge of the potatoes, he was forced to breathe in the delicious scent of the chicken fried steak cooking while he monitored boiling potatoes.

He'd also been put in charge of green beans, so while he managed those, they took care of the chicken fried steaks in the cast-iron skillet, the two of them talking to each other while he listened.

Claire seemed to be fine, which he took as a good sign. Claire left Sam in charge of the steaks while she set the table.

He drained the water off the potatoes.

"I need a masher."

"In there." She pointed to a drawer, where he found an awesome, ancient wooden hand masher. He mashed up the potatoes, added milk, butter, salt, and pepper, then covered that pot and set it to the side while he took care of the green beans.

Everything was finished at the same time, so they scooped it all into bowls and serving dishes. Reid refilled his glass of tea, and they made their way to the table to eat.

He stayed mostly quiet during dinner, listening to Sam and Claire talking about flowers. Claire was still very sharp and knew her flowers well.

Until she stumbled.

"Fall's coming. You'll need to make sure you have your order of ammonia." Claire stopped. Frowned. Rubbed her temple. "That's not right."

She frowned again. "I know what it is. The damya flower."

Sam reached over and touched Claire's hand. "Dahlia."

"Yes." Claire nodded. "Dahlia."

Sam looked over at Reid. He understood the issue. "It's a beautiful flower. We have some on the ranch. Martha loves to plant those."

"It's one of my favorites," Claire said with a smile. "You have plenty of those for fall?"

"Yes, Grammy Claire, I do. Molly's going to have some in her wedding decorations. A lovely orange, along with some calla lilies and roses."

"That's this weekend, isn't it?" Reid asked, doing his best to keep the conversation flowing smoothly.

Sam nodded.

"That Molly is so sweet. I love her mother, Georgia."

Dinner continued, as did the talk about flowers—and Molly and Carter's wedding.

He was happy to discover Claire had made blueberry crisp for dessert.

He was going to have to hit the gym for a workout. All this awesome food was going to cause him to gain weight.

After dinner, Sam made her grandmother sit in the living room, where she loved all over Not My Dog while Reid and Sam did the dishes.

Reid took a look over his shoulder. Claire was immersed in a game show on TV. Not My Dog was sitting on her foot and she had her hand on his head, scratching his ear. The TV was turned up pretty loud, so she wouldn't be able to hear him talking to Sam in the kitchen.

"How is she?"

Sam handed him a plate she'd just washed. "The doctor says it's Alzheimer's."

He gripped the plate in his hands, his stomach tightening. "I'm sorry, Sam."

"Me, too."

"Other than forgetting the name of that flower, she seems to be doing well."

She nodded. "The doctor said she'll have a lot of lucid moments, at least for now. The decline will be gradual, but she will decline."

He laid the plate to the side and put his arm around her. She stiffened.

"I'm fine. I don't want her to see me upset."

He understood that. "Okay."

He finished helping her with the dishes, then went into the living room and sat with Sam and Claire. They watched television for a little while—an old mystery on one of the classic television channels. They had fun trying to figure out who the murderer was. Reid guessed right and Sam accused him of having seen the movie before. He swore he hadn't.

Claire finally got up and said she was tired and wanted to go to the bedroom to get ready for bed.

"Do you want me to help you take a bath and get ready?" Sam asked.

"No. I want you to go home. I'm still able to take care of myself, Samantha. At least for now."

"Okay."

Claire went over and gave Reid a kiss on the cheek. "Thank you for staying with me. I'm sure it's not very exciting hanging out with an old woman."

He put his arm around her. "I don't know about that, Claire. I think you're pretty fun for an old gal. Plus, you make the best chicken fried steak I've ever had. I'm thinking of moving in here."

She laughed and patted his shoulder. "You're welcome anytime. Good night, Reid."

Sam kissed and hugged her grandmother, then they left.

He walked beside her across the street. Not My Dog stayed close to Sam.

"Thank you for hanging out with us tonight."

"I enjoyed it. And hey, I got chicken fried steak out of the deal."

She looked over at him. "Yes. Your radar must have been on tonight."

"My—oh." He laughed. "Yeah. It is my favorite food."

"So I've noticed. You ate two helpings."

He shrugged. "Can't help myself. It's a sickness. I've already decided I'm going to have to go for a run tomorrow morning before I start work. I've got a lot of calories to burn."

They had reached Sam's porch. She used the key from her pocket to open the front door, then walked in. He assumed he was supposed to follow.

"I don't know about that," she said, hanging the key on

the hook in the kitchen. "I'll bet you're sweating out a lot of calories working on the mercantile."

"A few."

He pulled her over to the sofa and sat down with her, drawing her against him.

"Rough few days?"

She sighed and melted against him. "Yeah."

"I know you think you have to handle this all on your own, but I'm here for you, Sam. If you need someone to talk to, someone to lean on—I'm here."

She patted his chest. "Thank you."

Sam listened to Reid's heart beating against her cheek, drawing in the comfort of his strong embrace even though she knew she shouldn't.

She had always been fiercely independent and had never relied on anyone but herself. Her grandparents had taught her to be self-reliant. But she'd always known she had Grammy Claire and Grandpa Bob to fall back on in times of need. And they had always been there for her—her rocks when times had gotten rough. From the time she lost her parents when she'd been so young, to struggling with having no parents, they had been there for her every step along the way.

Losing Grandpa Bob a couple of years ago had been a severe blow both to her and to Grammy Claire. But it had bonded her even closer to her grandmother.

Now, she felt those strong ties to her grandmother—to her only living relative—slipping away. And it hurt harder than she had ever expected it to.

She was independent and she knew she could stand on her own two feet. She would survive just fine.

But she loved her grandmother. Losing her piece by piece like this was going to be devastating.

And as she leaned against Reid, she realized that this—him—was exactly what she needed to soften the blow.

The only problem was, Reid was temporary. The support he offered was sweet, but eventually he was going to leave.

Losing him was going to hurt, too.

She knew better than to lean too hard on him. It would only be another knife in her heart when he was gone.

But tonight she needed this. So even though whatever she had with Reid was only for right now, she closed her eyes and let his strong arms surround her.

Tomorrow she'd go back to taking care of everything on her own.

Chapter 31

SAM THREW HERSELF into preparation for Carter and Molly's wedding. Fortunately, it had kept her busy all week long. The lion's share of the work was in creating the floral arrangements for the church and the bouquets—especially Molly's bridal bouquet. The floral décor for the reception wasn't quite so daunting.

She had been working nonstop for days—and a lot of nights. She'd been on the phone at least six times with Molly this past week, assuring her she had everything under control. She hadn't slept much and she'd put in a lot of late nights at the flower shop. She'd actually surrendered and called in help, punting some of her regular orders to a few surrounding shops, who'd been awesome and helped her out by taking on some of her daily orders. Every florist understood a wedding crunch, and she'd often assisted other shops who'd been under similar deadline pressure. When push came to shove, a big event was always a priority. And as long as her regular customers got their deliveries on time, everyone was happy. She'd return the favor to the other flower shops at some point.

Reid had brought her food several times this week. She

was so grateful. Otherwise, she might have starved. He'd also stopped by to visit with Grammy Claire. He told her she should work. He was on a gin rummy run with Grammy Claire, and since she'd kicked his butt several times already this week, he intended to exact his revenge. She didn't know what she would have done without him.

Faith had tended to her grandmother as well, taking her out to the store and to a doctor's appointment. She had also stayed the night a couple of times, and had told Sam to quit worrying, that she had her grandmother well taken care of. She was also bringing her grandmother to the wedding tonight, which was one less thing Sam would have to worry about.

"Will I see you at the wedding?" she asked Reid when he brought her a delicious croissant from Megan's bakery to start her morning off just right.

"Like it or not, I'm your date for tonight." He handed her a tall mocha latte to go with the croissant. "Oh wait. I guess I forgot to ask you. I did forget to ask you. Sam, will you be my date for the wedding?"

She laughed. "I'm going to be busy with the flowers. You need a date who'll have time to actually act like a date."

"Once the flowers are in place, your work is done, isn't it?"

"I . . . suppose so."

"Okay, so do your flower thing, then be my date. You'll actually be able to relax."

Relax. She'd forgotten what that word meant. "I'd love to be your date."

He brushed his lips over hers. "See you tonight. Call me if you need anything."

He walked out of her shop, leaving her with a latte, a croissant, and a mountain of work to do.

But she did have a date for the wedding. So there was that, at least.

After she delivered all the flowers to the church and to the reception venue and finished decorating, she dashed home to shower and change clothes. She was back at the church an hour before the wedding to make sure the groomsmen had their boutonnieres and everyone had the appropriate flowers.

Reid was there early, as well, to help out, and then he escorted her down the aisle so she could take her seat.

"Everything done?" he asked.

She nodded, finally able to exhale.

The church looked beautiful, decorated in hues of burnt orange, dark brown, and purple. The flowers at the altar had turned out gorgeous. The fall colors with the purple and white calla lilies and the dark orange roses were a perfect touch. And when Molly and all the bridesmaids—her friends—walked down the aisle, carrying their bouquets of purple roses and white calla lilies, everything was perfect.

And she could enjoy it all, because her work was done.

The wedding was spectacular. She teared up seeing her friend Molly marry her high school sweetheart, Carter. Reid squeezed her hand, and she turned to smile at him.

He looked so handsome in his dark suit, his green eyes sparkling. Damn, that man was handsome. Whether in dusty, dirty blue jeans or decked out in his finest suit, he made her heart squeeze.

A very dangerous thing, because she knew what they had was only short-term. She had to erect a guard around her heart, because she already knew she was falling in love with him, and she couldn't let it happen.

Her grandmother sat next to her, all decked out in her finest dark blue dress, wearing her favorite set of pearls, which Grandpa Bob had given her. Grammy Claire had been excited about attending the wedding, and Faith had already pulled Sam aside and told her everything was fine.

So maybe tonight—just tonight—she could let everything go and have some fun, especially with her oh-so-handsome-and-hot date for the night.

Just fun. Nothing serious.

After the ceremony, everyone waited outside for the wedding party, each guest having been given a container of bubbles to blow in their direction as they made their way outside the church toward the waiting limousines. Even though it was fall, the day had turned out to be beautiful—sunny, warm, and wind-free.

Molly was grinning so hard, and Carter looked at her like he had just been given the greatest gift ever.

Just as it should be.

Faith was bringing Grammy Claire to the reception, since it was likely her grandmother wouldn't stay for the entire event, and Faith insisted Sam and Reid be allowed to party a lot longer than the "older folks," as Faith said, so she and Reid climbed into Sam's car. Reid drove them to Tulsa for the reception, which was held at a beautiful, stunningly lit mansion that was rented out solely for the wedding. The stone facade was elegant and perfectly set up for the event, with tall trees lining the walkway leading up to the stairway and wide open doors. There were several floors and a balcony. It was so lovely and romantic.

Reid parked, and Sam grabbed her sweater and her purse, along with the gift she'd bought for Carter and Molly. They headed up the brightly lit stairs into the main foyer, where someone directed them to the ballroom.

"Look at the hearth," she said as they walked inside the ballroom.

The hearth appeared to be four times the size of a home's average fireplace.

"Impressive," Reid said, taking her hand and leading her over to it, where a wood fire burned. "And these floors. That looks to be some kind of antique oak."

"It's beautiful. Everything in here is amazing. I barely looked at it earlier because I was meeting my decorating deadline." Now she soaked it all in, from the colorful, medieval tapestry showcasing a warrior on a horse to the stained glass windows. It was a showpiece. Molly and Carter had chosen well.

Speaking of the bride and groom, they made their entrance to a fanfare from the live band and much applause from all the guests.

Reid and Sam found their assigned seats, though they didn't stay there for long. Sam wanted to see Molly's dress up close—it was a beautiful pale cream gown of satin and lace. It had cap sleeves and clung to Molly's curves. It looked as if it had been made just for her. Sam couldn't imagine a more perfect gown for Molly.

"You are gorgeous," she said to Molly, then hugged her close. "Thank you."

"You're also beaming. Congratulations."

Molly laughed. "Thank you again. It's hard to believe we're finally married. After all these years."

Sam squeezed her hand, so happy for her friend. Then she hugged Carter and moved off so others could offer their congrats as well.

The bride and groom had to start their first dance, so everyone gathered around to watch. It put a lump in Sam's throat to watch Molly and Carter, to see the love reflected in the way they looked at each other as they danced.

And then the bridal party all danced, and she watched all her friends dancing as well. They all looked stunning.

After the dance, she found Emma and gave her a hug.

"You look beautiful," she said to Emma.

The bridesmaids' dresses were a gorgeous burnt sienna with cap sleeves and tight-fitting bodices that were snug to the waist, then flowed out in very elegant fashion to the floor. All the women looked amazing. Molly had kept it simple, with Emma as her matron of honor and Jane as a bridesmaid, along with Des and Chelsea.

"I'm just happy they were able to alter my dress to fit my oh-so-quickly-expanding belly." Emma laid her hand over her lower stomach.

"Well, those things happen when you have a baby growing in there."

"Don't they, though?"

"How are you feeling?"

"Pretty fantastic, actually. And hungry—like all the time."

Des came over and slung her arm around Emma's waist. "I think we're fighting each other to see who can eat the most bacon."

Emma leaned against Des. "Oh, I'm definitely winning."

"We'll see. We can pound down some bacon on the ranch. Plus, you have to work right now, having to run your vet clinic. So you're burning a ton of calories. Me? I'm on vacation. That leaves more bacon-eating time."

Sam grinned. "I think you're both adorable. And you both glow, and you both look like you haven't gained a pound—except in your bellies."

"This is why I love you, Samantha," Des said. "I'm going to start dragging you to all my movie sets after I have the baby. So you can tell my directors how fantastic I look."

She laughed. "Well, the travel sounds fun."

She made her way around to say hello to everyone. It had been a while since she'd caught up with all her friends. Megan was there—without a date—and looking absolutely stunning in a black-and-white dress that fit her perfectly. With her silver heels that showed off her legs, she didn't think Megan would be without a dance partner for long.

"You didn't ask someone to come with you?"

Megan shook her head. "No. This way I'm free to dance with all the available men tonight."

"Smart move. And I see Brady is here—which makes him available. And he looks so good tonight."

Megan smiled as she looked in Brady's direction. "Since Carter is his boss, this is one event he couldn't turn down. Either way, I'm happy to see him again. And I'll force him out on the dance floor with me tonight. That man needs to have some fun."

"Did I tell you Reid and I ran into him at a biker bar a week or so ago?"

Megan slipped her arm in Sam's. "You did not. And what were you and Reid doing in a biker bar? I didn't even know Reid had a bike."

"He doesn't. We were out for a ride, and apparently the place we stopped at is one he used to frequent. It has very good cheeseburgers." She told Megan about Brady stopping in and having lunch with them.

"Good to know the guy gets out and around and doesn't hang out in his bell tower above Carter's shop like the Hunchback of Notre Dame."

Sam laughed. "I'm going to tell him you said that."

Megan shrugged. "Go ahead."

The band had started up a fun song—one of her and Megan's favorites. She saw Reid—and Brady—hanging around the bar. Of course. She took Megan's hand and walked over toward them.

Megan tugged at her hand. "What are you doing?"

"Getting this party started."

"Sam. No."

She ignored her friend and dragged her to the bar, where Reid saw her coming and mentioned something to Brady, who arched a brow.

Sam took Brady's hand and put it in Megan's. "Hey, Brady. Ask Megan about the Hunchback of Notre Dame. Also, she wants you to ask her to dance." She turned to Reid. "How about you and I hit the dance floor?"

Reid pushed off the bar. "Sure."

Reid walked with her to the dance floor and pulled her into his arms. The music was a little fast, but he had good rhythm and kept up to the song—and wow, did it feel good to have a partner who knew how to lead.

"What was that about?" he asked.

"What was what about?"

"That whole hunchback thing?"

"Oh. Something Megan mentioned to me that I thought Brady might be interested in."

Right now Megan and Brady were dancing—and talking—and Megan wasn't shooting her death stares, so she supposed her idea had worked out. She'd find out later, she was certain.

Sometimes people just needed a push in the right direction.

Like her friend Chelsea, who was on the dance floor with Bash, the two of them so wrapped up in each other they didn't even notice anyone else. It wasn't long ago that Chelsea was convinced Bash was the absolute wrong man for her. And now? He was the love of her life.

Yeah, sometimes people just needed a push.

Reid tipped her chin with his fingers, drawing her gaze to his. "What's going on?"

She smiled at him. "Oh, just thinking about friends of mine."

"Yeah? Thinking what?"

"About how sometimes people need a push in the right direction. Chelsea and Bash for instance. She was convinced she'd never end up with someone like him. And it all turned out perfectly for them. And Molly and Carter—they had their struggles getting together."

His lips curved. "Thinking about happily-ever-afters tonight, Sam?"

That thought made her smile. "Maybe."

"Everybody deserves one."

She tilted her head back, meeting his gaze. "Even you?"

"Sure. Why not? But I was thinking more of you. You do so much for everyone you love. I can't think of anyone more deserving of a happily-ever-after than you."

It was times like this that he made her heart squeeze. Being in Reid's arms, feeling his body close to hers, and hearing him saying all the right things made her realize how much she was falling in love with him.

Which only made her desperate to run far and fast away from him.

But she also realized it was too late now. She had already fallen—and he'd caught her. She was going to have to ride this out until he finished his project and returned to Boston.

And add another heartbreak to her list.

So she stayed quiet, not knowing how to respond to what he'd said. The best she could give right now was to be with him, soaking in his touch and the way he made her feel. She needed it, and she'd take it for as long as she could.

REID COULD TELL something was off with Sam tonight. Maybe she was tired. He knew she'd worked her ass off all week prepping for the wedding. It showed, too. The flowers were beautiful. Not that he knew a hell of a lot about flowers, other than they were pretty. But he'd hung out at the mercantile long after he needed to, watching her work late nights. He'd brought her dinner, making her take a break to eat. He'd stopped by her grandmother's house to check in and hang out, though Faith had been there as well.

Now all that wedding prep was over and she should be able to relax and have a good time. Still, there was something.

He sat with her and all their friends and family, and she should be having a great time. Her grandmother was having fun—she'd even gotten up and danced. That should have made Sam happy.

They'd eaten, and Sam had had several glasses of wine, which should have relaxed her.

But he sensed a melancholy in Sam that she couldn't seem to shake.

While everyone at their table was on the dance floor, he took her hand. "What's up?"

She pulled her gaze away from the dance floor. "What?"

"You seem unhappy."

"How could I be unhappy tonight? My friends got married, I'm hanging out with people I love. Even Grammy Claire is shaking her bootie on the dance floor with Faith. I'm having a great time."

"But . . ."

"No, really. It's a perfect night."

"But," he said again, giving her the opening again.

"But I realized that someday I'm going to get married. And Grammy Claire will either not remember me by that point, or won't be there to see my wedding day."

He saw the tears glittering in her eyes. He stood and pulled her to stand. "Come on. Let's take a walk."

He led her outside the ballroom and up the stairs, ignoring the *No One Admitted* sign on the second-floor balcony.

The night was clear, it was warm outside, and the super-sized stone balcony gave them a perfect view of the mani-cured lawns and full moon.

"We're not supposed to be up here," she said.

"So if someone comes, they'll throw us out." He pulled her against his chest and wrapped his arm around her.

"It's nice outside," she said, but instead of feeling her relax, he felt the muscles in her body tighten.

"When my dad died, my mom had been gone for a long time already," he said. "And I felt alone for the first time in my life. I still had my brothers, but I felt alone. Really alone. I realized— like you did—that there were going to be major milestones in my life that my dad wouldn't be a part of. Like me getting married—and if I had kids, my kids would never know how awesome their grandfather was. And they'd be cheated out of a grandmother because my mother was—well, you know."

She pulled away from his embrace to face him. "I understand."

"Life doesn't come with guarantees, Sam. And family is what you make of it. I got lucky that I had Ben and Martha in my life. And they may not be blood family, but they're like parents to me and always have been. I have Carter and Deacon and a lot of other friends I've made over my lifetime here in Hope. And when the day comes that I walk down the aisle with the woman I've chosen to spend the rest of my life with, Ben and Martha will be by my side. And my brothers will be there, as will friends I've grown close to—people I consider my family."

He swept his knuckles over her cheek. "Family isn't just blood relatives, Sam. They're the people who hold your heart, the people who know you better than you know yourself. You might think you're alone, but you aren't. You're well-loved, Samantha Reasor, by a lot of people in this town. You will never be alone as long as you're loved."

Sam held her breath. It was a beautiful statement. And while he hadn't put the two of them together in that equation, and not once had he said that she was the woman he loved, she could envision her future now in ways she hadn't been able to before.

He was right. She had so many friends, so many people in her life whom she loved, and whom she knew loved her in return.

And maybe she was going to slowly lose her grandmother—a fact that made her heart ache in ways she couldn't explain. But she wasn't going to be alone. She had Megan and Emma and Chelsea and Jane and Des and Molly and Logan and Luke and Carter and Bash and so many other people who'd always have her back.

Those people were her family, too.

And she wished—God, how she wished—that she had Reid, too. But she could wish as high as the moon and that wasn't going to happen, so she'd have to settle for what she did have—which was a lot. So much to be grateful for. And she had to concentrate on that.

She lifted her gaze to his, laying her palms against his chest. "You're right, Reid. I'll never be alone. Thank you for reminding me of that."

He slipped his hands along her neck and pressed his lips to hers. And for a moment, she felt like a princess, here on the balcony, stealing a kiss with her secret prince. She melted against him, overcome by so much emotion she didn't know what to do with all of it. She clutched the lapels of his suit, not caring at all that she was probably wrinkling him. She sure wanted him to wrinkle her, to touch her intimately. She needed to feel him close to her—closer than they were right now.

He pulled his lips from hers and she saw the need on his face, mirroring how she felt.

He took her hand and led her from the balcony. He stopped at the exit from the room, looking down the hallway.

"This way."

"You know your way around here?" she whispered.

"I might have looked up a blueprint when I found out we were coming here. I was curious about the history and architecture."

That was so Reid. He'd have to know all about the place they were going.

She loved that about him.

He led her around a corridor and down a dark hallway, into a very elegant ladies' room, the kind with wallpaper and velvet sofas. He flipped on the light, then closed and locked the door.

She arched a brow. "Kidnapping me?"

He grinned, moving forward to capture her in his arms. "Yeah. Got a problem with that?"

"Not at all. Though I have this fear of being arrested."

"Relax and only think about my hands on you."

He slid his hand down her spine, making her grateful that, despite the cool fall weather, she'd chosen a dress with an open back. Because his hands on her bare skin were just what she needed, coaxing that fire out of her that always obliterated every other thought from her mind.

He pushed her up against the wall, smoothing his hands along her rib cage.

"Your heart is beating fast. Still thinking about being arrested?"

"No, that's not what I'm thinking about anymore. I'm thinking about you touching me."

His fingers teased inside her dress, roaming ever lower. "Here?"

She moaned. "Yes. Anywhere. But especially there."

He led her over to one of those elegant velvet settees and sat her down on it, kneeling in front of her to remove her shoes.

"Let's get you comfortable," he said, sliding his fingers under her dress as he raised the hem and spread her legs.

She leaned back, so lost in him, in the way his hair fell over his forehead, in the wicked desire she saw reflected in his heated gaze.

And as he reached under her dress and drew her underwear down her legs, she was feeling more than a little heated herself.

He lifted her leg, kissed her calf, then the other, looking at her as he draped her legs over his shoulders.

And then she started feeling very hot as he shouldered in between her thighs, lifted her dress, and pressed his mouth to her sex.

Oh. The only word she could think to come up with for what was happening right now was *scandalous*. Here they were, locked in a forbidden room in this mansion, while all the wedding guests partied downstairs, and Reid was . . .

She lost her train of thought, because his mouth and tongue had become the most prominent thing on her mind, a swirling, delicious delight to her senses.

She gave herself up to his mastery of her body, not caring at all where they were, because all she wanted was the orgasm he led her to. And when she came, she lifted against him, needing more and more of the wild waves of climax that washed over her.

She'd barely caught her breath before he'd put on a condom and slid inside her, her body still quaking from the aftereffects of her orgasm. He cupped her butt and tilted her toward him. She wrapped her legs around him and met his thrusts, reaching for him, needing to hold on to him as she was besieged by a storm of sensation and emotion.

Reid leaned down to kiss her, a desperate meeting of lips and tongues as he held tight to her and ground against her. She felt the stirrings of another orgasm and moaned against his lips. He groaned in answer and slowed the tempo.

The sweet, slow, sensual movements, the way he pulled back and looked at her as he moved within her, were her undoing.

She looked up at him, reached for him as if he were her anchor in this wild maelstrom.

"Reid." His name fell from her lips in a whisper.

"Yeah. I know."

Her orgasm burst from her, making her cry out as she came. Reid gathered her close, took her mouth in a kiss and came with her, his body shuddering against hers as they both flew through these amazing sensations.

She was trembling. Or maybe that was Reid. Possibly it was both of them.

"I'm not sure I can move," she finally managed.

"I know I can't. You've got me in some kind of wrestling lock."

She laughed, and they untangled their limbs. He pulled her to a standing position, and held on to her, thankfully, because her legs were a little wobbly.

They righted their clothing, and Sam took a look in the mirror.

Not too bad a disaster. She fixed her hair and reapplied her lipstick. If her dress was a little wrinkled, she didn't much care about that.

Reid unlocked the door and took her hand. She tugged on his and pulled him toward her for a kiss, one that lingered longer than she expected. Long enough to reignite the flames again.

She finally, reluctantly, pulled back. "We'd better get out of here before someone really does start checking the upstairs."

"We'll continue this later."

"Definitely."

They left the second floor and Reid led them back to the

reception. She ran into her grandmother and Faith, who said they were heading out. So she kissed her grandmother, hugged Faith, and said her good nights to them. Then they found their friends.

"Where did you two disappear to?" Chelsea asked after Reid walked away to get them something to drink.

"We, uh, went for a walk."

Chelsea gave her the once-over. "Sure you did. I hope it was good for you. Truthfully, I don't even have to ask, since your cheeks are all rosy."

"It was cool outside."

Chelsea laughed. "Honey, I can tell by the look on your face you didn't even make it outside."

Sam shrugged. "Okay, maybe we didn't."

"As long as you had a good time."

She'd definitely had a good time. And she felt more relaxed then she'd felt in quite a while.

Thanks to Reid.

When he came back with a beer for himself and a glass of wine for her, she gave him a smile. "Thank you for tonight."

"You're welcome."

"You definitely know how to show a woman a good time."

He leaned in and brushed his lips over hers. "Not just any woman, Sam. I like showing *you* a good time."

And there went her heart, laying itself right at his feet.

With a sigh, she followed him over to where all their friends sat.

She wasn't going to think about her heart anymore tonight. She was simply going to enjoy the night with her friends. And with Reid.

Just tonight. She was doing a lot of that lately, especially with Reid.

But she had to, didn't she? She could only do one day at a time with him. And eventually that one day would be the day he was gone.

But in order to protect her heart, she had to enjoy him one day at a time.

There really was no other way.

Chapter 32

"FIRST FLOOR OF the mercantile is nearly finished," Reid said to Luke and Logan as they shared a beer at Bash's bar. "Bathroom is in, walls are up, and Loretta has given the okay on the final plans."

Luke took a long pull from his bottle of beer. "So Loretta's definitely committed?"

Reid nodded. "Yes. Lease is signed. She's coming in first of next week to make final selections on paint color and flooring. We should have the first floor finished within the next two weeks."

"That's great," Logan said.

"Yeah, it's all coming together. Better than I thought, actually."

"What about the other floors?" Luke asked. "I know last time we talked about some people who were interested in some of the second-floor space."

"Second floor is almost all leased out. We have several companies inquiring about spaces on the third floor as well."

"I heard from Max Claney about the third floor," Logan said.

"The lawyer?" Luke asked. "The one with the big firm over on Twelfth Street?"

"Yeah. He's expanding again and he might want the entire third floor. Thinks it's great space for his firm."

Reid grimaced. "Max Claney is a dick."

Logan laughed. "He was a dick when you went to school with him."

"No, Reid is right," Luke said. "He's still a dick."

"But if he leases the entire third floor, that makes him a paying dick," Logan said. "So do we care?"

"I might."

Logan looked at Reid. "Why? Because he wants that corner office on the third floor?"

"No. Why would I care about that?"

"Because you've turned down three people already who wanted to lease that space?"

Reid's gaze shot to Luke. "Who told you that?"

Luke hid his smile behind his beer, took a swallow, then set the bottle down. "First, I'm local law enforcement. I tend to know everything going on in this town. Second, everybody knows everything that goes on in Hope. You remember that, right?"

Well, shit. "They weren't the right fit for that space."

"If the check doesn't bounce, they're the right fit," Logan said. "So what's the problem?"

The problem was, Reid didn't exactly know what the problem was. "Cline's music studio would be too noisy for the other tenants. And we didn't build those walls to be soundproof. The last thing we need is a dispute among tenants right off the bat."

"Okay," Logan said. "You have a point there."

"We've already agreed to a lease with Miller Accounting on the second floor. Gail Miller is currently in divorce proceedings with Paul Miller of Miller Excavators, who wanted the third-floor corner office. I was at Bert's after I signed the lease with Gail, and in ten minutes I heard the story of how Paul cheated on Gail with their next-door neighbor. Could you imagine those two running into each other on the stairs or in the elevator? I didn't think it was a good fit and I kind of got the idea that as soon as Gail rented the space Paul probably decided to go after space in the same building just to piss her off."

"Hmm, that could be," Luke said. "I heard Gail and Paul were divorcing and that it wasn't going to be an amicable one."

"And what about the third?" Logan asked.

"Marshall Stevenson."

Luke and Logan both said "Oh" simultaneously.

"Now he *is* a dick," Logan said. "Don't blame you for turning him down."

The Stevenson family had been in major competition with the McCormacks for as long as Reid could remember. Their family owned the neighboring ranch, but instead of being friendly and neighborly, Marshall Stevenson had competed with Reid's father over everything, from cattle to horses to acreage to property fence lines. It had been a constant battle over whose dick was bigger, likely going back generations.

And Marshall's sons, Abel and Lex, were assholes, too, just like their father.

Abel and Lex were the same ages as Logan and Luke, but Reid had grown up around them, didn't like them, and he'd rent the space to anyone other than the Stevenson family.

"So Marshall approached you about leasing the space?" Luke asked.

"First Marshall called," Reid said. "Then when I didn't fall all over myself to immediately lease space to him, Lex came by to stink up the mercantile with Stevenson arrogance."

"That figures," Logan said, "since Lex handles the business aspect of the ranch operations. What did you tell Lex?"

"Same thing I told his father—that I had other offers on the table already for the space."

"Good," Logan said. "No way in hell are we ever leasing space to a Stevenson."

"I'm in agreement," Luke said.

"Glad you both agree, since I already told him no."

"Okay, so what are we going to do about that third-floor office?" Luke asked.

"I know what you should do about it," Logan said, his gaze fixed on Reid.

"What's that?"

"I think you've been turning down all these people inquiring about the space for a specific reason."

Reid signaled Bash for another round. "Really, and what's that?"

"Because you've always seen that corner office space on the third floor as yours."

Reid cocked a brow. "Now that would be a waste of the space, since I don't live or work here."

"But you could," Luke said. "You have the potential for business here. A lot of business."

"And your family is here," Logan said.

Bash brought their beers and a couple of bowls of pretzels. "How's it going?"

"Good."

"You need anything else, just signal."

"Thanks, Bash, we will," Reid said.

"Back to you moving here," Luke said, after Bash walked away. "You have the potential for a lot of business. I've heard the city is interested in expanding the police department. There's talk of having surplus funding for a new building. And City Hall is looking at an expansion, too. They're already talking about bids. You could get in on that."

"I could, if I lived here. Which I don't."

"Which you could," Logan argued, "if you pulled up stakes and just moved back."

"Not as simple as you make it sound. I own a company in Boston."

Luke shrugged. "So sell it. And start another company in Hope."

He laughed. "Oh, sure. You make it seem so easy."

"I didn't say it would be easy. But it's doable, if you want it to be."

"And who says I want it to be?"

"Nobody," Logan said. "But do you?"

He hadn't voiced it out loud—to anyone. He'd tried to

avoid thinking about it, to deny the feasibility, to leave the emotion out of even considering it. But here it was, on the table. And maybe it was time to discuss it.

"I don't know. I like being here. You know I love being around you two and Martha and Ben and everyone on the ranch. Boston has been great. I've built a successful business, but . . ."

He let the words trail off. He'd never been able to admit it before.

"But it's not home."

Logan had said it for him.

"No, Boston isn't home. But come on. I'm not a baby. I've done fine out there."

"Yeah, you have, and we're all damn proud of you, Reid," Luke said. "You've proved you can make it on your own. You built a business with no one's help—a successful business, too. But now that you've been back, we kind of like having you around."

"Yeah, kind of," Logan said.

Reid's lips ticked up. "I've kind of liked it, too."

"You know, at some point you have to start thinking about where you're going to grow roots," Logan said.

Reid frowned. "What?"

"The reason you're second-guessing everything is you're at the point in your life where you're thinking about planting seeds."

Reid slanted his gaze toward Luke, who shrugged. "He's gotten all philosophical since Des got pregnant. Just go with it."

"Okay, so I'm thinking about planting seeds."

Logan nodded. "Yeah. Metaphorical seeds. Not green beans or anything."

"Yes, I kind of get that we're speaking metaphorically, Logan." Sometimes his oldest brother was a pain in his ass. "Go ahead."

"You want to see those seedlings grow into a solid life—a future for yourself."

"Uh huh. Well, that's interesting and all, but I haven't been doing any planting."

"Haven't you? What about Samantha? You've grown close to her over these past few months. What about Not My Dog and your relationship with him? What about that third-floor office space that you haven't seen fit to lease out to anyone yet, because you see yourself standing in that office someday? What about all the people in Hope that you've helped out, talking to them about expanding their businesses, or the possibilities of designing new spaces for them? Isn't that rooting yourself into this town, into a future for yourself?"

Well . . . shit.

Luke leaned forward and laid his hand on Reid's shoulder. "Did I mention he was getting pretty good at all this philosophical shit?"

"No, you didn't."

"Well, he is."

"So when did you get so smart?" he asked Logan.

Logan's lips curved upward. "Hell, I've always been smart. Not my fault you never noticed."

"He's still full of shit, though," Luke said, grinning as he tipped his beer to his lips.

Reid had to let all of this settle in his head. Now that it was out there, he had a lot to think about.

After he finished with his brothers, he and Not My Dog piled into the truck. But instead of driving back to the ranch, he took a detour.

There was a piece of land he'd driven by nearly every day. He'd spotted the For Sale sign on the land when he'd first gotten back to Hope. It had sparked his interest and he'd stopped by once. Twice. More than a few times already.

He parked the truck, and he and the dog got out.

Situated at the midway point between the ranch and the town center of Hope, this plot of land was a little bit out of town, to give him acreage, which he'd always wanted. It was set far enough back from the highway to be quiet, but not too remote. He could see neighboring houses from the center of the property, but the copious amounts of trees afforded plenty of privacy.

He could already envision the house he'd design. A

two-story Colonial with four or five bedrooms, plus an office space, so he'd have his own area to work. A big yard for Not My Dog—and maybe a couple more pups, because he didn't want the dog to get lonely.

He'd always had a fondness for Colonial-style homes, with big columns and a wide wraparound porch. The back would have an oversized deck for entertaining.

Inside, there'd need to be a huge kitchen—with a dishwasher. Sam would like that. And an extra bedroom with an attached bathroom for Claire so they could take care of her.

They'd be close enough to town that he and Sam could commute together, if necessary, but still be near enough to the house to be there for Claire. And they could hire someone to help care for her during the day when that time came.

The idea had merit. It was a sound plan. A good plan.

It could work.

But as he wandered back and forth over the ground, he shook his head.

Was this really what he wanted? Could he see himself here in Hope for the duration of his life? Boston was a completely different lifestyle, a fast-paced city that he'd grown accustomed to. He'd settled there, built his career there. He had friends there, people he'd developed relationships with.

He did more pacing. More thinking.

But had he been happy there?

He thought even more about it as he and Not My Dog walked the land.

He'd been . . . content. He loved the work he did. Designing buildings was in his blood.

But as he stood in this empty pasture and looked around, for the first time in a long time, he felt like he belonged. This felt like something he could dig into.

This felt like a future. Like forever.

But was this entire thought process nothing more than a dream, something born out of a beery conversation with his brothers? Sure, it sounded great in theory while he was bullshitting around with Logan and Luke. But the reality of it?

It would take a major upheaval to make this happen.

Maybe it was nothing more than a dream. And maybe it was a stupid dream at that.

Not My Dog head-butted his leg.

"What's up, buddy?"

Not My Dog settled at his feet, then stared out over the land, as if to say: *You're overthinking. This place is awesome.*

"You think?"

The dog's tail thumped on the ground.

Yeah. Start designing our new house. And my new yard.

"Yeah, you're right. I need to pull the trigger on this. At least buy the land, right?"

Not My Dog thumped his tail and wiggled his butt, excitement in his dark eyes.

I can already see myself chasing rabbits through those woods.

"Okay, buddy, we'll buy the property. But I'm not making any promises beyond that."

He had a lot to think about, and even more to do. First he needed to finish the mercantile. And then he needed to go back to Boston.

Chapter 33

AFTER TAKING THE morning off to drive Grammy Claire to a doctor's appointment, Sam spent the remainder of the day catching up on deliveries. She was already thinking she was going to have to hire help. With Grammy Claire needing more assistance, and looking down the road toward the future, there was no way she was going to be able to manage the flower shop by herself anymore.

She finished sweeping the floor and tallying up the day's receipts, then closed and locked the cash register. She looked around, rubbing the ache in her stomach.

Reasor's Flowers had always been a family-run business. Her grandmother and grandfather had run this place by themselves, and when she had taken over, she'd managed it just fine. Sure, sometimes she'd brought in helpers when things had gotten hectic, but that had only been temporary. She'd prided herself on being able to handle whatever came up. And on occasion, like during the week of Carter and Molly's wedding, she might have had to shuffle off some business, but she'd gotten it back when other flower shops were under time crunches. It had all worked out.

But now? She could already tell she was going to need help, and not on a temporary basis. She was going to have to hire someone at least part-time.

It felt like she was giving up a piece of herself, and she hated the idea.

It was ridiculous to feel this way, but there was nothing she could do about her feelings.

As she put the last of the window display flowers into the refrigerator case, she noticed the lights were on in the mercantile.

She was here late tonight. It looked like Reid was working late as well. It didn't appear Deacon and his crew were still there, since the only truck she saw was Reid's.

Since she hadn't seen Reid in a couple of days, and since she knew Faith was over at her grandmother's house for dinner tonight, she dashed over to Bert's and grabbed a couple of sandwiches, along with chips, drinks, and dessert, then drove back, hoping Reid would still be there.

He was. She parked behind his truck and knocked on the downstairs door.

No answer. Of course not, because the lights were on upstairs. She tried the knob, and it was open, so she went inside. Not My Dog greeted her.

"Hey, baby boy. Where's Reid?"

Not My Dog wagged his tail.

"I'd pet you, sweetheart, but my hands are full. How about when I put this stuff down?"

She and the dog made their way upstairs. She took in all the details along the way.

It was almost finished. The banister on the stairs was polished, and it gleamed with a dark wood finish, while the wood spindles had been painted white, a beautiful contrast to the dark stairs.

She found Reid on a ladder on the third floor, working on light fixtures in the hallway.

"Don't you have people for this?" she asked.

"Oh, hey," he said, turning around to smile at her. "I

heard someone coming up. I thought maybe Deacon had come back for something."

"Just me." She held up the bag. "I saw your lights on because I was working late, too. I brought dinner if you're hungry."

He pulled a rag out of his back pocket and wiped his hands. "I'm always hungry."

After she gave Not My Dog some love, he found a spot on the floor nearby and promptly went to sleep. Reid laid out a tarp for them on the top stair at the entrance to the third floor, and she spread out the club sandwiches and chips. She'd asked for plates and a lot of napkins, and she'd brought two large iced teas as well.

"You have no idea how perfect this is right now," Reid said, digging in to the sandwich.

"Did you forget to each lunch again today?"

He nodded while he chewed.

"I managed a yogurt from the refrigerator at the flower shop, so I at least had that."

After taking a long swallow of tea, he shrugged. "We're trying to finish up by the end of the month so tenants can start moving in."

"Do you have it all leased out?"

"Most of it. First- and second-floor spaces are leased. Two offices on the third."

"That's great. I hear Loretta Simmons is going to open a bookstore and coffee shop on the first floor."

He smiled. "Yeah."

"How did that go over with Deacon?"

"About like you'd expect. Though he didn't say much when they ran into each other last week."

"Old romances. I imagine they're both probably over each other by now."

"You'd think. But there was a lot of tension when they occupied the same space."

"Hmmm, really? That's interesting. So maybe there's still something."

"I have no idea. I'm not big on recognizing those kinds of signals."

She wiped her mouth with her napkin. "Aren't you? You said you felt the tension between them."

"Okay, so maybe I am."

She laughed, then turned and leaned against the wall, looking around the space. "Are you going to be ready to say good-bye to this place when it's done?"

"I don't know. It's been a fun project. It'll be hard to leave it. There's so much history in this building. I'm so used to designing new. Having the opportunity to restore an old building, to blend modern with historic, has been the chance of a lifetime. I don't know that I'll ever get to do something like this again."

"I don't know about that. There are a lot of historic buildings in Boston. Now that you've got this on your résumé, who knows what jobs will come up for you."

He cocked his head to the side and gave her a quizzical look. "Yeah. I guess that could happen."

She had no idea what that look was about, but didn't question it. She ate her sandwich and enjoyed the ambience. The floor, while not exactly comfortable to sit on, was gorgeous to look at, with its dark, rich grain. "You had to put in new floor up here, didn't you?"

He nodded. "Yeah, but we matched what was downstairs on the other floors to give it an authentic feel. We stripped and restained the floors downstairs, then had to replace several of the old floorboards anyway, so we purchased new planks for those floors as well where some were worn clean through. We wanted the design to reflect the way the floors looked back when the building was new."

She ran her fingertips across the wood. "It's lovely. And the recessed lighting is modern here, yet you've added lovely historical charm with the wall sconces."

"Yeah, if you go too modern it's cold. Same thing with the exposed brick. We left it in certain areas to give people that warm, historic feel. You can do a lot with fixtures and chair rail and even paint choices. Even office buildings can feel warm and inviting."

She met his gaze. "I think it's beautiful, Reid. You've blended it all so perfectly."

"Thanks. I'm pretty happy with how it all turned out."

Sam could tell from the way Reid talked about the mercantile that he was in love with this building. She saw it in his eyes, in the way he looked at everything, the way he described each wall sconce, each brick, that he'd put his heart into this renovation. This wasn't a cold, austere office building to him. It was a work of art, and he'd poured his soul into making it beautiful again.

He was a man who put thought into everything he did.

She didn't know what she was going to do without him.

Tears pricked her eyes, but she refused to let this moment become sad for her. He didn't belong to her, and she had no right to lay claim to him. He had a life and a job somewhere else, and she wasn't going to make his leaving difficult when the time came.

The last thing he needed was some woman who had a life filled with baggage to cling to him and beg him not to leave her.

Even if that woman was in love with him.

Sometimes love just wasn't enough.

"So . . . when do you think you'll finish up?" she asked him, because she needed to shove the knife deeper into her heart.

"Probably by the end of the week."

"Then you'll probably head back to Boston, huh?"

Again, he gave her that strange look. "Yeah."

"You're probably excited to get back home. You've missed it?"

He shrugged. "I don't know. The weather's been nice here. It's fall in Boston. Gearing up for winter. Winters there can be a bit of a bitch."

She laughed. "They're no picnic here, either."

"That's true. But not like there." He picked up a chip and waved it around. "I've kind of enjoyed wearing short-sleeved shirts in October."

"So you've been spoiled. Time to drag out the winter gear."

She couldn't believe they were talking about the weather.

Why couldn't she bring up something of substance? Like telling him she was in love with him?

Because she wouldn't do that to him. He had a plan. She wasn't going to screw up his plan or his life.

"So what do you have going on tonight?" he asked.

She smiled at him. "Dinner on the floor with you."

"Thank you for dinner. Thank you for thinking about me."

She was always thinking about him. After he left town, she'd continue to think about him.

Probably for a long time. She wasn't sure she'd ever get over him.

Stop. Dwelling on this isn't going to help.

"I knew you'd be hungry. Because I was hungry. And because we're both workaholics who never eat."

He laughed. "You're right about that."

He bagged up their plates and napkins and then stood, holding out his hands to haul her to her feet. "And we need to stop working so much."

She brushed crumbs off her shirt. "We're not working now."

He drew her against him, and she memorized the feel of every part of him.

"No, we're not," he said. "Come with me."

He took her into the third-floor office space, the one with the amazing view. They stepped into the room but Reid left the lights off, which showed off the incredible sights of the city.

"I'm going to be so jealous of whoever ends up with this view. It's gorgeous at night."

He came up behind her and wrapped his arms around her. "You're gorgeous at night."

She closed her eyes and leaned her head back against his shoulder. "Could we stay just like this?"

"I'd be happy with that. Your body feels good up against mine."

She meant forever. She wanted to freeze this moment in time, to remember what it was like to feel his heart beating against her back, to breathe in the scent of him—that smell of male sweat and something that always seemed to smell cool and fresh at the same time. It was a scent she attributed uniquely to Reid, and as she turned in his arms and wound her hand around his neck to bring his lips to hers, she knew she'd always remember it.

He groaned against her lips, his fingers slipping low to grasp her butt and draw her closer to his quickly growing erection.

Passion for her had always been an iffy thing with other guys. Sometimes it had been there, and sometimes not. But with Reid it had been quick to spark and it had stayed that way every time the two of them had been together. She couldn't imagine living without that spark in her life. She wanted more of it.

"Ever make love in an office overlooking your home-town, Sam?"

He swept his hand over her breasts, inciting a hungry passion that wouldn't be denied. He could have asked her the same question in the grocery store at this moment and she'd have given him the same answer.

"No. But let's do that. Right now."

Since there were lights on in the hallway, he closed the door to the office, bathing them in darkness. Now they could see outside, but no one could see inside.

And suddenly Reid's hands and mouth were all over her, his tongue sliding along her neck as he pulled up her T-shirt and lifted it over her head.

Sam went along willingly, removing her bra so he could touch her. She desperately needed him to touch her, wanted his hands on her more than she needed her next breath. And when she felt his lips cover her nipple, she gasped. Not being able to see, only to feel, was a sexy, sensory experience. She tangled her fingers into his hair, holding his head as he plea-sured her nipples. Hot, fiery pleasure shot through her as he sucked and licked her, and when he popped her nipple from his mouth, the sound magnified in the empty office.

"Stand here. Look outside. I'll be right back."

"Okay."

He opened the door only partially and slipped out. She turned around and looked out the tall windows, enjoying the view of not only her hometown but the surrounding cities as well. If she had the opportunity to rent office space, this would be the one she'd want. She hoped Reid and his brothers would lease it to someone exceptionally cool.

He came back only a moment later, sliding a metal folding chair past the partially open door. He closed the door and placed the chair in the middle of the room.

Then she heard a zipper being drawn down and smiled.

She made her way over to him, making contact with his bare chest. "This could be interesting."

He touched her, his hands coming around her to snake down her arms. "It's about to get even more interesting."

He bent and held her hand while she kicked off her canvas shoes. Then he undid the button of her jeans, and this time it was her zipper that was undone, her jeans pulled down her hips and legs. Her underwear followed, leaving her naked.

He pressed a kiss to her hip bone. "I locked the front door downstairs, so you don't need to worry about anyone coming in."

She breathed in, then let it out on a sigh. "Your mouth is on me, Reid. Trust me, that was the last thing I was thinking about."

And then he did put his mouth on her, on her sex, and she was grateful for that chair as she held on to it for support while he took her on a wild ride of sensual pleasures, his tongue and lips sliding over her with hot, slow licks. She gasped and cried out as she came so fast it left her dizzy. But Reid was right there, wrapping his arm around her to support her while she trembled on her shaky legs.

She heard the condom package, grateful that he had thought to bring one upstairs with him. Because she wanted to feel him inside of her.

"I'm going to sit, Sam. I want you to straddle me."

Now she knew why he'd brought the chair into the room.

He had turned the chair around so she could look outside. And as she lowered herself onto him, she had him, and the amazing view.

But all she could really concentrate on was Reid, on the way he felt as he thrust into her, as he smoothed his hands over her hips and her butt. And though the room was dark, she could still see enough of him to meet his gaze, to see the passion in his eyes as the two of them moved in unison.

In the darkness, she let her senses unfold. She sifted her fingers through the thick softness of his hair, felt his skin rubbing against hers, breathed in the musky maleness of his scent, listened to the incredibly sensual sound of his voice as he whispered in her ear, and lost herself in the way the two of them were fused together.

It was so perfect she wanted to cry, but she'd already decided that she wasn't going to do that. So she let her love for him flow through her body, hoping she could communicate how she felt in the way she moved with him, the way she touched him, the way she kissed him. And when she tightened around him and cried out, she felt all of him when he took her mouth in a deep, passionate kiss, groaning against her lips with his release.

They stayed like that for the longest time, rocking together, sharing kisses and touching each other. It was almost as if neither of them wanted to let go.

But finally, they did, gathering their clothes and ducking out of the room to the attached bathroom.

She had red marks on her neck and breasts from his touch. From his mouth. They made her smile.

And when he looked in the bathroom mirror at her and smiled at her, then turned her around and kissed her, she felt that kiss all the way to her soul.

When he pulled back, he said, "Now you've been made love to in an office."

She reached up and brushed his hair off his forehead. "I'll say."

"I actually have some more work to do tonight. We have a prospective lessee coming in tomorrow morning, so I want to put some finishing touches on this floor."

"Okay."

He walked her downstairs, Not My Dog rising up from his resting spot in the hall to follow them.

He opened her car door for her, then pulled her into his

arms for a long, very drawn-out, extremely passionate kiss that made her wish they were back upstairs. But she finally pulled away.

"You have work to do."

"Yeah." He stepped back. "I'll see you tomorrow."

"Okay." The words wanted to spill out, but she bit them back. "Good night, Reid."

"Night, Sam."

She got in her car and drove toward home, feeling equal parts warm and satiated and also sad, because she knew the idyllic moments they'd spent together were quickly coming to a close.

She'd been drawn to Reid from the first moment she'd laid eyes on him last year, and now, she wanted him to stay.

But she wanted him to *want* to stay. It had to be his choice.

The problem was, she didn't believe that was the choice he was going to make. And she wouldn't ask it of him. It wouldn't be fair. Not with the way her life was right now.

She dragged in a shaky breath and made the turn at the traffic light, already knowing she was going to have a hard time sleeping tonight.

Chapter 34

————————

REID WAS DOING a final walk-through today with three of the tenants who were going to move in on Monday. He sat in Logan's ranch office and finalized the last of those tenants' lease paperwork.

The entire building was leased—with the exception of the corner office on the third floor. Logan and Luke had told him they were leaving that decision up to him.

He already knew what he wanted to do. He just had to finalize some things first. He couldn't make a commitment on some things without ending others first. He owed his people in Boston that much.

And as far as Samantha, he wasn't sure what to do about her. She'd made no mention of wanting him to stay. He really had wanted her to ask, or at least express interest. Instead, she'd acted as if him going back to Boston was a foregone conclusion. Then she'd seemed as if she was okay with it.

He hoped like hell what he felt for her wasn't one-sided, that he wasn't the only one in love, because if that was the case, then he was doing this for nothing. Because as much as he'd enjoyed being back home, and as much fun as he'd had restoring the mercantile, and making plans for some of the folks in town about future business, he could do restorations in Boston. And he sure as hell had plenty of potential for new business there.

The main reason he was planning to upend his life was because he'd fallen in love with Sam.

He looked up from his paperwork and found Not My Dog staring at him.

"What?"

Of course, the dog didn't speak, but he gave him that look. Reid was getting used to those looks.

So why the hell don't you tell her you're in love with her and ask her if she feels the same way before you turn your entire life upside down?

"Huh. Good question. Maybe I haven't asked the question because I'm afraid of the answer."

Not My Dog cocked his head to the side.

Bullshit. You're not afraid of anything. You moved across the country, the only member of your family to ever move out of Hope. You have balls of steel.

Reid let out a short laugh. "Yeah, sure. Right now my balls are quivering at the thought that maybe Sam isn't interested in a future with me. She might think we had some fun together, and that's it. Nothing more. So much for steely balls."

He could have sworn Not My Dog shook his head in disgust.

Get a grip. Man up, go over there, and tell her you love her.

"And what do I do if she just stares at me like I've lost my goddamned mind? What if she's more than ready to move on?"

Not My Dog growled at him.

Then you suck it up and go back to Boston. We've survived worse, haven't we?

"We? No, man, there is no we. But as far as me, then no, I haven't. My breakup with Britt was nothing like this."

He got up and went to the window, looked out over the pasture. "I've never felt like this before. What I thought was love with Britt was nothing compared to what I feel for Sam."

He heard Not My Dog's toenails tapping on the wood floor as he came over to sit beside him.

So what's the solution, dipshit? You say nothing, sell your business, move back to Hope, and then you ask her? What kind of a moron are you, anyway?

"A cowardly one?"

Remember—balls of steel. Let's get this done.

"Yeah, nice talk. But since you have no balls, I'm not relying on you for advice."

Not My Dog barked at him.

You're a dumbass. We don't want to lose her. We love her, remember?

"How can I forget? And I heard everything you said. I'll think about it."

Chapter 35

———

IT HAD BEEN a particularly tough day with Grammy Claire. She'd had two episodes of forgetfulness, she'd asked for Grandpa Bob twice, and she hadn't recognized Faith at first when she'd come over to take her to lunch.

The doctor had told Sam there would be bad days and good days.

Today had been a very bad day.

Fortunately, Sam had hired someone part-time to work at the shop. Chloe attended the county college nearby on a part-time basis, so she was only looking for about twenty hours a week, which was ideal for Sam. Chloe had been in training for a week now and was doing great, so when Sam had to drop everything to deal with Grammy Claire today, Chloe had been able to jump right in and handle the day's orders, for which Sam was grateful.

Grammy Claire had been cranky, too, telling Sam and Faith both that she could take care of herself, that she didn't need anyone there to watch over her like she was some child or addled old woman. She had finally—and firmly—insisted they leave her house.

It had been Sam who'd had to be firm but gentle with her grandmother and tell her they both loved her and it was for her safety that they were going to stay with her for the day. Grammy Claire sniffed and left the room, closing herself off in her bedroom.

Faith had told her it was going to be okay, but Sam had been devastated. If not for Faith being there, Sam didn't know how she would have gotten through the day. As a now-retired nurse, Faith had gone through this before with her geriatric patients, so Sam had leaned on her, had asked a lot of questions, and had gotten some very detailed answers. Maybe answers she hadn't wanted to hear, but she'd needed to hear them.

An hour later Grammy Claire had come out of her room, acting her usual sweet, happy self, with apparently no memory of her outbursts or forgetfulness. But Faith had told Sam that would likely happen, and would continue to happen as the disease progressed.

Faith could apparently handle this with a great amount of patience.

Sam wasn't so sure she could, but she'd prepare herself for it. She had no other choice. Whatever happened, she was going to have to be ready for it.

Later that evening, she and Faith had gotten her grandmother fed and bathed. Grammy Claire and Faith were playing cards, so Sam wanted to dash across the street and take a shower.

"Why don't you just go on home for the night, honey?" Faith asked. "I'm going to spend the night."

"You don't need to do that, Faith."

"I don't mind. Besides, Claire has the better coffeemaker. And a more comfortable guest room bed than my own."

Sam laughed. "Okay. Thank you so much for being here to help."

"She's my best friend, Samantha, and has been since her husband and mine became friends forty years ago. There's nothing I wouldn't do for her."

She hugged Faith. "We're both very lucky to have you. Call me if you need me or if anything happens?"

"Of course. But we'll be just fine. You go get some rest."

She went home and got in the shower, letting the hot water rain over her head and her body. She probably stayed in there for twenty minutes, until the water started cooling. Then she put on her pajamas, made a glass of hot tea, and grabbed her e-reader to finish the book she'd started.

Her phone pinged with a message. It was Reid.

You at home?

She typed a response.

Yes.

He replied right away with: Up for a visitor?

She smiled and sent back a reply: If you mean you, then yes. Come on over.

He texted back with: Be there in ten.

He must have been working late again. She hoped he'd eaten today. She didn't have much in the way of food, but she could always make him a turkey sandwich.

She thought about changing into regular clothes, but she was tired and he'd seen her naked multiple times. She figured he'd be fine with her pajamas.

He'd probably be fine with naked, too. That made her laugh, and God, she really needed that.

She answered the door when he rang the bell.

"Where's Not My Dog?"

"Luke stopped by the mercantile this afternoon. He had Boomer with him and was on his way to the ranch to meet Emma and the other dogs there. They were going to have dinner with Logan and Des and I knew I was going to work late again, so he took Not My Dog back with him."

"Oh. Well, I'm sorry I'll miss being able to cuddle with him."

He stepped closer and slung his arm around her waist, dragging her against him. "You can cuddle with me instead."

"You're not as hairy, but I guess you'll do."

He grinned. "Good to know I'll always be second-best to my dog."

"That's tough, isn't it?" She splayed her palms on his chest, then kissed him, needing to absorb some of his strength, the warmth and feel of his body. By the time he pulled back, she felt thoroughly kissed.

She took his hand and pulled him to the sofa. "Did you eat dinner?"

"Yes. I actually took time to grab a bite at Bert's."

"I'm glad. I was going to fix you a sandwich otherwise."

"Of course you would. Because you're always thinking about me."

If only he knew how much she thought about him. "How was your day?"

"Busy." He told her about the walk-through with three of the tenants.

"I can't believe people are going to be moving in soon. How exciting."

"Yeah, it is. How was your day? I saw your new employee running flowers out to the van. Chloe, is that her name?"

"Yes. I wasn't there today. Grammy Claire had a couple of rough episodes."

He picked up her hand. "Oh, no. What happened?"

She told him about Grammy Claire's day.

He tucked a strand of her hair behind her ear. "That's rough on you. I'm sorry. You should have called me."

She laughed. "So you could do what? Hold my hand?"

"So I could be here for you."

She wanted him to be here for her. Every day. For the rest of their lives. But his tenure here was finished. He already had one foot back in Boston. "Faith has been a great help to me and will continue to be. I think she's hinting around at moving in. She lives in the trailer park, and I know she'd be more comfortable at Grammy Claire's. And God knows I could use the help. Plus, with her knowledge of geriatric nursing, she'd be a lifesaver. I think I'll ask her to move into Grammy Claire's house. I haven't discussed it with my grandmother yet, but I know she'll agree."

"I see. You think that's the ideal move?"

"I do. Short of me selling this house and moving in with her. Which is another option, and I may do that somewhere down the road. But I still have to work, so long-term care will be something we'll have to consider at some point."

"So you have a long-range plan."

She nodded. "I do. I've discussed it with Faith, and to some extent with my grandmother. She's put her future care into my hands, because she knows at some point she'll be incapable of making decisions. She's already given me all her power of attorney, for both medical and financial decision making."

"You don't have to do this alone, Sam."

She gave him a look. "Of course I do. There is no one else." And she'd never, ever ask him to help her. She loved him, but you didn't fall madly in love with someone, then ask them to shoulder this kind of burden. It wasn't going to happen.

So while she loved Reid, she was going to smile and wish him well and watch him go back to Boston.

She had to let him go.

Reid had the answer he'd come looking for. She wouldn't ask him to help her because she didn't care for him in the same way he cared for her.

He knew exactly what he had to do now.

"I'm heading back to Boston on Friday."

She nodded. "I figured now that the project was finished you'd be heading back home."

"Yeah, I have a lot of things back there waiting for me to handle. Things I've put off that need to be dealt with."

"Of course." She stood. "I'm glad you stopped by. I would have hated not being able to say good-bye to you."

He hadn't come here to get a good-bye, but that's what was happening. He got up, feeling the chasm between them already. He didn't know what to say, how to end this.

Hell, he didn't want to end this.

"So before you go, I have something I need to say to you."

He held his breath, waiting for her to say something, anything, that would tell him how she felt.

"Okay."

She pulled him into her arms for a hug. "I've enjoyed every minute we've spent together, Reid. I wish you a lifetime of happiness. And whenever you're in town again, come say hi, okay?"

He held tight to her, and his eyes stung. Goddammit.

Balls of steel, remember?

Yeah. Fuck that. He drew back and kissed her, needing her to know how he felt, needing to sear her, to brand her, to make her understand in that kiss exactly how much he loved her.

And when he pulled back, she blinked, and he could swear there were tears in her eyes, too.

"Well," she said, her voice cracking. "I have an early day tomorrow, so I should let you get home."

He nodded and she walked him to the door. She opened it, took his hand, and held it, before finally letting hers slip away.

"Good-bye, Reid."

"Bye, Sam."

He walked out, and she shut the door behind him. He didn't even turn around to look as he got in the truck and drove off.

So this is what it felt like to really love someone and lose them.

It fucking hurt like hell.

SAM SAT ON the sofa and stared at the television that she hadn't bothered to turn on. She couldn't open the book she'd picked up to read, because tears were streaming down her face.

He was gone. She'd let him go.

It had been the right thing to do.

But the right thing to do hurt so bad she wasn't sure she'd ever be able to recover from it.

She laid down on the sofa and curled up, dragging a blanket over her, and continued to stare at the dark TV.

Chapter 36

IT HAD TAKEN two weeks in Boston for Reid to wrap up his life there.

He'd let his employees know right away, then put out feelers to sell the company. In the end, Tim, his vice president, had made an offer to buy the company. He couldn't think of anyone better suited to take his company to the next level. Tim would do great things with his architectural firm, and his clients were in good hands. They settled on a price, and the paperwork and finances were rolling.

He found a Realtor and put his condo on the market, furniture included, and had made arrangements to have his things packed up and shipped to the ranch.

It had been an incredibly fast-paced two weeks, but he was used to a fast pace.

When he'd gotten back to Hope, he'd been immediately greeted by Not My Dog.

"You thought I had abandoned you, didn't you, buddy?" He ruffled Not My Dog's coat, scratched him behind the ears, and, in the end, sat on the ground while the dog climbed in his lap and licked his face.

"Face it, bud, the two of us are meant to be together."

Not My Dog stared at him.

What about Sam?

"Yeah, I know. I miss her, too." He rubbed Not My Dog's neck, then went inside to see his family.

Martha greeted him with a huge hug, as did Des, whose burgeoning belly bumped him.

"Getting out there, aren't you, mama?" he asked with a grin.

"You know it. If not for all the walks Logan makes me take around the ranch every day, I'd be sitting inside getting as big as this house."

"It's not possible for you to get that big," Logan said, shaking Reid's hand while he put his arm around Des. "You're too naturally sexy."

"Aww, thanks," Reid said. "I never knew you thought I was sexy."

Logan rolled his eyes. Des laughed.

After they all had dinner together, he and Logan shared a beer out on the front porch. Despite the fall chill, there was something renewing and fresh about sitting outside. Besides, it would never be as cold here as it was in Boston. And he had a great coat.

"Everything taken care of in Boston?" Logan asked.

"Yeah. Company is sold and is in great hands. Condo is on the market, and my Realtor texted to tell me we already have two offers with the potential for another on the way tomorrow morning, so we might get in a bidding war, which will drive up the price. I'm hoping the condo will be sold by next week."

Logan took a long swallow of beer. "That's good news. All the tenants have moved into the mercantile."

"I'm glad to hear that. Including our third-floor corner office tenant?" Reid had hated leasing that space, but he'd had no choice. An accountant leased it. And was due to move in this week. Besides, that had all been a part of his dream. A dream he no longer believed in.

"He backed out."

Reid looked over at Logan. "What? He signed the lease."

"Yeah, well, we let him unsign it. He decided to relocate to Tulsa. Something about his wife and the kids and school district and her parents insisting they live where there's some private school and hell if I know. I was only half listening. He wanted out of the lease and Luke and I said yes. So the space is yours if you want it."

"Huh."

"You want it, don't you?"

Reid looked out over the land. This had always been home. And now that he was back, it was good to know it would always be here for him.

"Yeah, I want it. I'm going to buy a plot of land south of the main highway, halfway between here and Hope."

He explained to Logan where it was.

"I've seen the for-sale sign on that acreage. Good place to build a house. I suppose you already have it drawn out."

"I might."

Logan propped his booted feet up on the porch rail. "You let Samantha Reasor know that's where you intend to live your happily-ever-after with her?"

"Not exactly."

"Why not?"

"I don't know that she feels the same way I do."

"You ever ask her?"

"Well, no."

Logan slanted a look in his direction. "What kind of a dumbass are you?"

"Now you sound like my dog."

Logan frowned. "What?"

"Never mind. I need to talk to her. Really talk to her. When I left before, it felt unfinished between us and I let it go that way. I didn't tell her how I felt because I was waiting for her to tell me how she felt."

"Only way to find out what a woman thinks is to come right out and ask her. And you've got to stop playing those kinds of games with a woman's heart. If you love her, then you've gotta tell her. Trust me, kid. I speak from experience on that one."

"Fine. I'll go talk to her."

"You do that."

Reid took a couple of long swallows of beer and sat in the blissful silence with his brother.

"Hey, Reid."

"Yeah."

"Damn glad you're home to stay."

His lips curved. "Me, too, Logan."

Chapter 37

WHY IN THE hell was everybody getting married in the fall? Didn't every bride want to get married in June or something? It was getting cooler outside. Leaves were falling. It had rained twice this week. Who in their right mind would want to get married now?

This was Sam's third wedding this month, and frankly, she was tired of all the love and happiness spreading around Hope.

She didn't feel love or happiness right now. In fact, she felt downright grumpy. Having to do wedding flowers was not improving her mood any.

But she and Chloe had spent all week preparing burgundy and yellow roses and white lilies for Shauna and Phil's wedding. She'd delivered them to the church this morning for the noon service, and she had to admit Shauna looked stunning in her gown. Sam had even gotten a little misty when Shauna teared up as Sam handed her the bouquet.

Darn those happy brides anyway.

She'd gone over to the reception hall and made sure every tabletop had flowers. Chloe had turned out to be a lifesaver. If only she wasn't always in such a good mood.

They finished decorating the hall with flowers well before the reception started, so her work for the day was done. She and Chloe headed back to the shop, and she let Chloe take off while she cleaned up. She heard the bell ring while she was in the back of the shop.

"We're closed," she hollered.

The bell rang again. With a sigh, she headed out front, skidding to a stop when she saw Reid standing on the other side of the door.

She blinked—hard—needing to make sure she hadn't imagined it.

He was still standing there, smiling and waving.

She went to the door and opened it.

"Hey," he said when he saw her.

She backed up a few steps. "What are you doing here?"

"I was at the mercantile and saw your car parked behind the van, so I thought I'd stop by."

"No, I mean what are you doing *here*? In Hope. You went back to Boston. Like just a couple of weeks ago."

"Oh, that. Well, yes, I did. But now I'm back."

She was in no mood for guessing games. "I can see that. Why?"

He frowned. "Aren't you happy to see me?"

"Not particularly."

"Why not?"

Because I'm not over you yet. Because I'm still in love with you. Because seeing you again is breaking my heart. "Um . . ."

"Are you mad at me?"

"No. Yes. I don't know. No, definitely not."

He laughed.

She wagged a finger at him. "Don't you dare laugh at me, Reid McCormack."

He held up his hands. "Okay, definitely not laughing at you." He came toward her.

She backed away. "Don't."

"Samantha. Tell me what's wrong. You're upset."

"I'm not upset. I'm . . . Dammit, Reid. Why did you have to come back? I had a plan."

"A plan?"

"Yes. A plan to get over you." She turned around and walked away, going behind the counter, needing space between them. "And now you're back and you're ruining everything."

"You had a plan to get over me? Why did you need to get over me, Sam?"

She held tight to the countertop before lifting her gaze to his. "Don't make me say it."

"Is it because you might feel the same way about me as I feel about you?"

She refused to hope. "I don't know what you're talking about."

He dragged his fingers through that glorious, dark hair of his. "I should have said this a long time ago. I love you, Sam. I'm back here in Hope because I fell in love with you. Because I couldn't see my life being in Boston any longer. My life, my future, is here. In Hope. With you."

Oh, God. He'd said the words. The words she'd so wanted to hear from him, but had also been terrified to hear. Tears slid down her cheeks. "Don't say those words to me. Do you know what a mess my life is right now?"

He came around the counter and pulled her against him. "Do you think I care that your life is a mess?"

She tried to pull away from him, but he held her firmly in his embrace. "You should care. You know what's going on with my grandmother."

"Of course I know. Do you think that matters? I love you, Sam. I love everything about you. I love how you put everyone first above your own needs. I love how much you care about your grandmother. I love your grandmother. I love how you've always cared about me. I love that you love my dog."

She looked at the floor, at the big fat teardrops falling. "Don't. Don't love me."

He tipped her chin up with his fingers. "Too late. I already do. And I need you to come with me."

She sniffed. "Where?"

"I need to take you for a ride."

He grabbed the box of tissues on the counter and handed

them to her, then let her grab her keys so she could lock up the shop. Then he put her in his truck and took her for a drive outside of town.

She had no idea what was happening. Her heart was so full she could barely breathe.

He loved her. God, he shouldn't love her. She couldn't take this right now.

"Where are we going?" she finally asked after she'd wiped her eyes and blown her nose.

"There's something I want to show you. Someplace I want you to see."

The ride took about fifteen minutes. He drove off the main highway a short distance, down a gravel road, stopping at a for-sale sign pitched on a plot of land. He got out and came around to her side of the truck.

"What are we doing here?"

He put her in front of the For Sale sign.

"I just bought this land, Sam. I'm going to build a house here. A big house on a lot of land. For us. And for your grandmother. Plenty of space for all of us. And for Not My Dog."

"You bought . . ." She turned to face him. "For us? For all of us?"

"Yes. I know who's in your life, Sam. I know the burdens you carry. And I want you to know that you'll never have to shoulder those burdens alone ever again. I love you and I want to marry you. And when you love someone, their joy becomes your joy. Their sorrow becomes your sorrow. Their life becomes your life. Will you share your life with me?"

Sam could barely breathe. She had been so strong and so independent for her entire life. And here was someone offering to lend her a shoulder to cry on, a chance to share his life. Because he loved her.

And she loved him back.

"You would do this for me."

"Until the end of time."

She broke down then and sobbed, throwing herself against him and releasing that burden to him. Because she loved him and she trusted him.

He held tight to her and let her cry it out until she was finished. And then he went to the truck and grabbed the box of tissues and handed it to her. She wiped her tears and blew her nose—again—several times. And when she finally found her voice to speak, she knew exactly what she wanted to say.

"Reid, I love you. I loved you before you left, but I was too afraid to ask you to carry the burden that was my life. And I realize now how selfish that was, because being the kind of man you are, I should have known you would have easily accepted my life the way it was. And I'm sorry for that.

"I will absolutely positively one hundred percent marry you, with my whole heart. For now and for ever. And I will love this house that you build for me. But I think in the case of my grandmother, she would be happier in the home she lived in with my grandpa. Faith has offered to move in with her and care for her as long as she's able to. And when the time comes that Grammy Claire needs more care than that . . ."

"Then together we'll figure out the next step for Grammy Claire."

Her heart nearly burst with love. "Yes. We'll figure that out together."

He put his arm around her. "You'll never have to make that decision alone, Sam. I'll always be here for you."

She leaned against him. "And I'll always be here for you."

He tipped her head back and kissed her, and she knew at that moment this was their beginning. Their starting point.

And as long as they had each other, it would be perfect.

He took her hand in his and turned to her. "Oh, one more thing. How fast do you think we could put a wedding together?"

She frowned. "What?"

"You said one of the things that made you sad was that you didn't think your grandmother would be around when you got married. Let's make sure she is. Let's get married— like right away."

Her heart started beating fast. "Are you serious?"

"Dead serious. It might not be the biggest or fanciest wedding, but I'll bet with all the family and friends we have, we could get it done in a hurry and still have one hell of a great wedding. If that's what you want."

This was why she loved this man.

"Are you sure? Are you really sure that's what you want?"

"Absolutely. And we might have to live at your place for a while until we get this house built. If that's okay with you."

"It's totally okay with me." She threw herself against him, unable to believe she'd found love with the one man who really understood her, who could love her the way she'd always wanted to be loved.

She kissed him, hard, then pulled back and smiled at him. "Have I ever told you how much I love fall weddings?"

Turn the page for a preview of the next two
gorgeous Jaci Burton romances

Unexpected Rush

and

Don't Let Go

Coming soon from Headline Eternal.

Unexpected Rush

"MEN SUCK." HARMONY Evans tossed her purse on the kitchen table of her mother's house and sat next to her best friend, Alyssa. It was Thursday night—family dinner night at Mama's house. Everyone was coming over, as it always was at Mama's. Right now she'd prefer to be sitting in the corner of a dark bar, nursing a dirty martini. She was going to have to settle for sweet tea because, short of death, you did not miss Thursday night dinner at Mama's.

She'd already come in and kissed her mama, who was holding court in the living room with Harmony's brother Drake and some of his friends, giving her time to catch up with Alyssa.

Alyssa laid her hand over Harmony's and cast a look of concern. "And why do you hate men? Is it Levon?"

Harmony wrinkled her nose, preferring to never hear the name of her now ex-boyfriend again. "Yes."

"Did you two break up?"

"I did not break up with him. He gave me the classic 'It's not you, it's me' speech. He's doing so much international travel with the law firm, and he just can't devote enough time to the relationship, so it wouldn't be fair to me to lead me on when he knows he can't commit. He went on with more excuses but it was all *blah blah blah* after that." She waved her hand back and forth.

Alyssa's gaze narrowed. "What a prick. Why is it so damn hard to find a man of value, one who will respect a woman and give her honesty?"

"I have no idea." Harmony pulled one of the empty glasses forward and poured from the pitcher that sat in the middle of the table, already filled with tea and ice and loaded with so much sugar she'd likely be awake all night. At this point, she didn't care. She'd work it off in a gym session tomorrow. "All I know is I'm glad to be rid of him. It was bad enough his bathroom counter had more products on it than mine did."

Alyssa laughed. "There you go. What does a man need on his counter besides a toothbrush, soap, deodorant, and a razor?"

"According to Levon, there was stuff for his beard, trimming devices, facial scrub, moisturizer—separate ones for his face and his body. An entire manicure set for his nails, for use when he wasn't off getting mani-pedis, of course."

"Of course," Alyssa said, then giggled.

"Oh, and the scents. Let's not forget his entire rack of colognes."

Alyssa nodded. "The man did reek, honey."

"I think he owned more perfume than I do."

"Never a good sign. See? You dodged a bullet."

"I did."

Alyssa lifted her glass. "Let's toast to that."

They clinked glasses. "To men we're lucky to have not ended up with," Harmony said.

"What are we toasting to?"

Harmony looked up to find Barrett Cassidy standing at the kitchen table. He was her brother Drake's best friend and teammate, and since the guys both played for the Tampa Hawks football team and Barrett also lived in Tampa, Thursday nights meant Drake would drag his friends over to the house for dinner.

One of the nicest things about living in Tampa, as a

matter of fact. She'd often thought it had been fortuitous that her brother had been drafted by the hometown team. It had kept him close to home all these years, and of course, one couldn't beat the awesome eye candy her brother brought home now and then.

Especially Barrett. Most especially Barrett.

"We're toasting the end of Harmony's relationship with a man who was absolutely not right for her," Alyssa said.

Barrett arched a brow, then gave Harmony a sympathetic look. "Really. Sorry about that."

Harmony shrugged. "Nothing to be sorry about. Alyssa's right. He wasn't the man for me."

"Then I guess I'm . . . happy for you?"

She laughed, and she could tell this was uncomfortable for him. "Come on. Sit down and have a glass of iced tea with us."

"I'm not sure I want to wade into these waters. Breakups are not my territory."

"Oh, come on, Barrett. Surely you've dumped a woman before," Harmony said, pouring him a glass. "Or you've been dumped."

He pulled out a chair and sat. She'd never realized before how utterly . . . big he was. He'd always kept his distance from her, preferring to hang with Drake, so this was the closest she'd ever been to him. Both he and Drake played defense for the Hawks. Barrett was absolutely pure muscle. Just watching the way his muscles flexed as he moved was like watching liquid art. She could stare at his arms for hours, but she tried not to ogle. Not too much, anyway.

"I've been dumped before, sure," Barrett said. "And maybe I've broken up with a woman or two."

Alyssa leaned close to Harmony. "He's downplaying being the one who dumped the woman."

"I heard that, Alyssa."

"I meant for you to hear me, Barrett. You're just trying to be the good guy right now because we're roasting the not-so-good guys."

Barrett narrowed his gaze. "See, I told you I shouldn't be sitting here. If you're gonna want to bad-mouth my species—which you have a right to, since some asshole broke up with you, Harmony—then I should leave. Also, I'd suggest something stronger than iced tea. It helps."

So maybe he had been dumped before. It sounded like he knew how to get through it.

"It's okay, Barrett," Harmony said. "Me getting dumped is definitely not your fault. I'm not as pissed off about it as I probably should be, all things considered. So you're safe here."

Besides, looking at Barrett could definitely make her forget all about Levon and his prissy bathroom counter. She wondered how many items Barrett had on *his* bathroom counter? She'd bet not many.

She turned her chair toward him, determined to find out. "Actually, I have a ridiculous question for you, Barrett."

He turned his gorgeous blue eyes on her and smiled. "Shoot."

"How many items currently reside on your bathroom counter?"

Barrett cocked a brow. "Huh?"

Alyssa laughed. "Very good question."

"I don't get it," Barrett said.

"We're conducting a poll about men and their bathrooms," Alyssa said. "Indulge us."

Barrett finally shrugged. "Okay, fine. Uh . . . soap, of course. Toothpaste and toothbrush. Deodorant. Maybe a comb?"

Harmony smiled when Barrett struggled to come up with anything else. She knew he was an absolute male of the not-so-fussy-about-his-grooming variety.

He finally cast her a helpless look. "I don't know. I've got nothin' else. Did I fail?"

"Oh, no," Harmony said. "You most definitely passed."

"You should go out with Barrett," Alyssa suggested. "He's a nice guy, and he obviously doesn't keep thirty-seven things on his bathroom counter."

Barrett laughed. "Yeah, and Drake would kill us both. He'd definitely kill me."

The idea of going out with Barrett appealed, though. She'd had such a crush on Barrett when Drake had first introduced them all those years ago. And now? Hmmm. Yeah, definitely appealing.

"What my brother doesn't know won't hurt him—or you. What do you say, Barrett? Care to take me out?"

BARRETT WAS AT a loss for words. Harmony was his best friend's little sister.

Only she wasn't so little anymore. When he'd first been drafted by Tampa, he and Drake had bonded. Both of them played defense, they'd been roommates, and they'd become friends. It had been that way for the past six years.

He'd been coming here to Drake's mom's house ever since that first year, back when Harmony had been in college. Back when she'd still been a kid. Now she was a woman, and she'd just been dumped by some guy who was obviously too stupid to know what a treasure he'd had.

She was beautiful, with brown skin, long dark curly hair, and those amazing amber eyes. She had the kind of body any man would want to get his hands on, curves in all the right places . . .

And he had no business thinking about Harmony at all, because there was a code—no messing with your best friend's sister.

Absolutely not. No. Wasn't going to happen.

He pushed back his chair and stood, looking down at Harmony as if she were Eve in the Garden and she'd just offered him the forbidden apple. "I know the rule, Harmony, and so do you. I think I'll go check out what Granny made for dinner tonight."

He might be tempted, but there was too much at stake. He was going to step away from the sweet fruit in front of him before he decided to do something really stupid and take a taste.

Because going down that road would spell nothing but doom.

Don't Let Go

BRADY CONNERS WAS spending the day doing one of the things he enjoyed the most: smoothing out dents in a quarter panel of a Chevy. As soon as he finished, he'd paint, and this baby would be good as new.

It wasn't his dream job. He was working toward that. But with every day he spent working at Richards Auto Service, thanks to Carter Richards, he was pocketing money that got him closer to his dream. And someday he'd open up his own custom motorcycle paint shop.

Somewhere. Maybe here in Hope. Maybe somewhere else. Probably somewhere else, because this place held memories.

Not good ones.

A long time ago—a time that seemed like an eternity now—he had thought maybe he and his brother Kurt would start up a business together. Brady would do bodywork and custom motorcycle paint, and Kurt would repair the bikes.

That dream went up in smoke the day Brady got the call that his brother was dead.

He paused, stood, and stretched out the kinks in his back, wiping the sweat that dripped into his eyes. He took a step back and grabbed the water bottle he always stored nearby, taking a long drink through the straw, swallowing several times until his thirst was quenched.

Needing a break, he pulled off his breathing mask and swiped his fingers through his hair, then stepped outside.

It was late spring, and rain was threatening. He dragged in a deep breath, enjoying the smell of fresh air.

He really wanted a cigarette, but he'd quit a little over a year ago. Not that the urge had gone away. Probably never would. But he was stronger than his own needs. Or at least that's what he told himself every time a strong craving hit.

Instead, he pulled out one of the flavored toothpicks he always kept in his jeans pocket and slid that between his teeth.

Not nearly as satisfying, but it would do. It would have to.

He leaned against the wall outside the shop and watched the town in motion. It was lunchtime, so it was busy.

Luke McCormack, one of Hope's cops, drove by in his patrol car and waved. Brady waved back. Luke was a friend of Carter's, and while Brady wasn't as social as a lot of the guys he'd met, he knew enough to be friendly. Especially to cops.

Samantha Reasor left her shop, loading up her flower van with a bunch of colorful bouquets. She spotted him, giving him a bright smile and a wave before she headed off.

Everyone in this damn town was so friendly. He mostly kept to himself, doing his work and then heading to the small apartment above the shop at night to watch TV or play video games. He had one goal in mind, and that was to save money to open his business. He saw his parents now and again since they lived in Hope, but the strain of Kurt's death had taken a toll on them.

Nothing was the same anymore. With them. With him either, he supposed.

Sometimes life just sucked. And you dealt with that.

His stomach grumbled. He needed something to eat. He pushed off the wall and headed up the street, intending to make a stop at the sandwich joint on the corner. He'd grab a quick bite and bring it back to the shop.

He made a sudden stop when Megan Lee, the really hot brunette who owned the bakery, came out with a couple of pink boxes in her hands. She collided with him and the boxes went flying. She caught one, he caught one, then he steadied her with his other hand.

She looked up at him, her brown eyes wide with surprise.

"Oh, my gosh. Thank you, Brady. I almost dropped these."

"You okay, Megan?"

"Yes. But let me check these." She bent down and opened the boxes. There were cakes inside. They looked pretty, with pink icing on one and blue on the other and little baby figurines in strollers sitting on top of the cakes. There were flowers and other doo-dahs as well. He didn't know all that much about cake decorations. He just liked the way they tasted.

"They're for Sabelle Frasier. She just had twins." She looked up at him with a grin. "A boy and a girl. Her mom ordered these for her hospital homecoming. I spent all morning baking and decorating them."

He didn't need to know that, but the one thing he did know was that people in this town were social and liked to talk. "They look good."

She swiped her hair out of her eyes. "Of course they're good."

He bent and took the boxes from her. "Where's your car?"

"Parked just down the street."

"How about you let me carry these? Just in case you want to run into anyone else on your way."

Her lips curved. "I think you ran into me."

He disagreed, but whatever. He figured he'd do his good deed for the day, then get his sandwich.

He followed her down the street.

"I haven't seen much of you lately," she said.

He shrugged. "Been busy."

"I've been meaning to stop in the shop and visit, but things have been crazy hectic at the bakery, too." She studied him. "How about I bring pastries by in the morning? And I've never brought you coffee before. How about some coffee? How do you take it? Black, or with cream and sugar? Or maybe you like lattes or espresso? What do you drink in the mornings?"

He had no idea what she was talking about. "Uh, just regular coffee. Black."

"Okay. I make a really great cup of coffee. I'm surprised you haven't come into the bakery since it's so close to the auto shop. Most everyone who works around here pops in." She pressed the unlock button on her car, then opened the back door and took the boxes from him.

Man, she really could talk. He'd noticed that the couple of times they'd gone out. Not that it was a bad thing, but for someone like him who lived mostly isolated, all that conversation was like a bombardment.

Not that it was a bad thing. The one thing he missed the most since his self-imposed isolation was conversation. And Megan had it in droves. He just wasn't all that good about reciprocating.

After she slid the boxes in, she turned to him. "What's your favorite pastry? You know, I've dropped muffins off at the auto shop. Have you eaten any of those?"

He was at a loss for words. He always was around her. A few of his friends had fixed the two of them up before. Once at Logan and Des's dinner party, then again at Carter and Molly's wedding. They'd danced. Had some conversation. Mostly one-sided since Megan had done all the talking.

He wasn't interested.

Okay, that wasn't exactly the truth. What heterosexual male wouldn't be interested in Megan? She was gorgeous, with her silky light brown hair and her warm chocolate eyes that always seemed to study him with interest. She also had a fantastic body with perfect curves.

But he was here to work. That was it. He didn't have time for a relationship.

He didn't want a relationship, no matter how attractive the woman was. And Megan was really damned attractive.

"Brady?" she asked, pulling his attention back on her. "Muffins?"

"What about them?"

She cocked her head to the side. "Oh, come on Brady. Everyone has a favorite pastry. Cream puffs? Donuts? Scones? Cakes? Bars? Strudel?"

He zeroed in on the last thing she said. "Apple strudel. I used to have that from the old bakery when I was a kid."

She offered up a satisfied smile. "I make a killer apple strudel. I'll bring you one—along with coffee—in the morning."

He frowned. "You don't have to do that."

She laid her hand on his arm and offered up the kind of smile that made him focus on her mouth. She had a really pretty mouth, and right now it was glossed a kissable shade of peach.

He didn't want to notice her mouth, but he did.

"I don't mind. I love to bake. But now I have to go. Thanks again for saving the cakes. I'll see you tomorrow, Brady."

She climbed in her car and pulled away, leaving him standing there, confused as hell.

He didn't want her to bring him coffee. Or apple strudel. Or anything.

He didn't want to notice Megan or talk to Megan or think about Megan, but the problem was, he'd been doing a lot of that lately. For the past six months or so he'd thought about the dance he'd shared with her. The conversations he'd had with her. She had a sexy smile—not the kind a woman had to force, but the kind that came naturally. She also had a great laugh and she could carry a conversation with ease. And that irritated him because he hadn't thought about a woman in a long time.

For the past year and a half since his brother had died, he hadn't wanted to think about anything or anyone. All he'd wanted to do was work, then head upstairs to his one-room apartment above the auto shop, eat his meals and watch TV, and on the weekends do custom bike painting. Keep his mind and his body busy so he wouldn't have to think—or feel.

Women—and relationships—would make him feel, and that wasn't acceptable. He'd noticed that right away about Megan, noticed that he liked her and maybe—

No. Wasn't going to happen—ever. He needed to get her out of his head.

He only had time for work, and making money. He had a dream he was saving for.

And now he barely had time for lunch, because he had a Chevy to get back to.

Welcome to Hope, Oklahoma.

*The small town that's sure to warm
your heart.*

*Full of big hearts, fiery
passion and love everlasting . . .*

Jaci's Hope series is available now from

headline
ETERNAL

Jaci Burton's Play-by-Play series

... what's not to love?

Irresistible, ripped sports stars – check ✔

Smart, feisty women – check ✔

Off-the-charts chemistry – check ✔

Intimate, emotional romance – check ✔

Available now from

headline
ETERNAL

headline

ETERNAL

FIND YOUR HEART'S DESIRE...

VISIT OUR WEBSITE: www.headlineeternal.com
FIND US ON FACEBOOK: facebook.com/eternalromance
FOLLOW US ON TWITTER: @eternal_books
EMAIL US: eternalromance@headline.co.uk